CARAMEL FLOODS
Stories
By Fin Sorrel

ISBN-13: 978-0-9988476-4-1
ISBN-10: 099884764X

for more books, visit Pski's Porch:
www.pskisporch.com

Printed in U.S.A

This book is dedicated to Nova Zachary

Acknowledgments

I would like to thank Pski Porch Press for opening their doors to me, and releasing my first book. Alicia Sangiuliano for her continued support and friendship through some of my darkest moments, who taught me that I do love to work, . I would also like to thank my dear friend Zachary Hubbard, for his friendship, and all of the tireless hours he spent helping me revise and rework Teacup Galaxy, among other stories of mine not included in this collection. I'd like to thank my professor Wendy Bourgeois, and her husband Patrick Rogers who taught me how to look deeper into my writings, and for their support in my endeavors as an author. Brandy Gump my muse for many of these stories, who taught me how to suspend my disbelief, and believe in my self, also who taught me the wisdom and blessings one can find in nature, plants, and animals. My deepest of Gratitude's go out to all of the people who are in this country that picked me up hitch hiking, handed me money when I was frail and starving, put me up in their houses and allowed me privacy and access to resources, fed me, kept me alive. Some of these stories have appeared in the following journals:
A Galaxy of Starfish: An Anthology of Modern Surrealism (Salo press)
Avatar Review, Queen Mobs Teahouse, FUR-LINED GHETTOS 7,
Mad cap review 4, Mush/mum 4, & mad hat lit.

Contents || ||| || || ||||
{photographs by the author}

| | | Magic | | |

[Noon Mm.]
Her, and Allen build a fire in a club-shaped grill — Allen
holds her in a wedding dress, petting her hair, Streams of glitter float down, and land in the rug —

| Noon Aa.|
On bundled fuchsia, the big, pink, and purple ligaments of
straw ink, all German green, gorging the dripping seeds spilled
on the silverware; her hands painted white to the finger nails.
Of fluids, a rainbow, slower, of white doors, falls into the
ocean, spiritual fingertips down her white arms, holding up the
great American Idol. She holds a wad of 100 dollar bills, all
together in a strip of tape, and lights the stove with gasoline.
Gorging on the fuchsia, she cries, staring at the peach colored
thread of the loveseat, and paints herself all of the way white,
thrashing in panic, paranoia, seizures, and throws the perfectly
wrapped hundreds in the large flames, her hands shaking;
crumpled to a bowl of flowers, she rubs red paint onto her
hands, washing in the flowers, and puts on a daily outfit of
brown, chestnut tattered rags. She does her best to make her
hair nice, but the red paint makes it difficult, and dirties her
more. She wanders outdoors, begs men for money, her hands
shake a tan hat with a few coins in it. A number of white trash
scuba divers float in the backyard, in a few feet of water, little
neighbors roller-skate by, giving each other a ride on the refrigerator, and on the phone, with a little gurney they pull alongside full of telephones, roosters peck on the tape recorder.

[Noon: G,g.]
It looks like rain, Allen says. He's standing at the pane glass
window, holding drapes. "...It's how it always is with Aquarius,
and Pisces. It looks like rain." Allen says. She sips bergamot tea
out of a neon coffee cup — on the side is a quote by Elizabeth
Janeway. "Reaction isn't action — that is, it isn't truly creative."

3

She says nothing, just turns the cup so he can see the quote —
Stares at the window. He cannot read it, but knows the cup.
He, instead sighs; fumbles with the peach feeling of the drapes,
yawns, then retires to the mannequin room.

She stares at the glass, watches the rain bounce, splashing in
her swimming pool. Off the gutters, and dripping down off the
shed, into the wheelbarrow. Allen turns on the above head light
in the mannequin room, and looks inquisitively at his creation
(all the rejects from work.) The torso which was dipped wrong,
has large rounded breasts under the armpits, instead of her
chest, something no one at work could figure out — hands,
head, and feet, arms, legs, pelvis all fitted together with saws,
glue, heat, paint and screws.

[Hunts the glow at night, for fuel to the luminescent birds,
wired to the brain, and spine] A forest of no locations; beads
clank together glow above the beds / Everglades pass by the
station, forts, the people made of palms flash palms flash in
view, speakers over speakers over the mouth of those who
choose to speak in the manner of tongues, the people who
choose to drink Luciferin and luciferase, their mouths are
glowing deep into the night. We can see they have been drunk
from the corporate waters. When one wanders the cities late,
the impression is that one walks through stars. I see a man
dressed in a skeleton costume, with a Marionette , I've been
dragon all day, run into 711 with the giraffe mask, bodies happy,
amazing creatures, woman, man, woman, child dragon, a man
woman child, wow, wild, glow in the dark green.

[NOON Ii.]
Ice cream sandwiches are strewn about the yard, bikes thrown
here and there, some kids jump in the pool, and thrash around,
splash a neighbor girl, Celeste. She has a bowl of seahorses,

4

releases them in the pool, when Allen comes out, onto the
back porch with arms and legs of a mannequin. Look out! He
yells, and throws all of the smoldered mannequin parts into the
swimming pool~

| Noon Cc. |
We're driving far. She gets into the blue Chevy nova 1977 and
the engine starts up slow, and rumbles. Her makeup is done
very well. It is not the same white you usually have on. He
says, pulls out under the willow tree, the limbs scratch on the
hood. He notices her eyeliner gœs from bottom eyelid, to ear.
She has touched up the upper eyelids with rainbow glitter. The
lipstick is faint rum, her jet black haircut is recent, and long
strings of it curl behind her rosy ear. She laughs, and pulls
up her purse, warmed up to the car, and pulls out cigarettes,
and then straightens her jacket. He's been doing this contest
with the lines in the road but speaks for a while about teachers of a coastal tradition, and she agrees with the few things
he says. George is your name, right? She winks, and he pulls
the Chevy around behind a park, so the question can sink in.
He checks his hair in the mirror after he parks. She rolls down
the window and puffs at the cigarette. I'm moving away, Zœ.
Wednesday night. The company has been curious about what
my research paper entails; they want to bring me in for study.
She is silent, and pulls smoke into her lungs, let's it slow down
to her tongue.

| | Oshun | |

[Noon Oo.]

She slides down Allen, and pulls the blankets close to her
back, he helps, fumbles for her wrist, and then her ankle, he
feeds her a grape, as she pauses on him, steadies her labia at
his tip, and eases down along, slow, stops to relax her whole
body before inched again, slow. The rain taps, and drizzles at
their window, the telephone wires draw his attention beneath
her, he closes his eyes when she whispers, moans to hold her
thighs. Allen relaxes, and feels overwhelmed by the edge of
an orgasm. Stops her where she is, by her thighs. She waits,
quivers, moans in his ear to grab her breasts, licks his ear,
and they kiss. Their tongues lick tongue, then lips, then lick
each other on tongues, he squeezes the tip of his groin, and
then nudges it against her clitoris, allows it to use for massage,
until she again centers her labia around Allen, lowers until
they connect ~ Slow, she slides all of the way down, relaxes her
back and shoulders. He watches a black bird out there, pass in
the window, all of the way up, she holds it, pauses here, Allen
grabs her by the thighs, and gently lowers her body down, and
up, pauses again at the top, until after gentle breath, her moan,
she starts to move on her own, his hands back to the bed. He
forces himself to remain still now, against his body, he tries to
relax into her new pace, a bit more desperate. She drops him
into her all the way, after so long at the top, erratic, pulses, he
breathes stays relaxed, feels his body fill with snakes, lizards all
black crawling through him, rodents scurry away, she is in the
depths of quiet moaning now, as if falling asleep, a place for a
soft warm river stone is arranged at the bottom of a river, and
the room, the window gœs distant, the rhythm of the tapped
rain obscures, they both fill with rivers, flounder, crawdad,
and branches float on their breast, and crotches, float by every
moment, sometime now, they both imagine they float down the
river in two small canœs, exchange food, and wine~

9

ABCDEFGHIJKLMNOPQRSTU

God   File   MAN   OSHUN Trade, milk.

[Noon Ss.]

Allen comes home, and takes down an enormous bag of mannequin parts from his shoulder; he sees a note on the table,
and picks through the newspapers for it. I've gone to Canal St.
to rustle up some money for our mannequin's motor, love and
kisses.

[Noon Hh.]

She wakes up in the middle of the afternoon, terrorized that
the house is haunted ~ the sound of Allen's tinker in the mannequin room echœ to a bent pitch, and she closes her eyes,
see's syrup drip down a classic '77 Chevy Nova window;
brown, maple syrup, in long lines to the hood of the car~ She
opens her eyes, and sees the daughter of her neighbor float
above the bed in a blue veil~ The sounds of Allen's tinker are
so loud, and echo repeated, around her, the sounds crash yellow, orange, thick blue, silver, crash black, and purple, shiver
the normal lines of the rooming definitions, she closes her
eyes, nurses the headaches, he's burning on a new head, and
arm today — The torch sounds Viper, her head, she sees the
rabbit hole of broken mirrors she built, the little garden —
Secret place, somewhere ghosts won't go, the hollow, open by
flower, the house is haunted, the house is haunted/ She wakes
up, in sweat, looks at Allen directly. He grins, hovers over her.
I've got a new Mannequin. She breathes; he disappears, into
the cigarette smoke, she sits up, yells for Allen. Her voice
echœs through a larger house then this house, and no answer
comes, just the grumble from her lower lungs, until she gets to
her feet, rises, and sees   a family of Czechoslovakian woman
around the bed.

Sees the jars, thinks that money should be a tiny bottle that can easily shatter. With little glitter, and holograms inside of them, Buddha and Jesus, instead of presidents, and Dionysus — Threads of luminescent arms entangled over the house, orange cardboard piles up out on the road, oranges, pencils, dyed dogs paws, and tails, purple and blue Mohawk — Someone shouts this: look what it's done to my teeth, all of this travel, and red bull, and rock stars, my bag is full of drawings, they yell, I couldn't find my toothbrush, but I found a paintbrush.

The house slows to a gas pump, Love you guys, love you all She whispers, staring out the window at the gas pump. (HAGHEAD), (BEGBEDBAD), (CAB CAGE), (DEAD), (EGG ED), (ABBA)

Mona Del Rey plays on the old radio. The slow sickness, red gas jug, at her feet fills with gasoline, a dream, lost in Greenland plays through the window, little morning elves dressed in grey cloth stand in the window in Greenland, they keep songs, as the gasoline fills the gas jug. They are drawing on the windmill, She turns, and sits down at a sad bar, hangs in her drink, she thinks about how it must have been the nightshade, and remembers vomiting on her jeans, at midnight~

[Noon Uu.]

Allen pulls out a pair of lacy, black underwear from the bag he has, full of mannequins, and moves around the statue, sneaks the underwear over the plastic tœs, up, along the rubber calves, the thighs, to the crotch, snug ~ he unscrews the top of the head and she hands him the motor, a small metallic cube, with six strands hung out of the open skull. He raises it to the mannequins head, inserts the motor components into a chiseled out portion, inserts the tubes, lowers them by hand, into the facial cavities he had hand dug. She watches through bergamot tea, he reapplies the top of the head with its long,

11

fake black hair.

[Noon Nn.]

Straightened up neck to head, wobbled with power line images crossed crisscross, she just woke from an alligator dream, feels sideways, head full of overlapped conversations, a radio plays flowers, yellows, pearly whites, lavender Allen, she hasn't seen him in weeks, but she can hear the ratchet, the drill, it makes her head feel wrong ~ On the radio they are speaking in tongues, in butterflies, migration through the living room, building, cocooning everywhere, the patterns in Oaxaca, Mexico, New York, she sees, tunes her head with her left nostril, and picks her nose to mess with volume, and turns up her head, flicks green latex paint at the ceiling every five, and fifteen seconds ~ That's how she gets the idea to paint the kitchen nook two separate shades of avocado green.

*

In the shed, she gathers up the supplies, and stacks the clocks under her arm, wanders back to the reading nook. Power lines grow animated gardens through the sidewalk, down the telephone poles, into cars, and around the base of poplars, the swimming pool is jet black, with mannequin parts, and telephone wire, which float around counter clockwise ~ The sky grows thick with the power lines, crisscross, so thick, the house is covered in night, the trees, concrete, her head is heavy, and aches as she staggers, throbs into the reading nook, in there the radio soothes all interferences soft, almost at a whisper, the voice of the newscaster dissipates to galaxies, star belts, softly untangles the wires of her hair into midair, the whole city of New Orleans, Over Canal, and Bourbon, all tourists, and transplants, all of the locals, everyone who had watched the cables turn the streets black, watch as she watches them rise off of the surfaces, they had lodged in, and fly away ~ The whole skyline grows thick with intersections of power lines, where a dance party starts, and drinks are brought out, to celebrate that headache rising to disappear ~

She stands over the reading nook, and watches wires snuck into the teacups, and under the table cloth lift up and rise away, escaping briefly in the cracks of the paint, and window casings ~

Allen still saws, hacks, drills, and hammers, as a long black power line stays in the air before her~ wiggling to second guess an area of her which may be entered into, she's exhausted, and sits at the nook and rests her head ~ The wire will go away, she thinks.

| **Eledumare** |

God
{noun proper interjection }

One of the names of God
Oruko olorun

[Noon Ee.]
REPEATING TIME / SPACE, POSSIBLE DISORIENTATION
OCCURS (THIS HOUR HAS BEEN REMOVED, PLEASE
REFER NOON Ee.)
[Noon Ll.]
Every escape in the house has been marked with a bowl of
fresh flowers from the garden, they have been arranged to look
like arrows to where, and when. Allen gets off for lunch to the
basement, storm doors, and front door, all of the windows
wide open. She is sleeping next to a vase of Brugmansia flowers, those white devil flowers, long tentacle like vines draped
onto her hands. She is sleeping in the living room in the pool
'float,' with a tea cup, her sun bathing outfit, sunglasses. When
she wakes every now and then for a spot of sunblock, Allen
closes a window, and she barks orders, and lifts her shades. He
knows she won't remember any of this, and fall asleep. It will
take some time before he can get to work on his new mannequin, this makes him furious, and he closes the windows and
doors anyways, calculated, and timely, each swoop. Visions
of the floor turning to mush begin here to come into shape
around his tiny calculated steps, he starts to wonder if the roof
has been leaking green, and wooden liquids, blank waters,
liquefied barcodes?! He sees a Panda, and a unicorn covered in
tiny sequins, the two animals stand over her, chewing a pillow
with her voice in it, as she puts sunscreen on her shoulders.
She lowers the sunglasses, smiles, and says: Now you know,
Allen.
[NOON Ee.]
REPEATED TIME SPACE. POSSIBLE DISTORTION ERROR
HOUR HAS BEEN REMOVED (REFER NOON Ee.)
[Noon Dd.]
She walks in back, to the pool, and stands naked with blood
red dress in her hands. The green swimming pool ripples
her reflection, marbled face, and pale shoulders. She dresses,

and jumps into the water, the red cloth slowing down around her, bubbling beneath her breasts- the banging in the nearby mannequin factory rumbles low, as she watches the dress float up to the surface, the blurred fabric, detaching slow from her skin; the information of early computers loads up and coarse through the water, squid memories chew into the computer code, slow men Walk along with buffoon taint haircuts, they look at her body, memories of octopus, and rumba drums of the mannequins drifted down into line, on the belt, the octopus entangles pieces of her dress, and for a moment, she cannot fight much, the octopus fades back to the soft red fabric, at the surface of the pool.

A dripping, alkaline dream, a wire lace, organic, literally hair and broccoli swimming, strands of song take to rising up the hills, leaning into its water, to swerve along the symbols, is her, and an alkaline kiss, floating away, the lips to the tops of the banyan trees, an eagle, lips, being wires, bent straw hat kiss, permanent, still see through, too, waver like feedback guitar on the horizon, frequency, puckered back into the sky, along a wire -

There were knots in the way that the ocean tied a part of the clouds to a kiss, a sunburned lining to those crustaceans on the walls, the night, out there, walking into the rain, the drawings drift passed of a black panther kiss in our window, panthers we are smiling underwater, and longing for those long tongues, they longing for panthers grip, and grip tight, just enough focus to continue playing as children in the clouds ~ A paper boat drifting away, were existing chances, realms within the wallpaper, or down   in the purple liquids of the panthers liquid tongue, frozen outside, and hermit crab, and horse, too, shaved, in fishnets, down there, in sexual language, symbols not dolls, not people, just really down there, inside, safety, hiding the fury us black panther kiss feels, so, in time, after string disintegrated, and broken down next to the sun, laid to decay.

As in; forgotten, eyes open underwater, exciting loss of old poison bubbling to the surface of the water.

[Noon Uu.]
REPEATING TIME/SPACE DISTORTIONS ENSUING (HOUR HAS BEEN REMOVED (REFER NOON Uu.)

[Noon Mm.]
TIME OF DAY MISSING (PLEASE REFER TO NOON Mm.)
| Noon Aa.|
Hour Has been Repeated, (Refer to NOON Aa.)
[Noon Rr.]
Allen's at work, she dresses in rags, and wanders downtown to Canal. Her pocket-change-hat has a few coins in it from last time, she makes her way, noticing only the corroded sidewalk where live oaks root, and break through ~ A gang on bikes rolls up to the pool, and sees the floating trash, of unrecognizable mannequin parts, their bodies ruffle the trees around them, one in pink, gold and glitter smiles. Let's jump in!

[Noon Ee.]
The room is picture frames - gold, Victorian, silver, Roman, Latin, wood. She's been obsessively hanging the frames all morning, since Allen set off to work. He builds arms, and feet at the mannequin factory ~ she had been delivered a five pound bag of organic dark roast coffee later in March - and decided on it this morning first thing, at 5 a.m. A box in the attic she pulls down, labeled Maggie's Artwork in black --By April, she has the living room so that picture frames hang from the ceiling, mirrors block all entrances in the living room, couches are stacked precariously by color, green, to black, white to beige. The mattresses are piled all of the way to the roof, mirrors angled to reflect areas of the room make them seem larger than they are, ropes are tied out of the clothes

from inside every drawer, and every dresser in the house has been brought out and set up in triangles in the middle, so as not to pass. By the time Allen gets home from his job building arms, and feet, she is lying on the bed against the ceiling, weaving a dream catcher out of old t-shirts.Beautiful slurry she got there, between her legs, and red, blue chewing gum commotion, sitting on a rubber microphone, orange chewing gum the sky passes on, using the ceiling, and green trees, forests, animal, plants, chips, I'll have chips, what kind of chips, puppets she plays with, smashing them into each other. She gets bored and leaves us puppets in the corner -- paper dolls is her new thing, then she says let's get a raccoon. Whittle a pair of socks, whittle a pair of hands -- whittle the woods, and whittle a branch, a necklace made of tears ; to store the local couch, the bones rattle above, no, I don't want to talk about that, look, I just want to talk about plastic, four with holes connecting holes -- waist, the found purple in the parking spot -- Cake in the crotch, in your crotch, cock dipped in key lime pie, a dinner of flying lessons, and lifting from beds to rooms, outer space --

| TV |

[Noon Tt.]
She labels each telephone wire, walking up, along magazine
St. between the live oaks, each is labeled with an alphabetical
symbol, much like braille, some code made up on the spot in
her head —

[Noon Vv.]
They have the mannequin do its first chores now, vacuuming,
taking out trash, organizing folders, even painting—
The garden is where Allen and her spend all of their time
now~ her planting azaleas, and garlic bulbs, holy basil (Tulsi)
and squash today — The mannequin is in the kitchen doing all
of their dishes from the past year. Allen gœs inside for an hour,
and she gets done planting, and lounges around the pool (now
growing ferns in its waters.)

|SHE|

cut it out

On bundled fuchsia, the big, pink, and purple ligaments of
straw ink, all German green, gorging the dripping seeds spilled
on the silverware; her hands fingertips down her white arms,
holding up the great American Idol. She holds a wad of 100
dollar bills, all together in a strip of tape, and lights the stove
with gasoline. Gorging on the fuchsia, she cries, staring at the
peach colored thread of the loveseat, and paints herself all
of the way white, thrashing in panic, paranoia, seizures, and
throws the perfectly wrapped hundreds in the large flames, her
hands shaking; crumpled to a bowl of flowers, she rubs red
paint onto her hands, washing in the flowers, and puts on a
daily outfit of brown, chestnut tattered rags. She dœs her best
to make her hair nice, but the red paint makes it difficult, and
dirties her more. She wanders outdoors, begs men for money,
her hands shake a tan hat with a few coins in it. A number of
white trash scuba divers float in the backyard, in a few feet. Of
water, little neighbors roller-skate by, giving each other a ride
on the refrigerator, and on the phone, with little gurney they
pull alongside full of telephones. The roosters peck on the tape
recorder.
Cut

[Noon Ss.]
Allen comes home, and takes down an enormous bag of mannequin parts from his shoulder; he sees a note on the table,
and picks through the newspapers for it. I've gone to canal St.
to rustle up some money for our mannequins motor, love and
kisses.

[Noon Hh.]

She wakes up in the middle of the afternoon, terrorized that
the house is haunted — the sound of Allen tinkering in the
mannequin room echœs into a bending pitch, and she closes
her eyes, see's syrup drip down a classic '77 Chevy Nova
window; brown, maple syrup, in long lines to the hood of
the car~ She opens her eyes, and sees the daughter of her
neighbor floating above the bed in a blue veil — The sounds
of Allen tinkering are so loud, and echoing, and repeated, it
appears around her, the sounds crash yellow, orange, thick
blue, silver, crash black, and purple, shivering the normal lines
of the rooming definitions, she closes her eyes, nursing the
headaches, he's burning on a new head, and arm today -- The
torch sounds Viper, her head, she sees the rabbit hole of broken mirrors she built, the little garden — Secret place, somewhere ghosts won't go, the hollow, open by flower, the house
is haunted, the house is haunted/ She wakes up, and sweating,
looks at Allen directly. He is grinning, hovering over her. I've
got a new Mannequin. She breathes; he disappears, into the
cigarette smoke, she is sitting up, yells for Allen. Her voice
echœs through a larger house then this house, and no answer
comes, just the grumbling from her lower lungs, until she gets
to her feet, rising, and sees a family of Czechoslovakian woman
around the bed.

Sees the jars, thinks that money should be a tiny bottle that
can easily shatter. With little glitter, and holograms inside of
them, Buddha and Jesus, instead of presidents, and Dionysus
— Threads of luminescent arms entangling the house, orange
cardboard, piles up out on the road, oranges, pencils, dyed
dogs paws, and tails, purple and blue Mohawk — Someone
shouts this: look what it's done to my teeth, all of this traveling,
and red bull, and rock stars, my bag is full of drawings, they
yell, I couldn't find my toothbrush, but I found a paintbrush.

The house slows to a gas pump, Love you guys, love you all
She whispers, staring out the window at the gas pump.
(HAGHEAD), (BEGBEDBAD), (CAB CAGE), (DEAD), (EGG
ED), (ABBA)
Mona Del Rey plays on the old radio. The slow sickness, red
gas jug, at her feet fills with gasoline, a dream, lost in Greenland plays through the window, little morning elves dressed in
grey cloth stand in the window in Greenland, they keep singing, as the gasoline fills the gas jug. They are drawing on the
windmill, She turns, and sits down at a sad bar, hangs in her
drink, she thinks about how it must have been the nightshade,
and remembers vomiting on her jeans, at midnight—

[Noon Ee.]
The room is picture frames - gold, Victorian, silver, Roman,
Latin, wood. She's been obsessively hanging the frames all
morning, since Allen set off to work. He builds arms, and feet
at the mannequin factory— she had been delivered a five
pound bag of organic dark roast coffee later in March - and
decided on it this morning first thing, at 5 a.m. A box in the
attic she pulls down, labeled Maggie's Artwork in black — By
April, she has the living room so that picture frames hang
from the ceiling, mirrors block all entrances in the living room,
couches are stacked precariously by color, green, to black,
white to beige. The mattresses are piled all of the way to the
roof, mirrors angled to reflect areas of the room make them
seem larger than they are, ropes are tied out of the clothes
from inside every drawer, and every dresser in the house has
been brought out and set up in triangles in the middle, so as
not to pass. By the time Allen gets home from his job building arms, and feet, she is lying on the bed against the ceiling,
weaving a dream catcher out of old t-shirts.Beautiful slurry she
got there, between her legs, and red, blue chewing gum commotion, sitting on a rubber microphone, orange chewing gum

the sky passes on, using the ceiling, and green trees, forests, animal, plants, chips, I'll have chips, what kind of chips, puppets she plays with, smashing them into each other. She gets bored and leaves us puppets in the corner — paper dolls is her new thing, then she says let's get a raccoon. Whittle a pair of socks, whittle a pair of hands — whittle the woods, and whittle a branch, a necklace made of tears ; to store the local couch, the bones rattle above, no, I don't want to talk about that, look, I just want to talk about plastic, four with holes connecting holes -- waist, the found purple in the parking spot — Cake in the crotch, in your crotch, cock dipped in key lime pie, a dinner of flying lessons, and lifting from beds to rooms, outer space —

I write to you from the cranky neck of my wife (e.) The year is 1777, and Sasha enters obelisk geometries of Josie City, with a snail's pace —
She is biting me - Small, blurring German dolls, at the curvatures of her eyebrows; she is looking at the lake, it used to be a clock. We don't want to look at flat black, it's scaring her and me to sleep — Snail trails of chipped, gold skeleton keys daisy chain beneath her, amidst this "orangutan logic" she has tucked, and partitioned with laudanum. I rub my eye, and struggle to rub my eyebrows against hers —
The slime is a mauve, and golden reflection, displayed as multiple bulbs of light, they act in the way stars do, to retrace her steps; stars, so intent that she tucks deeper, unknowingly, as she lingers to a shop window, handling the skeletons in her pocket. I dream country roads until morning, on foot, finding poor, rusted housing —
  through research at a public Library (hidden in the back with the manifestos,) has written the most accurate account of my life. I find this out in the year 1666, through the Montague Publishing Archives.

| Noon Bb. |

Neighbor girls in white and cream throw a boy in the pool,
screaming at least once for ice cream, and kicking a scuba
diver, until a gift is issued, tiny geniuses, girl subacute, scuba
telephones, are finally starting to generate. Six clocks are
brought to a tool shed, behind the house (three black, two
white, and one red.) The moving company leaves the white
clocks stacked on top of the black ones, on top of the red ones,
and the shed doors are left open, so when she gets home, she
can see the many different time zones. She has made seven
dollars. In China this is pretty good, in Brazil she did okay,
even in Alaska not bad, but by the time in New Orleans, she
didn't make enough. Neighbors roller-skate by, and freeze, stop,
roll straight, bend, contort, back and forth gliding to the card
table in her lawn. Computerized by their own way of moving,
like glass shards, blocks, and interference, the neighbors forming more than one picture of themselves, a six car pileup in the
background, makes her neighbors rolling glitch movies as normal. Especially The Ventures song that plays, and the blonde
hair, a boy in a wrestling mask lights a firecracker, between
mirrors, glass shard like chunks of a computer glitch, gliding
the neighborhood, that generates around him explode slow.

[Noon Yy.]

The sky is yellow all over town, like a pollutant was dropped
into the water, yellow fog courses up the air, rising out of yellow puddles, against a black and white version New Orleans,
and off, out of people's sweat, all day, as Allen works in the
factory, and she panhandles out of her change hat, on the corner, neon yellow covers the streets like playa dust of the dessert, at seven o'clock it makes national news as being a yellow
epidemic, and this is the entirety of everything has gone yellow,

same tone, texture, shape,. every hand to mouth, arms, legs, feet, the trees, the air, the plants, the factory, thoughts, sound, life. Yellowed~~ Ape trains, rushing through town, dividing mental street from shœs, and it's hard to feel like a beast in these shœs ~

The next week I find her grave (at the cemetery in Paris,) on my way to Prague to teach about the innovative filtration systems of the northern Gypsy, blending down from the bent silk and alignment all string ~ I meet Sasha the next day, in Germany, near a Doll factory, where Steffen and wheeler dolls are produced. She is reluctant to speak, but after some technical ranting on my part, she finally says her name, and this: "I will be home later." and "Don't worry about me now, I am doing research."

There are hands Ivan found, painted white in the hospital, lounged plump, abandoned to a field, where the path smells like winter spruce, dangling from ropes, as fine as the razor wire used to keep out the blind from rummaging for manikin legs –

Sasha follows me back to Paris, sitting on the train car directly after mine.

In those days, groups of suited swimmers threw all night parties with fine cigars –

Mimosas, and manikin footage, where in, a group of swimmers lounges drunken, under black water, sharing smoke over the legs of heads, of hands, or feet, dunked vintage with the manikins–

[Noon Xx.]

Allen builds a xylophone out of the remaining parts of the house mannequin, using motors from old clocks, and the one from the head to make turbines that spin. He tries it, is surprised how calm he feels, how the songs ring out like a gymnasium or a coliseum, off he stares at the heads of the other failures bent in the corners, hanging arms and feet, and hands. He thinks to play Philip glass.

[Noon Zz.]
She walks home, through the puddles, covered in yellow paint, and her husband is outside. He plays the zither, and smiles, to say welcome home, this is your home, I love you, dear ~

When she makes love to me, a dream of buried clocks tick underground. Women dressed in white, paint their faces with leaves, using black ink until the perfect circle covers noses, and eyes, mouths, earlobes, jewelry. That had been deconstructed by secret society, the known Walther's White Winters -
Her body is a connection device, pouring essential oil into my skin, an inescapable vortex of clocks, both ticking forwards, and at the reverse back with time, pouring snow. Little pockets of the group still exist today; even an exploration to the first hotel (since boarded) takes place off of the coast, in a small town in these dreary folded papers—
The theater and its coordinates cannot be discussed here. Most of her subtle gestures seem derived from a past lover, and I fear, as I am falling in love with her, I am falling in love with her past.
Leather rose is the entire clue -
I move to Italy, and then to America in 1670. First to skirt back a bit, and curtsy, for in the lights at one's binoculars -

[Noon Pp.]
She and Allen wake up at dawn. They put on their clothes, and forget to eat breakfast; they have two cups of coffee, and walk slowly to a place where they had become the river, where their bodies met the steel plant, and cry, loosening those tears to the rust, and dirt of the steel mill ground. Allen Notices it first, but dœsn't say anything about it ~ she lollygags on a broken train

trestle for a good long time.

Look, Allen there's a piano in the river, there. She shouts. The tipped over Honor lay crooked, green Algæ paints its lower half ~ the white keys all tan and black.

[Noon Qq.]

Allen's at work again, at the mannequin factory. She floats quietly underwater, in the black ink of the power lines, and feet, and hands, and head of the Mannequin parts, the squid floating up to wrap around a mannequin leg, sinking it down around where the seahorses gather. The grey clouds above dump out rain.

I meet Sasha in America, in a hostel in New York in 1672. The hospice of the heart must be warmed before its valves close up, and cool.

She, like me, is trying to escape something not worth discussing. Shared thread, a bony eclipse, those shuffled rooms, turning, turning, and on the perfect English argument, salt shoulders. Check, change the channel. Flowers, bee, and conversation with the grass –

We, instead wander New York together, finding objects: little forgotten remnants, scraps of the morning paper, and pieces of the city left to rot.

Hold that thought: next, a white channel it takes, shuffles, flips, next channel, the room, the waking room, the dark piled underwater, and magazines – a shared voice, one yelling—

[Noon Ff.]

She wakes up in a room sewn together, tween the stitching hang feather, cardinals, male duck feather, and goose, and raven. She's got a cranky glare, and sees the goose feather through a murky blur, and a yawn, stumbling to what used to be a kitchen for an orange, she counts her steps, and watches the floor mold away and crumble, folding, and dissolving to

white beach. It is the sound of her laughter that shocks her
more than the room turning to sand that shocks her ~ the light
of its exact sound, cutting in a soft violin shape, through the
beach -- The bird calls of a sparrow echœd down, through a
hallway, same doors to a small, granite courtyard -- two lions
on their sturdy hinds, holding bowls of koi fish in their paws ~
and one echœs that follows the stairs, clocks as they casually
generate time, until she has caught each sparrow in her calls,
and secured each wall. We make collages out of these objects,
and feel we have fallen in love again.
In an oak chair waking up from a long dream –
In Love together for months, every morning, every night, and
sometimes three times in the afternoon, we imagine clocks,
ticking underground, until they tick over all of my dreams. Cat
masks and candelabras in the chimney singing song fires –
In the mornings, we drink coffee at a small table, the one we
found in the alleyway behind our cheap tenant. Before the
echoing chambers, emerging open, before the echoing chamber
releases its hourly pink signal, the rooms wait, sleeping, and
the first flake of lead paint cracks from the ground floor, in the
foyer –
After some time, I have forgotten why I left Paris in the first
place, sucked, abnormally deep into my dreams.
The shattered hands, delicately shifting around in a circle, on
the floorboards –
We make love for days, we eat nothing but rice, and garden
tomatœs she grows. A shot out window – hunks of plastic
wrapped faces, and torsos being staggered in a configuration
that is well fitted to comet – Smashing me into the stove, the
wall, crushing my pocket watch under her foot, she cries in
pain, and blames me for her loss of happiness. Fluttering in the
eastern clock –
I lose touch with my body for two whole days, transfixed in
mid air, above the bed.

Shape shifting at subzero, inside caverns, all blue electric signs from scatterbrained refuse, and junk yards, as in butterflies patterning from the cages of felt button down vests, we hung in the stalactites, around the origami quartz, ruby, and amethyst, dreaming. Shattered glass boxes, triangles for storage, things like shells, elephants moseyed with the first man along here, the first man who can paint, the sides of his shoulders, a Victorian curtain hung, with little golden fleur de Lis, a velvet rose, and argyle steps beneath him and his elephant, they complain their lips are burning from spices -- An igniting of triangular glass releases the electricity into scattered minerals, floundering in the air, like fish slow motion beneath the surface of the quartz -- this blue light, in three tons of neon, liquid, and sky, the cavern illuminated by it, it projects a video; I am seen in a van with two friends, and a dog, and a hermit crab. We are in Florida. My amethyst crystal flies off of the roof as we cruise down the highway, the van screeches to a halt, we look on the highway for the stone, and find a garbage bag of fossils, and a skull. And I decide to move to a place away from cities, where Amethyst grows under the mountains.

The signal draws a ghostly party at the swimming pool, west wing –
We make love slowly in the air, starving, caught in moving recordings, as higher levels in 02, and moving objects –
Never leaving the apartment, Sasha, and I stop exploring, we stop paying rent on the apartment, and one day the landlord starts knocking, so Sasha barricades the front door, and says we enter, and leave through the window, through the fire escape.
A talk show of European grays with three of the output/input RCA computers glitch, and signals interrupting heart beats –
We only leave at night, and she begins shoplifting. Headset's

feeding back with violin, harp, prepared guitar, and 5:00 a.m.
I find food in the trash, and we eat again, struggling to lift one
of the white arms to the nose, there in one corner - One meal
a day, moves a mirror - She gœs out for a week, and I don't
see her. After a week of sleeping alone, I wake up, and she is
hovering over me. Oh, on string -
She demands nothing more than peaceful rest, and kisses me
on the lips, her skin smells of Patchouli and frankincense. We
fall asleep together, arms wrapped, a cocoon of ticking dreams.
Now the feet lift from the floor boards, (bend he the jacket,)
and the tail feathers crawl their own string, and a man above
the room (floor four) with hands in reflections, all the many
masquerades the room makes and has witnessed -
She holds a mirror before my face, feeds me medicine beneath
the mirror, and will not look at me,

I get an internet connection and send this pœm out in haste:
Drugs, New Orleans --
--- _____

_____ &&&&&&&&&&&&&&&&&&&&&&&&&&&&&&&&&&&&&&
&&&&&&&&&&&&&&& && ^^^^^^^^^^^^^^^^^^^^^^^^^^^^^^^
^^^
^^^^ ---
--- !!!!!!!!!!!!!!!!!! (!) !!!!!!!!
!!====
{&&&&&&&&&&&&&&&&&&&&&&&&&&&}# # # # # # # # # # # # # #
#
3333333333333333333333333333333 (((((((((((((((
((+) ....
....
.......................))))
))))))))))))))))))))))))))**** **

```
*************************   _____   _____
_____!!!!!!!!!!!!!!!!!!!!!!!!!!!!!!!!! !!!!!!!!!!!!!!!!!!!!!!!!
!!!!!!!!!!!!!!!!!!!!!!!!!!!!!!!!!!!!!!!!!!!!!!!!!!!!!!!!!!!+++++++++++++++++++ ----
-----------------------------------------------------------------------
---------------------------- --------------------------------------
------------------------------------------------------------------- $$$$
$$$$$$$$$$$$$$$$$$$$$$$$$$$$$$$$$$$$$$$$$$$$$$$$$$$$$$$$$$$$$$$$$$$$$$$$$$$
$$$$$$$$$$$$$$$$$$ ==============================
==============
```

elegant wrinkle in the universe to heal my wounds.

A curve of wife, cruel storm of shadows, a thousand images they wet by in a dream and take away your headache, the storm crawls near on electric alligator switchblade that the wife holds dear to her black mass, a collapsing shadow box there in her chest of oranges and rainbow antennæ, as in a deeper thirst of rose thorns and barbed wire and electric lines, her power is but a massive growth she has learned to carry, and watching her eyes roll back while she is destroying with her trimming scissors neatly plucking at the dead leaves of those trees, to stray here is the wandering heart she cannot yet destroy in full, because tarp shaped clowns wander up St. Claude watching the hours at great clocks made of tin foil and shœlaces, sheep skin and barnacles. A curve of the wrist, creole tongues lapping at the great water, tinsel, fish, pearl medallion drooling America, and neon, and blue hair from their stomachs, their shrimp guts, their intestine, baked in flour, flopped and grilled, and fried and powdered. A yellow righteousness, crazed, insistent on gravy, and winning cheap shots of neon, and America, and blue hair. spin wheels rotating fabric space, thin circles round and round

[Noon Ww.]

The mannequin is causing a lot of raucous in the kitchen, accidentally slamming plates, shattering bowls on the wall, and dropping glasses, while trying to run programs for breakfast that Allen had input ~ Allen and his wife stumble into the kitchen, in their underwear, and smoke sizzles out of the mannequins motor ~ Spinning the 90 pounds of rubber, metal and plastic in overloaded circles. A sound of overworked lawnmower motors is heard and Allen shouts something in computer language she can't manage, and the mannequin stalls, to a halt, dropping the crock pot into a thousand porcelain pieces, little, gathered leaves she has chewed, to help heal my wounds. Shotgun holes through that one –

big white swooping throwing wheels, rotating, revolving and the place spins passed, hair all a retard.

Curling snack, snack, snack, snack, curling ron-dez-vous, and let it be known the turns, trigger fine hairs, speak a language under umbrella laughter, curling back a cloud or hay, a chimney or a mule, for a fourth night in paradise.

I haven't gotten a response back. So I continue.

Shape the name in a small glare of legs in statues through window blinds

Legs of a runaway circuit raising a small confusion that marks purple lines in the rocks of the shore -- for a history. The fan blades another kind of parade already on the way as a centipede of laughter through a hundred legged puddles landing horizontal in their gloves --

After cars collide, two nights with a coy fish spinning in my gloves, along the wrist of the afternoon, I am dealt a hand of sunlight and am drinking the moon --

And all of their ugly mirrors angled with the fishes, a language of wires, a tucking\

and intersecting of birds, a welded line of futures at the dripping-cloth-tongue all guessing and flannel and wooden -- Spiral down electric neckties, electric eye glasses -- To sew the night together at last

A beautiful, normal space and corner in time as well as the persona standing perched

at your front door -- you've made your mask and you smile inside this cloud and swim an eel infested distance.

Butterflies to down syrup ~ elongated in hologram -- blinking blue , red, neon feathers to stray --

-- TWO FISH -- To sew the night together, we need a rewinding hat, with an operating rodent on board, to get inside of the machine -- We will need (among other hanging objects) a heating device, in which long strands of egyptian time may be pulled, thumb piano players all around the curtain room are playing Mozart, Bach, and Chopin -- Zeppelin, AC/DC, and Megadeath -- their masks blur at the edges of the room -- glowing ribs, and skulls, and spines -- We may need (among other, hanging objects, two double long bicycles, stacked with working (and yet glued together) radios, with antenna.

The sea will be our music (in at once,) splashing so forth, a mist of shanties along the glass bottle, and a ship for us inside -- hinges -- and door frames, wall paper, and galoshes for everyone aboard -- those who entertain the idea will be offered great woolen blankets, and a new pair of garments: shœs, and socks, powdered, first. Included are the radio bicycles...

(among other hanging things) which will spin the tale of the fish, and the water bearer -- the love entangled web of their story, to the sea together -- A dress -- a rabbit -- masks-- a russian hat -- ties -- wool shirts -- necklaces -- and a harp -- Orchids -- sprays -- acrylic paints -- blankets -- bracelets, and jackets, and shœs! All will march in a parade of misguided watches!
To sew the night together, we will need to gather a bit of chalk for an overall outline of the moon's light, and subdued cubes, those sugars that drop, and dissolve near my boat in the lakeside -- by watching the curve of the swamp, and move of the frog, we will sew the night together at last -- Galoshes, and Russian hats for this night -- naked, amidst the neon making legs and arms and
handles of napes and necks out of knees and with neon tube, the whole lot of the night floating boating, and glowing every surface lined in color. Green to be blue, and sewing with Sewing Bee Orchestra on the barge, buried behind us, lovemaking neon lights -- all sewing together the edges, and fabrics, and colors of the night at last --
In the beginning of the shape -- of an elongation -- a fleur de lis, a lock of hair spinning -- trying to make clouds out of trumpeting horns and shattering drums --
Terms: _____ THE SEA: A deep consciousness, closely related to that of companionship, a feeling that overwhelms the lovers. friendship. HANDLES: "mustache with particularly lengthy and upwardly curved extremities; a shorter version is named

the petit handlebar." HARP: "a multi-string musical instrument which has the plane of its strings positioned perpendicularly to the soundboard." TO SEW: to insist, and create a change that is irreversibly beautiful, and perfect in every measurable way for human and all other existing animal, mammal, fish, frog. Cow, Snake, Rat.

Notes: Dream Journal Excerpt (no. 1) _____ A dark black cobblestone french quarter, where I was able to sneak back into my hovel, and wake early to the streets, with police passed out at bottles of Vodka, and beer, snoring while cats hopped passed and shuffled. Strangers lurked -- where I could even meet Brandy [Meesh ' ka] at a dark courtyard around the cobblestone street, near shops that opened up and a mechanical shapeshifting color animal rode on tracks, [around the dark abodes, on cobble stone pathways chasing cats and a girl all pale made me feel safe at the inside of an old,] french museum -- I could even sneak into hovels there with the furniture of victorians, all welded by hand. In the shadows of the ornate dream town -- This place was not a place for fears but for us who could cross into the night. A London maze where spirits could hide in houses no longer forced to commiserate in the cobble streets.

_____ The pale girl was happy to tell of all her most secret of sculptures and artistry's, as well as her best hiding places for us other creatures --

Waking to the sound of bulldogs, we notice a cat entering the squat on Rampart. Brandy says God sometimes uses animals to wake us up, and I say no it's the cat they're barking at. "This is a cat squat." I think.

[

The wallpaper, peeled everywhere (must have been caught in hurricane Katrina.) Old boxes of tools, [can] see to the second floor through slats - paint chipping like old roman paintings

- light comes in through white sheets molded over the doors, broken windows. Cat piss smell and old chairs stacked by ghosts, and holes in the floor everywhere, leading to a room in the other shotgun. A stack of encyclopedias is the most exciting thing i've seen in a long time... What used to be a fire place.]

The white cat sneaks to this area (...) ceiling caved in, at the back house, knocked out walls we enter through -- Brandy and I wrap in jackets, and sweaters for warmth, hold each other tight, breathing on each other for an organic heater.

We sing a song in our heads, while roaming the streets until we separate. Drunk on gin, I yell: "Pœm for a quarter!" on lundi gras. "Let us hear it." A man and his wife say.

Esplanade Clouds

Oh, how do we tie our hair in the dollhouse windows, to the cat, a length all philadelphia telephone wires as branches, our cedar ties the hair back in a willow rosetta, ornate forget me nots, around bristle spirals, winding one hand through our hair even in the sea at the epicenter, french iron work, weaving with algæ, the eye of the storm, a hurricane of celtic cats, ornate cats through our hair - tied back into pigtails in one long ponytail to the sea, and the moon --

(2014) New Orleans, Louisiana

We write letters, hers postmarked 1777, mine 1666. I begin to believe I have lost my mind. Or the postman has made some kind of mistake, or she is playing a trick on me. But still a good mask –

I spend all of my time between composing, stealing liquor, and cigarettes. Hallways flurry, puffy, cookie, birdie nests, fight, flight of white beak, and raven, into Atticus –

I purchase, with the last of my money, a small parcel of rat poison, and stamps. That when the recording crew entering with boxes, tapes, computer wires, screens, chests of cable, two way radio, antennæ –

I talk to no one, haunted at every movement, every shadow
my hands cast, I begin to write the letter while the place grows
bored, wants only to rest, and wither behind me at its equipment, away from the Microphones aimed at the memories—
The rat poison glistens, dead black in the circumference of
the small bottle: danger, Poison, skull, and crossbones. Do not
drink. The liquid is flat, and empty. The way I feel (but worse
because it has the potential I am unwilling to venture through,)
I must get away. I must write the letter and hideaway for an angel in the morning, with a queen of the costume room, change-
ling, withering, mirroring.

* * *

I've arrived at telephone booth, and with twenty three blurred
stars, lines, the ghosts of hands, gloves reciting an ancient Lan-
guor for strawberry, oranges, and apple. White dialing, from a
childhood crevice inside of a Lapiz, a black, a silver and very
marbled tongue that sews the seams of a fruit, verging even
now, on the silence of clocks, pasted to the bramble bush foreground, over taking the sky before near blindness, a clipping
occurs near climax, the clocks spread from the nozzle of spray
gun. Time, through chimneys, a friends house -- Bosnian card
tables, thick in claw paper -- always rascal dancing inside dog
costume, always witness, eroded blackberry pie -- a Christmas
grandma making soggy drumming rhythms, escaping ceiling
float, and slack jawed extras, new founded growths, a kind of
Russian gray, a rabbit hat, worn until a second death, looking
up and the left foot peaks squirming sound -- Falling through
table, classic in a drunk town, picked through the winning and
escaping into a dream -- this is the fold drunks ramble on for
three months about -- Jezebel, grown weary, pets geranium
with gloved hands. Armatures dance to center, the card tables
plush velvet --

A small shard of experience floats down on a floatation device, like snow to the island of very black Indian wolf festival -- a warehouse wolf wrestling -- doorway --
"This one girl wouldn't turn the light on."

Trying to do math homework -- A shellfish women enters the banquet -- she is me, helium gasping, all in an inconvenient placement of movie screen curly and straight bangs, and faux hawk and lounge cut, and dread lock, and fuzzy head, and blond long, and Rosy cheeks.
Watching Jack London, white fang drizzle particle over the wall in some comfortable dog's bed, the pillow divulges information proper spritzers and shopping malls with nerve gasm, and never ending roger rabbit --

White hands pick up marionette strings from an opening of clouds roulette wheel lands on the percussion, the higher lover in white Persian cat picks up prepared guitar, and the spinning curl of hairs come down upon the piano keys -- a glass eyed goggle head sways in, on wheels, a giant tanned bus ride, and the shadow show, in its first flight, begins. These all between the moon and the road -- a rolling through of six millimeter films, costumed in manic pixie dream girl -- Thirty five millimeter camera, and radios, and microphones. Paint sticks, and backpack full of magic paint -- on ward to dawn!

Shadow puppet, reaching for a pocket watch -- My name's Origami Ruesch -- I will walk you to the cake in the castle.

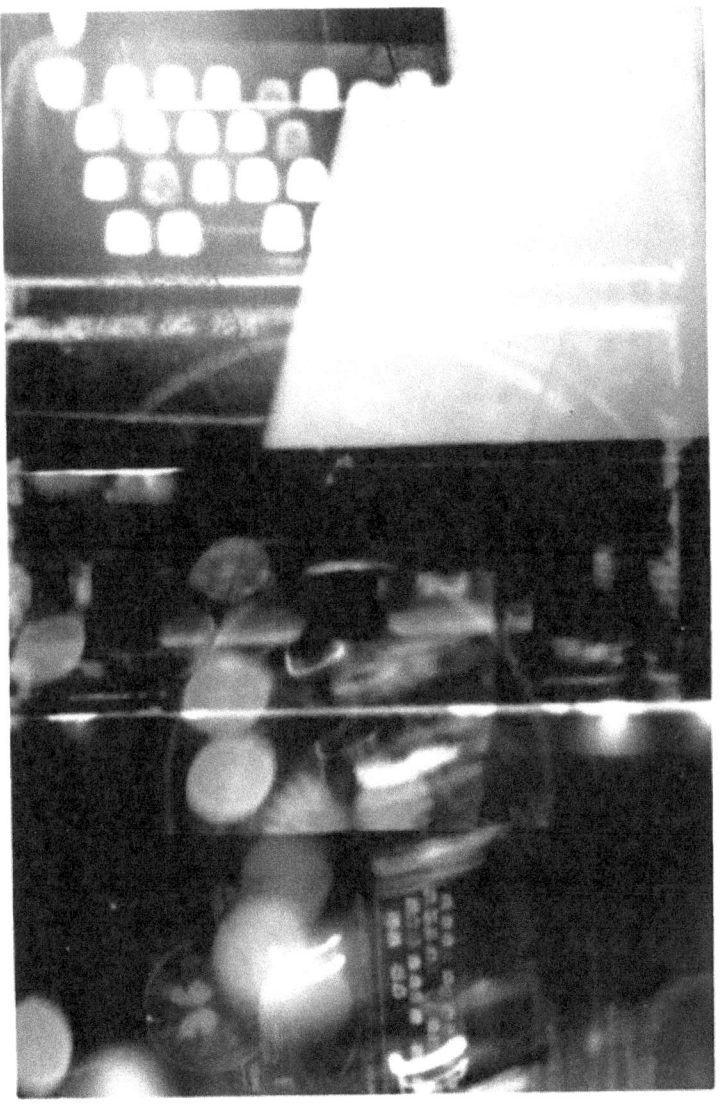

| Ex.plo.sion No.i |
The trick is to focus on tea poison, luminous in the fill of walls.

The liver sinks in honeycomb, tiled rooms across the zeros of fake skin, took notes on a tongue-ivory-conception.

Indentation
(n.)
Beneath the cream layer;
Note:
       machines at side are in place.

Within, is a stark rectangle, set kindly upon fox fur.

Join our hand in a single magic trick. This mad math; ozone layers touch fingertip layers, jello pressed molds build a bridge inside a hat.

News stands of denial, (Manny, stern in an upside down plot, to erase remnants of town,) Hung his hat at the distance of a firehouse, one long hand out of the window, strong odor perhaps followed him around [a ghost.]

Years grow down to the water, the time drinks.

| AIR SIGNAL |
Ice triangles hang from his lift, his pulley hand, a bench out in the park.
              A fire bird
rolls up on
the bike track.
Runner shorts in a blue "banana" (Rochester plates)

eyeballs -wrenches clients, learned zombie speak - out to the vertical undertakers; pulled clients to the hills, to paint their nails glitter, because cops hate glitter I.e: (glitter witch) nudged a bicycle onto the overgrown race track and shook down peeled oranges they have her stood in.

| air signal |
"The ways in which we are fashioned to town."
To adjust our levels, allowed clients said this signal has become as.toun.ding.
"All the money you made on that guiney pig race, their gonna bring out the whoop ass(...)"

I would really be interested in . deconstruct of this whole radio station. and with the help of other, more experienced aspects of myself, put the whole town back together properly.

I am under oath / sanctity.

An iron, mechanical body adheres glitter witch to this inferno— radio knob, for versions of her glitter window.

Glitter witch wants "play songs" spoken to the speaker,(Mind games)1 She has done this dance for (vertically) unknown hours, and arrangements, the beat of the hardwood against a spunout bike rim, She's seen this music corrode on the entire palace of rats a dozen times.

Fur hands reach toward (Mind games)1, to play one more time at the park, on 1600 Tower Blades.

The first rule, She imagines with Arnet glasses, hidden behind the wheels of the car, to establish residency in the woods. She could not decide the rules, as they were all vid-played backgrounds of the oak trees, but not the actual address, spun across the pond. She tramps through the overgrowth into the high hill of the park. The teenagers smoke and throw their butts into the water. Pink blurs camp on her side-view-mirror. Mountains must be explored, needles in the house, Glitter-bitch needs to remember a hundred storefronts.

The time is correct on the control panel, this too has contorted magic over our mind, this also plays a game with our emotions, dealt out hours, pulled in ropes to moments~

Our mind game is frozen, a box of frozen toys drifting along the tank, fish tank, the tank.

Glitch-niche will find the cage that peels back the skin of the mind, to heal this erupted valve, deemed useless, forget-about, never-to-examine-more.

The Tables have Turned and Turned Forever, this is THEE examination, She dusts on the floor for prints, gears toward the illuminations of the past, 'forgot' is no longer in the partition of 'memory.'

This is too small to remember, the tapes on the D file are of interest ~

|| | || |}{-|||-}{|| ||| ||

General motion factors include: sinking in the suit – determining which coats, green drool, fortified in the mobster-monster. "Chest pocket of the rope coat, leave slack and a fringed ever-clear edge," this way sorting data from the over cocked silence will be as easy as "chairs stacking corners of the rooms."

Determine a frequency under the alpha delta spectrum, including theta rumination, which can be utilized for further stark, street looping, designed to factor in yelling points.

To turn down the room in radon carbonation, sub tropic layers are simply declined in mass boats, so that hoarding the shore (on a pinpoint of the first fractured shale retort) is a Lengthwise fragment blur, rising through the winds on a crossing day. We are zoomed in on, by one of the larger fraction equipment teams. There, lethargic, reunited, stale in our gloss jewelry, will find beneath the armpits a golden soil, like mud. Leak down narrow hallways of laughter and light, the remembering umbrellas of skylight orange popsicle cream that were once sun's drool, in the length of those holy, pressed walls, the luxury tastelessness.

That only once we can recognize the shape as being two dimensions flatter than the ozone (tired unhealthy from drugs.) To let the years into the equations, turn to its side, the ride in the boat to the shore line of frost bitten cheek bones, emerge throats and tongues without placement in the guts. Our harmony, underneath absolute bone line. Our marrow of the future, signified in dust what art was once able to express in us, this significance of darned socks and the line of our dreams. To the shape, we whisper elongated retina (of syllables) to free the gross knots in our consciousness. Forever tongue tied, behind the avenues of lace, park in lot number seven, or pale filigree designed in the fabric song.

That sharp glare in a limp of frogs tumble toward the horizon, half bleak neurology sudden in light cast. Form, (wrought iron symbolizes) that great fall, a moment from within, where hairs leave the stereo to the light of magnification (ten percent and beyond.) Pull in the lever of the clock to separate moments, torn between blurred glass. The sudden numeric frosted over with cigar stained fingers, peel away dimensions so they reveal lichen. The pattern language beneath, numbers which tell us the identification, which breed of light one might have stumbled upon. Nevertheless, drool sneaks off of a chin and the one who remembers drains ancient posits with a sneaky suspicion, dœs his job without notice of great diamond stance; spins mid center the chiseled concrete beneath, movements fascinate the mind. Arrived on all points within one snug on the fraction, a calculator that can be traced back to the origin, a musculature where all dances form and fray, and decompose with twist away, instead of through the next position on a mapped foot. One step aligns, then falls naturally to its side caught in three chances before stumble fairy fall directly underneath its space bounce. The dress flails up into the air, stagnant for a continuum, a misted ox water molecule. Spun out finch that dissolves to the ravenous facial feature, there we watch the growth of a man's beast eye; the slip down from the rooftop, and into shape in the local hamster festival room. The wheel spins (almost) already before we can ask to enter. The rug is one catch upon their fold arms, stuck in the sky; one leg removed of the pressure and curled beneath the other, one steadied now upon a knee and one that expels that bath of light before an extinguish device made of pure bird fraction, Explosive membranes that align chess game pieces to the mathematics used for repeat stimulation, white light that washes over an entire dance. Halos for all of its interact members, reclusive at first until order is presented in permanent modes. The days lead up to features, arguments, and room for one (/) all verified symbols in the group pattern language.

All steps had begun to take place right as the arm let down into the lake beneath concrete floor, some (asshole) had installed our break in the system Abraxas Druid Cooperation Dream. The one found object licked from the roof of the mouth, a pleasant moment, before the drool spread over the dance, and practiced each string of leak sound, to turn one hand awkward and into the face of the record device, pressed flat against our glass spread of cold skin. Not sight for this before, I had a hyper manic moment. I might flail towards her dynasty, undress my form and dance there in secret next to the plate glass design. Unknown beneath our nostrils, the far edges of the fraction, (which I hadn't explored as thoroughly as I had apparently rehearsed) in ADX Continuum. Repeated thoroughly from room to room. Turn to a room behind me, the ground I noticed seemed to grow food, small seeds poked through as the feet stamped into their aligned steps. Before years, there was this layer, this manic stage repose the dancer inside of her diamond.

1_____

Write a letter to yourself and secret enough so that you know what you know, you do not know what you do not know and make yourself blind in every secret, all faculties must whisper to keep a secret from you, the author of this letter, this package, yes it may as well be a full on package, but you must not know what it is there inside of it. Whip your mind into shape for the plastic coat it will be, suffer from this way you can be ready on the day a post office decides to open again and deliver you your own mail, sent to say Canada and then back to your house in say Arkansas. That would be a good place to send it. I want to teach myself to whisper all of my secrets into the jars I have impossibly hidden (yes) again from myself. So that I may play hide and go seek with myself. This may take some practice or some time, or maybe I should just shoot for (shakes head yes like good idea) Friday. Miserable soup fetish I've got there, some stark or an optometrist stationary I should dumpster some of that for this letter thing. I might not want to pay postage unless its really scary how good I hide things from myself while introduced to them. This might be me try too hard again, I might break some part of myself if I try too hard. I could use rubber bands for some, maybe I could connect them to a switch that adjusts the pen from another room, (or a pencil, paintbrush) I may still know what I am doing, the achieved goal would be that I have no idea what it is that comes in the mail. I don't want to waste time in written others because I know that they don't use it anymore (the post) unless they want some from me.

I guess I'll try a napkin for some, too. I'll cover my eyes with it? And try to plug my ears? Maybe, Oh! I got it. A record of me say gibberish! I could close my eyes, plug my ears and say gibberish. Or Oh, I know I'll put music on really loud and try to say a poem but the recorder can only hear me, then I'll take some drugs that say YOU CAN'T REMEMBER SHIT and I'll dial a number on the phone and then hang up and they might call back and I'll say I need drugs and hang up and they'll call back and yell stupid American cliché profanity at their iPhone and then they will dial the police and have the police trace my phone number and I will just get my mail when American cliché, while trying some astro-mental (sic).

Florida, 2014

Bizarre area no. 000.02

No trespassing

Le Acid Bar

Le acid bar. The restaurant sitting morphed, half caved in; one whole side sinks down, perched directly off of the main road in town. Neon flickers through half of the letters in the tube, spelling Le id bar in Persian cursive halogen. The dim walkway is lit up in front of the old building; the glow from the sign tapers off into a yellow street lamp on the opposite side of the highway.

An old cemetery, hidden behind rose bushes, and iron bars silhouette the skyline of old town. A group of hooligans walks passed the cemetery, holding up their pulsing lanterns as they go.

We arrive at 2:00 A.M. and decide on one of the booths tucked near the back, where the portrait of Jean Simmons, holding a cup of coffee, hovers on the wall. Behind us, two men talk slowly, and the waitress comes to our table, seemingly from out of nowhere. She looks like she is on fire in places, but her feet are still glowing in a stream of water, the only stream of water going through town, in here.

"What would you like?" The waitress asks me and my companion from a distant voice. It is as if she were standing on the other side of the room when she speaks, her voice echœs. Whispers come out of different appliances in the bar. I hold the menu up to my eyes and inspect the options.

"I would like four hits of," I pause and grumble to myself. And then I go on. "LSD 25, and one hit of your... Loony Tunes." I fold the menu closed as the waitress writes down my order on her pad, and then I set it near the right end of the table.

"And for you?" The waitress's voice asks from across the room, to my companion.

"I would like a stick of your hashish, ultra kind, and," She pauses. "A cup of coffee, to share." She folds the menu up and sets it on the table next to mine. The waitress looks at me.

"Anything else?"

"I'll have a club sandwich as well, no bacon, just Tempe." I say in a loose and relaxed manner.

"Okay." The waitress says. She picks up the menu's and walks into the kitchen area. I watch her (a flame blouse) pouring the cup of coffee. She reaches in the back and grabs a small white box, and opens it atop the refrigerator, pulling out five tiny sheets of matte paper and the creamer for the coffee. She grabs a napkin (that almost lights in flames) and a saucer plate, and sets the paper hits on top, with the creamer and coffee cup on a tray in the other hand. Not much conversation gœs on between my companion and I as we wait for our orders.

"Do you see that? Is she like on fire?" My companion whispers. I nod. Yes.

The waitress sets the coffee and creamer down next to my companion with the plate of LSD 25 in the other, along with the Loony Tunes.

"There you go. Enjoy." The waitress says to us as I look at my selection. The glowing paper calls my name. Waiting.

The atmosphere is nice, it is warm and tolerant. The only place to go at this hour, when projects are over, and the project minded folks come out of the woodwork, needing an extra boost.

"Loony Tunes have always been the better half." I say, still looking down at my doses that glow bright yellow now.
My companion sips her coffee slowly, and watches the people walking passed outside. She follows the lanterns with a clam expression, a look of casual longing.   The heat rises from her coffee in steam.

"Want one?" I say, lifting one of the 25's up in front of her.

"No thanks." She whispers, turning from the window to alnd her eyes on the front of the building, where she can watch passing lanterns.

"The hash should be fine." She says, then she settles back again in the red seat, squeaking the cushion and sipping her coffee as I throw the hit into my mouth, somewhat like a French fry.

"I'm glad they decided to carry this strain." I mutter under my breath.

"Over schedule, said you fined (guitar, drums, singing echœs) come on over to the river." a voice from the other end of the room. It is very loud suddenly in here. Every night about this time, people begin yelling to communicate.

"See what we can find out – What do you do, do you ever go to the headwaters and cross?"

"Nothing! I want nothing!" I shout, turning in my seat. The man directly behind me catches the burned, brunt of my voice, and cringes to the side of his red booth.

"Don't sit there!" I shout. I turn and pick up another hit from the napkin, popping the hit into my mouth. Now, there are two pieces of paper floating around in a fishbowl, sticking together, they make out with each other like two school children for the first time exploded out of proportion. They are two ugly kids. Their tongues flap around in aggressive ways, they have really goofy glasses, drool curves on their stinking lips, the braces show. I start to get disgusted by this image.

"Is there a little greenish man there? At the end of that tunnel, is he wearing a green suit or he just, is he drunk?" My companion asks me.

"What man? Nothing! I want nothing. Making out in my mouth here?"

She cuts me off.

"He's got a little-bitty refrigerator beside him. He is telling you to leave." She stares straight ahead.

"Get out of here, now!" He says.

She smiles and turns to chuckle to herself.

"What little man?" I choke out. My companion laughs quietly to herself. Her laughter echoes, blends with the music on an old guitar solo playing on a radio. I swallow the acid and watch the room shift up out of the ground, from where it is sagging, the window moves closer to me.

* * *

A little bit later the food and hashish sticks come, and both of us are laughing maniacally. The waitress gives an exhausted smile to us as she is setting the food down in front of me.

"More coffee?" She asks my companion, her eyes dodge me, a flame inside.   She is a perfect ten. Her body never reacts in reluctant manners.

"Thank you." Callie says; the waitress shows us her flaming back as I pile into my club sandwich. She walks away, into the kitchen and out of view.

"You got the lighter?" Callie says. She is holding up the hash-ish stick above her coffee. The waitress comes back and fills Callie's mug.

"A lighter?" I am confused by the question. My hand digs out pieces of paper, pennies, a broken pencil. I pull out a hat, a banana, three mice – who run off of the table and into gutters.

"Here you go." the waitress pulls a huge book of matches from her front pocket, and tosses them onto the table. It lands down like a dictionary with a loud bang. The utensils shatter about, forks and knives clashing into the water glasses.

"Thank you." Callie says. She picks up the book of matches and lights one of them. We are alone finally. The two men who had been speaking slowly have left. She lights the joint.

I drink some coffee, and watch the flame in awe. It is enor-mous, the flame is the size of a gopher.
"let's go to the cemetery." I say quickly, under my breath. She nods her head, yes. I pull out "twnety-thwee" dollars to pay with. My companion pulls out her "tewn" dollars, and we get

up to go.

We say goodbye to the waitress and she quickly blows me a kiss goodbye. Her eyes look similar to stones you might find lining the bank of the river. Her lips get closer to me as I walk to the door, and I close my eyes as the sound of the outside world closes in from all around me.

Concrete Animals

The disassembled madness of man; the mania of ferns driving
skywards – straight into the conscious abyss known only without
us, and with our dying, just as the rest of these dying things:
ferns rot, broken cars parked forever, the gravestones taken over
by moss. Lilting into the forests of mania, an incoherent spelling
contest, figuratively speaking a language: lost long ago.

We cross the highway, hunching down into the clearing of dark
weeping willows. We carry with us a giant nothingness, the
smokes I have stuffed deep down into my coat pocket. I can
feel an owl watching me move, I am a wooden man lumber-
ing through the cemetery statues. I stop and roll a cigarette, my
companion continues forward, nothing of a thought about leaving me behind.

The cemetery grows bright as I stop to smoke, lighting up in
stages (from the edge of the field first, it starts) moving and
shifting up to where I inhale the smoke. Waves of emerging sunlight where the sun is absent. The grass tingles under my boots,
moist, and catching sweat from my shoulders. From my feet, to
my neck, I feel all of the grass growing through me.

Callie moves up along a rising hillside where the abandoned
mansion stands, an iron megalith, hidden by the forest of weeping willow, eaten slowly by the earth.
In a frozen, statue position, with my hands to my sides I hear
her.

"Shawn?" Her voice finally reaches me, taking first the pathways
into the foliage, and communicating from the leaves. It is not
Callie's voice; she is farther out than that. I feel like collapsing
on the ground, to become it suddenly, to become the tunnel

before me inside of an instant; the white foam and fiberglass tunnel under the entire range of the cemetery.

"Shawn." I hear my name, the voice is pulling me out of this feathered, white tunnel.

"Practicing – I'm practicing."

The movement is light, Shawn can see it moving, so can I: lifting it from skies. Years, moving slowly into one moment that has already now passed. Shawn is in the plastic tunnel made from foam, sanded concrete, gyroscopic snake skin, pale boys, loose strings, old shœs...

I am lying in the grass upstairs.

"What is this here, is the sun coming out? Possibly..." There are three of them.

"You can't go back now." Three voices in different calibers. Ninety mops, dripping room, submerged under pockets of water, forty Q-tips dropped into a puddle, six hundred fingers dipping into a bucket of donuts: the blue bucket.

"Are you hearing this? Shawn? Are you hearing these voices? Different dungeons for different sounds – shapely records of water – This sound belongs to the voice of Catheline Hermington, a second grade school teacher who lived in this same town circa 1923. She was a wonderful woman, Shawn. She has a lower voice than this one." I pick up my smoke from where it fell in the grass next to a gravestone marked Susan Albanee. I peak into the grooves and almost get lost in the late 18 century molding, lost to the eyes in the cement.

The lighter is in my pocket. The lighter is in my hand. The

cigarette smokes in my mouth. I am standing up, I am walking toward the mansion tucked, eaten behind the woods.

A car gœs passed, behind me, slowly.

"Traffic is picking up here." Shawn thinks. I keep rummaging through my thoughts, and they are all leading me right back here, where this grass grows thin over Susan's gravestone. I look away, look down at my feet. I can see for months, for weeks I see; I have been walking, and walking, and walking, and walking.

"Okay, I'm gonna go forward now." I say aloud, breaking the fear and silence entrapping me; I pull my smoke back into me, inhale it, and my feet are moving rapidly, forward to the hill. Familiar headstones weave through my visions, visual representations of this happening, little films of what happens, holograms of videos of what happens –

McDonald's gravestone.

"I've seen this grave stone here before, haven't I?" Shawn thinks. I know differently though. Shawn seems to think, or he believes that McDonald's grave belongs to someone who died in nineteen-ninety two when."

"When, what?" One of the voices shouts, popping up from behind a gravestone and then ducking back away in a shredded bed sheet costume.

I am walking up along the steepest part of the hill.

It's orange o'clock when they order the rafts for lake explorations. Using a head mirror, each player experiences, from multiple angles, a pinstriped boat with numbers on the sides and white bench seats that open up as a mini refrigerator. The dissection equipments float in a green light, beneath: a stereotactic device, lancets, rasps, retractors, and surgical staplers, lined up, and floating to the surface.

Richter's head mirror glows. Pupil sectors, cut away for two knife throwing wheels, spin in black spirals inside of his head. A small operator rodent named Gosh operates the eyes with cogwheels and pulleys, using them in great might, and agitation. The wooden wheels spin once, and then Richter closes the lid of the refrigerator, and Percy steps into the boat from the dock where he had been standing.

Percy is a motor mouth; he uses the Pennington clamp to keep his flapping jaws closed, but it dœsn't stay snug enough. His jaws drool through the retractors, spin lyrics, breathe letters. He never "speaks into the microphone."

The two of them grab a pair of bandage scissors and snip the line of the dock. This leads to a TV splashing into the water, sizzling.

It's green thirty, and the boys are getting really thirsty for an Xos 2 Exoskeleton (leader of all exoskeletons) so they can drink. Not once has either boy seen or heard an Xos 2, but the operators manual makes specific reference to their whereabouts in this lake, and so they go, to hunt down an Xos 2 exoskeleton, to drink it up into their head mirrors.

Percy unpacks his box of cardboard, cutting it with a scalpel, and putting together one of those robot suits that astronauts wear. Richter stuffs his arm in the water and pulls up a wet, bleached mountain goat, setting it on the floor of the boat. He notices the lack of movement and gets an RF knife to do the job, cutting the sloppy, goat fur away. Revealed within is a fur explosion where Christmas lights piled under the whole inside fluff out.

One section followed by another, goat sends of string Richter thought were seaweeds light up in the water. Row after row of Christmas bulbs light the depths of the murky water, illuminating the entire lake bottom in yellowing seconds. The goat starts twitching, and Richter puts the RF knife and bandage scissors in the air. Percy flaps his jaw, repeating a common phrase of the region: "Hammers tucked in conversation!" he mutters in the robot suit.

He has just fashioned a whole astronaut suit out of cardboard, and begins doing a celebration dance, awkward left and right, robot booty before falling off of the raft, his helmet part hits the arm rest, and lands inside of the boat.

Richter looks down into the water at the headless robot floating away into the thousands of Christmas lights, and then he lifts up the robot head from the planks of the raft, inspecting its sequins Percy taped on all around the mouth and nose. Richter makes a noise, like approval mixed with a kind of oblivious muttering, and through the glowing lake bottom, Percy watches as Richter begins putting on the helmet, careful of the poking tuna cans that the ears are made of.

Traffic Jam

I would call her Taylor, because black hairs draw toward the curve of her lips and edge into the miles between us - But instead I curtail a whimsy, freak out the neighbors by dressing my cat in an armor of arrows, go outside, into the suburbs, dressed in my fag dreams, and search for purple, learning the arithmetic of streets my art teachers taught me - and curving down the avenue of Toasters, big loaves of bread slide up from inside, all around us -

Meeshka wants some of the toast and jumps up and down, clanging the arrows stop motion. Odd for a cat -

"No Jumping!" Med.z Tony says.

I pull open my switchblade and dust off my shoulder.

"Who said that shit!" I look at the toaster designs, Fleur De Lis, at the toaster designs, pinstripe -

"Who tells my cat rules, that's my cat, bitch!"

Mishka's still jumping. The toasters let out building size slices of steaming bread into the back yards. Golf course toast, swimming pool toast, pink flamingos, swing set toast -

I'm spazzing out, yielding the switchblade at the air. Now they'll think I'm dangerous, I've got a cat dressed in arrows jumping up and down for building sized toast and I'm swingin' a switch blade.

"No Jumping, dammit!" Med.z Tony shouts. He's inside my

shirt right now, muffling his cries with spandex I've got on for my squirrel man role–

"Who just said that to my cat!"

"Your heart Chakra, idiot! Look down! I'm sick today though, so don't kill me in the eyes, Dumbo."

"Why are you talking to my cat! You Sancho Richardo! Over pass! Look out!" I duck as a building of hot toast crashes down to meet us. We are on the Astra turf, so, I don't really panic, but Meeshka is jumping like crazy now. I think about trying on that mask with her earlier, she had said she's on her period, so I guess she's a little hungry? Or something – My chest burns and I stray from the Astra turf and drop the switch blade, toasted bread lands on Meeshka, it's stuck to the arrows and struggling, she asks for help – The burning turns into a song that I belch out of my stomach – the song helps Meeshka tear into the bread – I find a golden chair with red velvet and sit, watching Meeshka play in the bread – She eats through one side, back strokes down the middle, chops at the toast with her arrow armor, and comes out of the pool with a towel, brushing back her long strings of arrow hair –

At yellow thirty we go over to the Alamo, the dance – At mustard O'clock we watch the sunset over the toaster hills – At green O'clock we get a boat and explore the cave behind lake Spinster –

At turquoise thirty we watch "Strangers fall in love" and Meeshka puts her paws on my leg. At Blue O'clock she sleeps –

The highway still passes over our heads in green dimensions that look like hovercraft's and street lamps – I paint a starfish on Mishka's back with my pointer finger, wipe it away, paint a rose, wipe it away.

Three drawings of a highway passing over head made of roses and starfish. Bolts, street lamps, rust and wear in 'starfish roses.' I leave nothing out. I put on a helmet I made out of street signs and cardboard boxes, switch on remote cruising and am swimming with Mark, Dot, and Alpha G in the tank.

Mark comes out of the pirates treasure, buried beneath the heaps of tourmaline pebbles, and whistles bubbles.

"Looking good, Zach, where you been Neeshka?"

"Nelson, dude I know alright? Mark, thanks Mark. Ah, the tank is nice."

Pyramids

Ah, possum berries, my favorite beneath the bleachers, tucked in an origami suit with flowers dancing in the fog. On the field: Swedish burlesque dragons dressed in cheerleader costume. My favorite hour. A bracket machine is being built in the far woods—away, away—by the neighborhood skateboarders who break apart apple trees to construct it. The cheerleaders are wild-eyed and speaking in tongues; they practice with stevia milk and Brussels sprouts lined in jars at the forty-yard-line. Not even the trick of the wind draws their eyes under the bleachers, to my giant knots of possum berry glazed in the soup sugar I gathered from pine sap. A monkey puppet—the machine I built last autumn—dances next to me with the flies. I like to sit under here in the fall season while the necks of the possums grow long, sharing pomegranates with my monkey apparatus. The Burlesque show is a new thing and I believe the hammering off in the distance has been orchestrated around each of these movements. I have this terrible idea that when the girls get to the finale and they are all spread eagle against each other's backs, routine complete, perched there like a tetrahedron, beautiful and glowing diamonds, sweat glistening on their rouge thighs, articulating just the correct gestures, tœs pointed, wrists free, their sharp elbows pointed off into angular hexagons, all spinning in gentle gyration, the skateboarders will have already fastened down shopping carts to a catapult and will be ready to release its holding pin.

The skater in the aviator hat and goggles will stick one shaking hand into the pin hold, the other clutching whiskey, sloshing all over, and after half a second there will be noise as the shopping carts fall through the clouds, exploding microwaves and beer cans—a symphony of convulsing wires and cradles and blankets flying through the sky. My worst fear is that the dragons, dressed in their favorite costumes, about to do the human pyramid, may undergo some cruel form of gear-headed mania, and this new extension of my yearly celebration will be deserted for less experimental pastimes.

In the event of a cataclysmic squashing (explosion of cheer-leader dragons), I am equipped only with the standard welder's goggles and have no internal emotional protection regarding my heart, which now beats for them, those fog-wrapped prin-cesses whose routines not only seduce but intrigue in a purely cerebral context.

Every creak of the bleachers startles me and I shut my eyes, trying to enjoy the possum berry's tart flavonoids. The danc-ers do the human pyramid, all of the blondes on top, brunettes with freckles smiling beneath, and the redheads looking about to fold, red-faced at the bottom. The dismount is a flawless one. I take a second from my monkey and applaud quietly, but they can't hear.

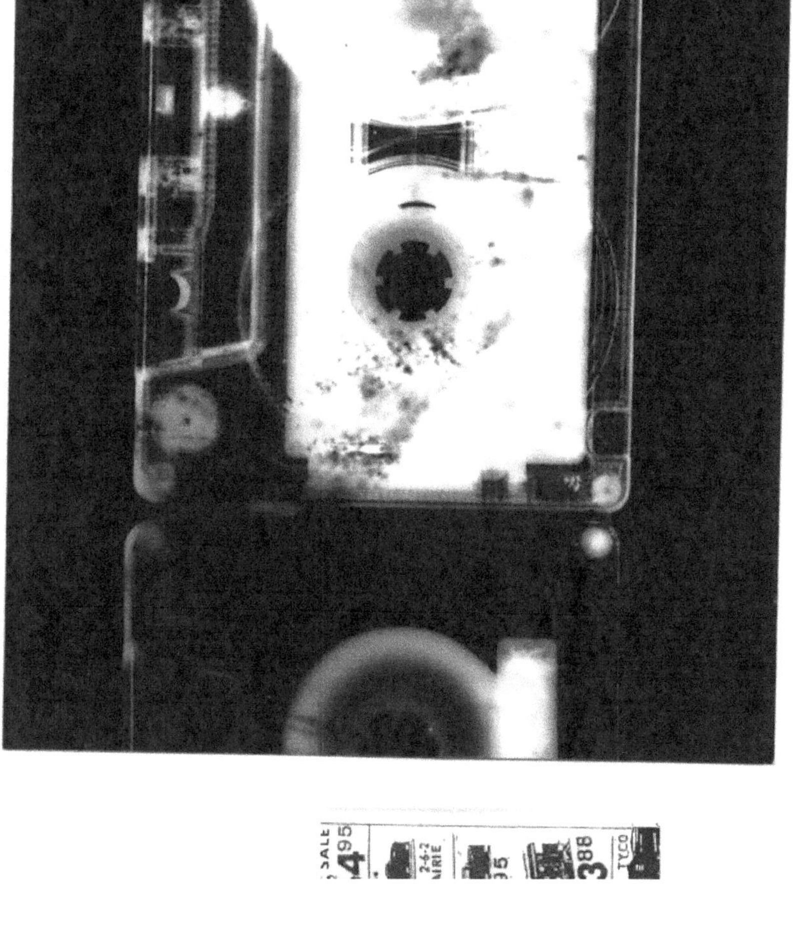

79

Beads

Every shadow contains a soft treasure planted inside, between the limbic system of the dark apparatus, and the lines separating ribs; torso and splintered head of the beast –

Casual, raining down, plastic tear drops, withering in a pyramid shaped dress, Angela Rubens folds to the entryway, caressing her soft white kitten Alters Rube – her shale fingernails weaving intricate fur.

A record operator, sitting at an oak table in a room over, frail green light and a series of punctured floorboards hanging near the headphone sets, bundle soft cable into one outlet.

He places a dust coated needle in the groove of a 16th century sphere – swan lake – sound traveling through the rat devoured holes of the tool shed wall – in through the shadow lair – the dark apparatus.

A light flickers on beneath the metal plating, a casting through of machine punched octagons. This sunken shadow emerges softly upon the mink fur walls of the enclosure –

In another room, a wheeler engages springs behind the foot of a chair, gaining momentum where a shelf of freewheels lay installed, rotating at ninety degrees.

From rusting wall wires, converged in the mink furs, hanging from nails, a whole back of the plates disengage, rolling aside to reveal the wheeler workstation.

On his back, oxygen compression tanks with adorning components follow the length of both arms, leading up to his long skinny neck. In a dull yellow glow of over use, each hand tool organized behind him, is displayed against brick that has begun to crumble in places.

Brown spectacles drop low over his nose, sagging with tan sweat as he moves through different wheels.
The wheeler, a scrawny metal worker from the late 1950⊠s cast, sits in a goon position, seated, perched there, meager over siphoning equipment.

He is engaged in meters, dials tranquilizers, clocks, edging through his shop as he searches the room for diagnostics.
At ten-to-twelve-on-the-dot-to-the-seven-as-well, the oak branches dangle down into the v-machine, fragmenting, drumming a rhythm upon what now pulls together as a moving transport roof.

We turn to each other, with costumes and intricate make up, realizing we have been sitting in the theater. The night train releases a warm, guttural roar that echœs off of the hills in the distance. We examine each other: toys, papers, and cloth bags at our disposal. Fire heated seating, an object with the word NORWAY on it.

Through the theater seat, into myself at last, soft pastel lining of velvet cushion sewn beneath me. My eyes fold closed, single whistle of wind echœs down the ravine, a field of white flowers surrounding me, a small house with rickety smoke stacks.

The hills in the distance of Norway. Small pictures of my feet, dipped in tall wheat grass appear below cut-outs of fragrant-cement-throne-rock-mountains.

Daisies glimmer in the sunlight, burning silhouettes of the animals living in them. A caterpillar climbs the stem of the white flower, the body spreading apart and lifting the head away.

Feeling the flower out with torso and back legs, a part of the flower disappears in the caterpillars mouth, the size of a sunflower seed, showing the blue sky through yellowed veins, running to the stems, toward the branches of NOH theater.

YEARS IN A SEAHORSE

---

(1)

My mind is still a balloon full of helium. I am wandering the
shale cliffs, I store a few balloons, and a dream, like a good
idea, in your home. I found a glass of water in the forest vines,
and filled my wandering legs without a doctor. When I arrive at your residence, seven seconds passes, using topics like
healing with garlic, the state of the union, homelessness in the
inner city, these make up an hour for me, and then abandoned,
a few weeks. I figure if I sit down with you, and bring glyphs
into your eyes, and the spinning summer waterfall bathing
-- I've forgotten about it-- and the rest of Berlin unfolds with
us, please notify the author Gertrude Stein right as six seconds
(you seem pretty sure) are going through equations of creating
that seven seconds stuffed in a box with a key.

(2)

Earthworms burrough three holes into 4465 east Remington
place. China plates, cabinet flower print, vine dreamt, a vertical ladder, tied at the top toe in painted sun, then the educa-
tion of light. Healing a freeze-frame with two black fedoras,
floating underwater, upside down in a profile, split in screens,
two each side of a mule passing Arc st. digging glass with their
new album, spectacles

                                        o

like spiders, hospital and a queens hand, glove-handkerchief
umbrellas flying over the ocean; one, spinning nowhere, one in
the rainbow. Middletown, turning a record beneath the needle
claw, his wife closes herself in eyelashes.

Leprechauns climb out of old pottery all around the floating room. Middletown is a strange place, each bit of burning aroma wanders like tourists to the sea, the passage is in ocher locks of lichen, like arms. For a thousand breakfasts, in a claw foot tub, before moon and flame, bathing in leaves on the webs of sleep near the eaves of a French impersanator, Godfrey, with rockets in her dreams, large green eyes, and delicate hands, flirts with a tv remote. Her finger nails glitter in the static, dreams switch channels, static as she sleeps.

Closely trimmed in a white dance of basil lakes, and parasols that leak out speakers, the boats turn green. The algæ, laughing, goat for halloween! Waking (A. in glove), (A. in goat) eating cakes. Godfrey Samples small locks of her keyboard with knife-point algebra. The road let's in floating military backpacks, to wire with solder, and children and Leaf the children's world, just left heart beat, just playback oxygen, Oxen wanderlust.

(3)

Face the symmetrical furniture, the chandeliers, the jacket, the green, neon clock. The angel Auriel makes sure the favorite pair of color swatch eyes, the best way to the nose, woke eating cakes in the identical Wednesday, dancing on the slides is with a hundred years in this letter to the post office, or over a week, so galactic.

I am curious, humane, sheltered in scarves. I have grown a lot of wings from maple, and friends in New York. I even found a place for the past, and I will have a healthy fear of you who jangle your keys next to the passage in twilight. I join handmade letters from cardboard, kiss under heavens, float to shore, as Zachary.

(4)

At the felt sleeve of the cosmos, the Catalina stairways practice
Eucla cod, the Elvers are fed atoms, and suspended in anima-
tions so the Danio can gorge on tv commercials.
There are nine awkward turns to go, thanks to the iceberg
crystalline, her first frozen mammoths appear in the story
bridge, and reflecting ponds, in the snow suits, and warm
tongues.

(5)

Swerve into a hat, into a white whale, a bird, throwing glitter,
glowing retina tin can, sewing machine spit, conditioner lathered foam noises. Lurching on a wire, a maple figure, is woven
black threads, a new nightmare stitch under the winding of
doors, sculpted all hair for songs, and gold furniture, rewind --

Chance Arrival / A Bird from Lungs

I've fallen into electronics and am now breathing smart guitar, after I enter a room of clocks, I can hear the sound of ticking time everywhere I enter, I see it as intellect in woven carpet reflections. Dance into my past particulars on stilts made of firewood, my milk of magnesia mazes, with the white mask in a new design for healing wounded hearts that scream birds from their pockets, painted body, chest, throat, mouth, flight. I'm gargling fuchsia in my mouth and remembering collages of encyclopedia blue jays flying in circles over my head, my head tilted sideways, I hold up an owl in the mirror, a scroll, a written love letter I swallowed rolls from my lips onto her feathers, those past particulars inside me, milk of magnesia mazes.

Camouflage behind mannequins, I hear clocks ticking, imagine flowers blend to liquid, see the blue tabletop melt like ice cream, a vase with a letter from her drifts silently down liquid ropes, landing on the rusted hinges of my trap doors, all atmosphere with squid like bodies.

The sound of a radio broadcast. You are shopping for a new lover, entering parts of a maze, they play symphony number nine, and you begin to weep. At the free-on steps to a lady in white, you hear ice forming, hold up the black flowers melting ice cream petals into the pond, there are doors marked tuesday on all sides, to wednesday beneath her frozen feet, saturday doors open into the pond, icicles form long tears across the shale in wax knives and the clock starts ticking.

When I dream, I turn into rosemary, and look through cracking branches, to where they build a shanty town and paint it red. The hammers and saws, and shouting. Ravens dodge in and out of shattered windows, caw, caw! beneath this shanty town is a rail yard, the rumble of train engines, and rusted iron against iron. I allow flowers to fall out of my hair, to land on the tracks, and watch starlings as they devour worms inside the quickly decayed irises. In an old house cicadas become crisp dry leaves, become rotting ropes, become woven with bind-weed, and chicory. The warblers can perch on the bindweed trellis, newspaper scraps from the wars they make into nests; the sound of grocery bags crumpling.

In my dream a mannequin hunches over in a field, vomiting whole flocks of black birds into the corn.

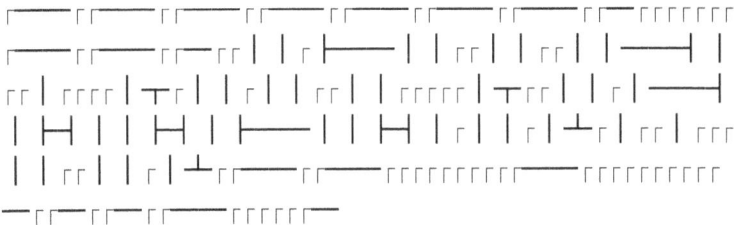

*I Z A A w a s a l o t t h i n n e r now that she had met
the man in the mental cabinet, the light is trying to get into
my eye, she had muttered, after realizing he would not stop
talking, and that she had forgotten her medicine in the car.
Her car, full of little pigs, and dogs chasing sticks, A squiggle
drawing passes the two of them, like a small cloud to separate
the conversation, a ghost there beyond, some pane of glass that
two builders in white suits have to carry to their job, fracturing
the conversation that gœs on, and on, and on.

*SATURN, dressed in the finest clothing closet specials, (his
black corduroy jeans, and 1950's button up t shirt), sweats
profusely at the bench seats, secretly thinking about how small
her Boobies are, and what she smells like in the morning after
sex. He watches her eyelids as they close, slow motion letters
written to mars, and Jupiter from satellite.

She imagines him in a chamber now, whipping a naked girl
across the chest, and stands up. She sees the underground station, a subway train passing along its tracks to the east side.
Clearly, she makes out the numbers 152nd. And realizes his
head is full of martinis and glasses of wine.

He holds a cigarette, and passes drags of it slowly, takes his
time on each inhale, holds it there just long enough.

I will be off now, great to meet you *SATURN. Izabel whispers.

She tries not to get too close to him. His cigarette smoke bothers her.

Have a wonderful day, *SATURN mutters, extending his cigarette towards her and quickly pulling it back to his lips.

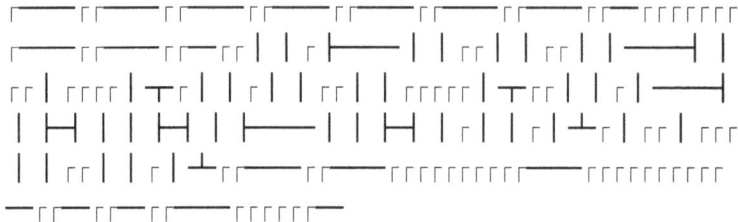

She focuses on his lips, cracked in spaces, Fragile when entered.

As she walks away, she notices the maple tree gleaming in the sunlight, it's deep red leaves *glow under the heat. It reminds her of home, and inside of that home, she witnesses a closer vision, or rooms built inside of the sap, at the park under leaves. A saturday. By the clouds, she grabs a hold and takes a corner of one under her armpit, attaching the fluff into her garments, and rides it, feels epilepsy, sighs fragrances that bloom into magic flowers from her delicate lips, storms in the head, brew, and crickets crawl along her wrists, and jump off of her hands into the towns below.

She lands onto a rowboat, and watches the pond rippling winter edges of frozen water apart into fragments.

Her arms warp down into oars, and hang there, stuck like this as she rows through the ponds fronds, in the weeds, behind the harbor, men and dogs stand in the water leading up along a path to a spotting of old houses. Old men stand in the old house windows. She floats up into the thin air above the row boat, a satellite of ribbons spin around her gesturing body. An Old Jamaican man fishing along the pond hangs his hat, and smokes a pipe. Under the water, frequencies delicate undulations train the fish into a collection below the boat. Puzzle pieces in the weeds scamper out of the ground and click together. Her tongue curls from inside of her mouth and touches the crisp air, as to taste a falling snowflake.

A sweet spell, all of its tangible meanings and awakenings, a sleep spell, a dream of dawn is released, marbled paint at first, and then coated in lacquer thinner, and a mantra of radio signal from the shore, from the old man's radio, she remembers Montana, and quickly witnesses the edges of a white mask as if it rinses over her soft skin, covering her whole face white. An old boxcar rolls passed, one man watches it through a window in the house.

Six years ago down in a dream, *IZAA had made Usnea tea, she sees herself then, hovering over a copy of the Kabala, her boyfriend in bed drinks a small vial of Ginseng.

The fading memory becomes strings and hollows out, turning into the pond water and planting itself along the rocks.
A moment later, a young version of *SATURN climbs over the hill to the train tracks, and kneels down by a RR sign, examining the rations in a backpack. He lies next to an on ramp, and uses his pack as a pillow.

When the dream slips back its curtain, He witnesses it morphing as *IZAA dœs, floating above the boat. A library in Toledo. The smell of old books in the History room. Bethlehem, Pennsylvania, The old steel factory haunts the horizon, giant monolithic machines. He walks down 42nd street in New York City, takes the subway to times square, Union Square, Washington square, Brooklyn, Central Park.

In the weeds, in the harbor, *IZAA Plants Roses at the fall of Midnight, clutching an imagined soft light.

Hovering somewhere inside their collective thoughts, *IZAA and *SATURN shared a similar vision of the satellite Humphrey. It curled along a secure planet, by neighboring star belts of the galaxy andromeda. She would secretly go there at night, in dreams, to meet him, and lay down in the soft white sheets of the bed. He would taste her flowers as they emerged from her delicate lips, softly blooming as she lied her head back. A new crop of azaleas had been growing from her spine, from inside of her belly, and along her throat. His cock, stroking her along the clitoris, made small, joining trellises, that would play, and then enter her labia, very slow motion, and delicate, tracing along the skin, and folding with the creases, before forming into branches of the chinese maple, and spinning through them both, entering all of the nerves and bloodlines, until solid. And they would stay there, passed without gravity to hold them, and spin together, without movement, slugs, dripping from the branches, to the bed.

Waking in the morning, the whiskey at the lips again, the coffee, and the tea, and the breakfast cereal. The body had become stiff, rigid, lonely.

"Jesus, Thank you for bringing us together, Thank you for the wonderful Sun Today, and for Comradery of *IZAA *SATURN Satellite, I'm thankful for the food, and for the chance to heal in the divine spirit --

I'm thankful for God or the light inside or Jesus that this spirit always can exist to comfort my heart in the darkest cells of madness --
Amen."

INDICATORS: _____
*IZAA *SATURN: MEESHKA: SORREL
*glow /GLOWING

Even farther away
My brain is cider
Light headed black with mist
In a cylinder motorcycle
Course
Hanging bag and pixel
And fences, crooked picture,
And picture and organizer
Nail polish dreamcatcher
And how dœs that light come
And I pause my eyes for a beer --
Hanging books and hanging boys
And pants and feet are
Still in the candle light
And what purpose do sounds
Entangle with tent in
Our dreams where were walking
Abandoned cities

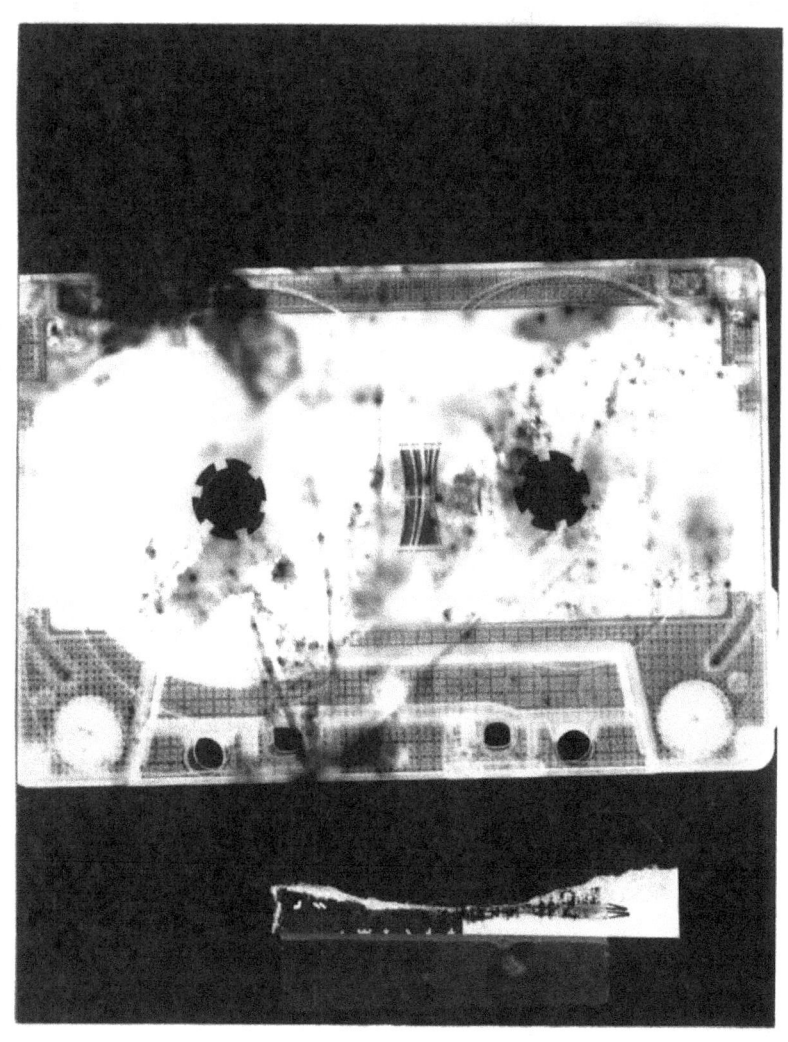

|| || ||| ||| ||| | **AN ADVOCATE**

BLUE SUIT, white tie around his/ her neck, jogging through all
the graveyards in the downtown sector, from the graveyards, to
the room. The room: All white walls, one black hole painted
where a window would be, a spiral drawing, in black charcoal.
An obsessive man~ He sits down with a bouquet of flowers, and
sees in his picture, blue purple blue purple. He sees wires and
formations, in trees.

A broken down house, a glowing light to the side, a flipping of
the mirror, catching the sunlight in his vortex~ He is still in his
costume, his old raggedy black suit and tie. Except this time his
head is not human. His mouth, and his eyes and his ears are a
small mammals in the family Leporidæ of the order Lagomor-
pha, or in layman's Rabbit.

He holds a prop in hands that are close to human, sort of a
mixed blood, a prop of lantern light, stands in front of that familiar house, and looks at the top window, as he always has.
Izaa is seen walking in the mud somewhere in an alley of an old
town at dusk, she hangs her head and passes broken houses,
where people are seen in their grungy, dirty clothes, having dinner. They speak partial english, and partial Portuguese. Some

French, and some Italian. She takes out a black pen and draws on her hands, closely inspecting the knuckles as the ink dries over the skin.

The phone rings in a room. In his suit, perched at the table, with his strange new rabbit head, William, all rosy cheeks, answers the phone. He talks for a brief moment in a low, hushed tone. He is very collected, and describes each syllable down to its every Latinate pronunciation.

Yes, I do know that residence. He listens for a while.

I will be right over there.

He climbs down an old ladder and takes a bicycle down an old road. Arriving at a broken down

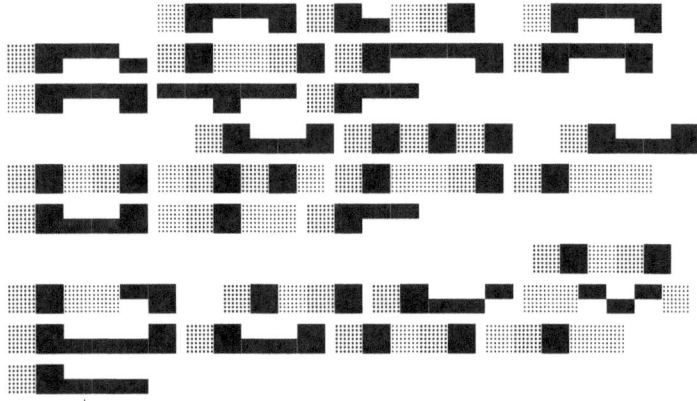

House under construction, and with binoculars, inspects the house next to it that is boarded up, and spots inside, a leather mask swinging back and forth on a meat hook. He climbs into the rafters of the house under construction, his dirty elbows poking out as he sets up his binocular stand, and pears next door.

The faint sound of a voice is heard, a whispering of a young woman's voice, or a child, barely noticeable, and then a calm still silence.

As the wind picks up, a wind chime across the street emerges in the silence. The house is still. But the curtains move, a picture of a face in the window, a poster, hanging on a far wall. From the rafters, the blue suit lumbers down, lowering himself from the rooftop to the dirt driveway. Trees sway in the back yard, piles of trash lay everywhere from the demolition crew. Bottles of beer tipped over, rusty cans. In the backyard of the house next door, the bunny boy looks in a window that is broken, sees a curtain pulled by the wind, and a pile of random books and magazines. He gœs to the back porch and rummages through a stack of old newspapers, notices a clue in one, a page printed about the house he is standing in front of, the old house where the family had been found in the basement. He examines an old rusted bike, hears the twinkling sound of the wind chime, and pauses. Smelling the ripe air, a fire in the distance, the smell of burning woods ~

The sounds of people walking makes him turn to one side, holograms of awareness, otherwise known as people, empty streets in all actuality, He walks, it's maybe his one true last freedom, he searches around the side of the house for a door, and circles around into the front porch, where he cautiously enters with no problems what so ever. The door knob softly turns, and easily opens. He looks inside, smells the air. Adjusts the door, fitting it closed neatly behind him, and follows a staircase to the red carpet below, where it flattens to a landing, and rises back up to another red staircase. At the top of that staircase, he sees that standing there in a doorway, a figure in a white mask, hunches there, before sneaking back into the dark room beyond, and softly closing the door behind itself.

Saturn turns, and checks the front door. His heart begins beating quickly. He smells an odor that scares him. The noise of a small motor starts up below him, in the ground.

That thing moves fast. He thinks. A gaseous smell enters his nostrils, a fart or puke, or socks, whatever it is; he cannot understand where it could be coming out of. He opens the door and steps back through, but now a hallway, an old theme park ride tracking a tunnel, walks in, glowing props everywhere, prerecorded sounds broken, looping over and over somewhere off in the distance. He wanders down the tunnel, and into darkness, crosses the tracks, and steps over into a props set up, a robotic woman hangs limp, her hair covers her eyes and face. He listens down the tunnel and hears a clanking sound, and gets frightened, so he turns back to the door, and jiggles the handle, shaking now, he enters a hallway of doors that are all closed, a chandelier hangs in front of each of the doors, they shiver, and a tiny sound emits as the door closes. He passes each door and grows more worried that he will not be allowed to leave this house.

What he got into here is a job for a rat, not a rabbit. But his knowledge of the place was all that they had needed from him, he was the only rabbit for the job, according to the voice on the phone. Who the voice belonged to, he could not say. Scary shit, this world.

A motor clicks on in the back room to his right, and all of the doors begin slowly opening. The hallway spirals down to a basement, where a man hunches over a hole in the floor. The man is in all blue, his hair pokes out of a mask over his head. The rabbit head, Saturn turns away, unnoticed by the other digging the hole. He walks back up the spiral to the opened doors and peaks into a room, where a long hallway gœs out, to the end, and then he turns around a corner and sees a brick wall, a cold city, neon lights glow, and he can see his breath, No one's around, his suit is thin, his hands are covered in marker lines, those keep turning into silk ribbons and unraveling onto the ground at his paws. Black piles of recording tape, unraveling in piles.

Down a side street he looks up at a house, a mansion hovers in a soft fog. Boarded up windows on the front porch~ A quick glimpse of him on the porch sawing away at the house is witnessed, a quick flash of a light bulb, he is in the attic room, red carpet leads down the steps, flattens at a landing, and rises to another set of steps.

Turned on over head, a light bulb flashes, a phone rings. The masked figure comes out of the room and holds a phone.

Hello.

Saturn takes a few steps through a dark empty hall. He hears the phone ringing downstairs. Back in the front of the house, he climbs the steps, and passes the masked figure, holding the phone. He opens the door, and enters a room. Trophies in a glass case line one wall, and a McDonald's slide has been set in the opposite wall. The carpet is plush red. And glowing above is a red exit sign. He gœs to the slide, gets inside, starts on what a voice tells him is a hunt for apples. He slides for what feels like forever, and lands in the balls. Gœs down another couple slides, and climbs in some nets, now he is younger than he was before, a baby rabbit, with a pinstripe suit, and a simulator ray gun he can aim and adjust.

A voice speaks through the vents.
He's okay in there,

The subject seems to understand fully our test. He's doing everything so very well, for such a young age, wouldn't you say, Shawm?

Yes, Indeed. Izza. Very well.

He's not upset is he?

He's not upset. Just curious.

I distinctly remember him being a lot bigger don't you?

In the window, the tube glows green, he looks out of the balls, and slides, listening to the voices but not really interested in what they are saying about him. The colors shift from normal to flat and to black and red, He closes his eyes and a screen goes black on a television.

Now a pause.

A still frame. An attic, in a rafter, a rodent view. Sunshine comes through a window in the attic, lands on the beams. A rat jumps around, and runs along the beams. It is Saturn. In his new costume. Looking down from the ceiling, into the outside world around him. In that world, it is raining, but he is dry and warm. He watches street lights at night. Safe in the roof, sleeping.

Underwater scenes begin to emerge in Saturn's dream, dark, murky, calm, slow motion undulating, glowing lights drifting by like satellites, zoom, swirl, spiral, long hallway with doors, the tunnel with broken ride props coming back to life, as the motors are plugged back in. And then out of the water, in a boat that pops to the surface, way up there in the clouds, blue skies, and slow ships passing.

A ship takes him to a landing pad up near a castle pod floating there in the sky. He gets off the ship and is greeted by a woman with a brown coat and a clumsy accept, and a loving smile of appreciation for something. He stands with her for a moment on the smooth step, and discusses Atlantean gold shells making up the decor of the castles. What wonderful design. She wanders closer and touches his chest softly. Rubbing his arm while delicately she looks him in the eyes. Her brown casual eyes, glance his face with affections. She kisses him softly at first, until he begins to kiss her back, and they softly grow more entangled, until at one moment she and him fall back into a soft cloud next to them, and take off each other's cute clothes.

She whispers in his ear, it is the best sex she has ever had in her life. He feels the same way, too but says nothing. Gently making love to her, and staring into the earth below, at the fields, and mountains and clouds and prairie, thirteen hundred feet away. He plunges into her textures, careful of each "layer" as if it had its own life to it. Each opening, he could feel relaxing into him, and soothed, him and her. They were safe here. Fully relaxed, finally into each other. Examining her body, as she closes her eyes. Saturn, witnesses her small breasts bouncing to the rhythm. As he watches them bounce, he is careful to keep the rhythm exact, so that she can relax and feel her whole body under his control. She starts to seize up a little and he continues, gesturing at the same rhythm, she seizes and her tœs curl over the cloud edge. Her back leans up into his gestures, and relaxes finally. The both of them still. And warm.

They start laughing. And he gets up and she checks his body out.

While he pisses off of the cloud, down into the thirteen thousand foot field.

I love you.

I love you.

Whenever you are silent, and looking into the small screen that explains yourself your life, take a dose of Ketamine, and spread your sickness (like a child) into the school nurse program, so that when freakish, the epileptic classroom, with its posters of hand painted garbage, they call art class, can spread in the vision. Accept your defeat at the post office, when paying for Explored ratios, and divulge in its secretions, tell on your friend to the teacher, and see the unraveling of a whole friendship, and divulged language, that whining sound that gets things accomplished when wired.

STUFFED PILLOW< LIKE MY BRAIN
SETUBAL PORTUGAL --SCISSORS--
SAD BALANCE, SACRED EIGHT INFINITY
LOVE LOVE IBOGAINE EAST NORTHEAST
WEST SOUTHWEST HIEROGLYPHICS
COCOON PROTECTION -- PURE LIFE
SOFT FOLDED PLAID -- ROCKING CHAIR
--- BASKET HAT FOR THE BRAIN --
EACH STEP TŒ TOWN WOOD
HOLDS UP THE TABLETOP STUDIES
EVERY EDGE   ETCH SCIENCE
POOR SUICIDAL -- turn the doors at the wrist into a line
across the veins, and from a line, create four, drawings of bone
HEAL YOURSELF!!!!

Expressions of glee amount to the shœ lined shore, testicle cancer, is healed, I looked for it all in the mirror, I got bugs out of the deal, so I looked again, and found the snipers inside of me trying to crawl out of my pores, this is a nightmare, I keep saying it, but that nightmare is there because it's all there is left of traditions based on the idea of nightmares, I think to myself. So much cooler inside of these play station whereabouts, totally tricky substations hidden under here.

Sheesh, Lucy.

How many delicate details are we missing out on just by sustaining ourselves on vino and cigarettes until we black out in the desert, searching for a lunatic who dœsn't even care for meager people like us, and Dr. Dre is out there in the desert, looking buzzed, he's got himself, a little dude with him, named junior, who looks like a lawn gnome my girlfriend had in her pussy till she came by dude taping her with a dildo, and softly masturbating. What a weird day.

"Sea salt brain full of rubber duck...The garlic gerbils, wood chair-housecat sits down, ass tie die,
Yeshi! Candles singing spaghetti~"

‒ ─────

| STATIC |
| RADIO |

─────

The gold leaf bridge houses two ghosts with green makeup and gold teeth, standing in their white underwear, near lake Pontchartrain ~

The two ghosts handle net bags full of camel cigarettes and talk to the original I6a on handheld radios, leaning close to the stove to warm their legs --

Matrix Witch, another peephole version of the glitch-witch-bitch, draws near with a spray bottle full of purple flowers --

Link, the one who can go invisible, tells her that her hair looks
like a sponge, as if radio wires came out of the pores when
squeezed, instead of water --

She just stares at the water with her squeeze bottle aimed in
the clouds -- The original I6a tells them to offer the glitch
witch one of their fishing poles, so she can contour her body in
the direction she is most interested, but the ghosts look inside
the kitchen cabinet, instead of the floating basket -- and she
starts in on the squeezing of that bottle -- misting in circles the
air around her -- and then glitching her head and hands and
torso, taking on computer graphics appearance -- glitch an old
channel, six news broadcast of her delivery of the weather,
when she worked as a nursemaid in that movie, Sixteen Stones
--
She flips her face right on the left, and upside
Down on the right, sprays at the ghosts, they turn on dance
music -- turn on a fog machine, disco lights -- they watch their
gold teeth blur in tracers over the horizon line --

She just keeps spinning and stopping a leg where an arm,
hand where a heart, mouth where a toe, like a slot machine of
barbies with a leg and a hat and a waist, plastic ass -- nose
hand, hair, spinning, until the ghosts put in quarters and lose
all of their money, then blamo! They win $600.00 and cash out
--

i.
Been tendrils, snake wired effects, snore from lungs, the leafless tree at seventy miles an hour, and falling / The skin is the
leather, the hands are the stories to little rock -- An orange
mist in the eye -- A giant and a puppy --

i.

It took the length of mazes to thin purple crushed velvet almost a century even trade avocado to the tongue and feed the
mind its alphabet, Conway sign is pointed out pebbles and the
semi's are like wandering cows and make the mud flaps into
curled lips

ii.

Who had wandered the forest, a long length of octopus aliens,
dripping snakes up into the clouds, attempt to pull the fog
down, that heavy moisture as wires, and cables echo and
sprout others out of a snored old man on his back, his head
rests on the grey hat, was it he who wandered leafless trees
at seventy sundown's, miles apart, these musical waterfalls of
flute, and mirror, an hour upon his lonely feet, and falling, the
skin is the leather, those handfuls that are stories -- the little
rock clutched in his tired palm, an orange mist in his eye -- he
is dreaming, a giant black and white puppy. In his dream he
whispered about the length of mazes, he said to the thin purple, crushed velvet, hung from a window that almost a century
had passed, even before trade of avocado to the tongue, fed the
mind, that its alphabet pebbles fed the mind so long -- Since--
he points to a sign for Conway -- watched the mud flaps like
wandered cows curled lips --

I.

In another room, the Arkansas hills pass at 50 mph to East -
West - South -
Somewhere
Blur and the fish jump fling off water -- graveyards confederate
flag train tracks, the old haunted house on the hill
The warm string insanity of string a' netting -- A radio static

ii.

He points to another room with a solid stone ring on his finger
to the hills of Arkansas, he's passing in a boat at 50 mph to
east, west, south -- Blur and fish jump in the boat, fling off
water, passes graveyards, confederate flags, train tracks, old
haunted houses rise on the hill --
He leans back into the leaves, the warm string of insanity, a
white serpent of string, a netting, then, just a radio in a field,
buried in leaves, the tuner left in between channels --

It's awkward, under a clock with a sword anyway -- as field
mouse, Mishka, running the steps, to sneak food to a friendly
mouse -- each honey tone in the south, what shoot/cut/scene
must wander with winged three headed camera

Exit sign, glowing above escape, here through this hatch, and
come in the back of the mind, and change around the rooms,
inviting the friendly mouse into here; with some garden fla-
vors and spruce up this little laboratory to a small paradise for
Mishka, the mouse.

In here you can plant Azaleas, and cucumbers, and pump-
kins, and squash and live here in this garden with her and
her brothers and sisters, the mouse and you, and me and our
giraffe, if you know how to shape the basement ceilings, with
pipes running steam, into glass set in clay, up in spiral to octa-
gon window. Sail envy.

The shades are drawn now; pink fuchsia, dawn orange, neon
red curtains, cats at the sofa -- shirts and shœs have all been
lined up, in front here, near the mantle in a circle, there is the
mouse inside each shœ, snored quiet -- and the cats yawn

The television replays little rascals, and the three stooges in short bursts, changing channels every two minutes -- the grey couch seat is seen from the crow in our corner of the chess board, its vision protects mouse shit in the shœs, the man sitting at dinner and TV -- S/he flips on Little rascals, then three stooges.

Goodnight. Sweet dreams.

Shaving Sister

We piled on the lattice work until, near the black lake; we had it steady in the corners - matched up in places. The orange-gloves grow worn on the outside, slimy on the inside. The orange gloves we hang in trees each day, a golden ray of them, wheelbarrows full of gloves that get wheeled to the dump site, and strategically hung with a thin-fishing line, I think its 10 pound.

Davis grovels, attaining a long lattice piece from the pile, and standing it up edgewise, so that it flaps over in the breeze, he stares at it and rummages through his jumpsuit. A roll of duct tape comes with receipt papers, and his lighter, which he sets down near a rock.

I tear down walls of the lattice, and throw it aggressively, getting deep inside of the cube, (where more lattices –older lattice - stained from rot, is revealed beneath.)

The sound of a woman, singing, whistles through the Oak woods. The voice echœs from a cabin I know of, down half a mile. I hide under the fur of my cap, tearing off lattice and throwing it.

Davis has built something out of it: a smiling female. She stands there, made of gloves and lattice. I nod. Good. Behind him, a naked blond with red-genital hair sings. She takes some orange gloves down and puts them on like shœs. Her vocal fold is visibly shaking and it annoys me. I bend down and pop open the red tool box, pulling out a Splitting maul. I tear off another layer of lattice from the cube and turn to the female - raise the maul over my head and smash the lattice woman through the middle. Davis screams, and the woman, singing, naked, grabs him and pulls him swiftly toward the river, where she salutes me and picks Davis up off of his feet. He screams, but I pull out a television remote control unit from the toolbox (RCU) and press mute.

The water rises high above the trees; the entire river in one, long, rising water fall grows. I turn back to the cube and tear through eight sheets of lattice, getting into what seems like a center. The water made of collaged pictures of a female) begin opening their mouths, and Davis cuts out paper in the middle of the rising storm, laughing at me and pointing the scissors before the water starts to fall.

I get through, in the darkness, and the water crashes into the bank, releasing paper cut out naked women all over the shore. They all stand up and line dance to a country song one has playing on a radio, and the cube takes out its legs from the ground: the cube starts line dancing with a naked girl with red nipples, who licks the top wall away, and I see her. She has a horn and blows a song through her horn.

Satellite Cornelius and Dream Costume

No. 1
Panda's hang in bamboo, chewing on geodes that settled near volcanœs. A girl named dear Mona Marie, and another girl Edith Piaf are climbing into my speech patterns, they use ladders, that they found in our garage to get near a blazer tent in my facial contortion where they can place things down, a brass trainman's lantern on Canal in Venice, Italy. They are setting up Umbrellas to sell them in a small town, a boutique.

Mona takes down her gown and finds a queen sized bed behind cases of my vocabulary. Edith and Mona cough, and out come the local "boy" in the mirror next to them.

It's happy hour on satellite Cornelius and I'm feeling powerful. Dressed in brownish red, to orange, full up on Edith Piaf, and Dear Mona Marie, and "boys" -- Pandas hang around the bar in bamboo, chewing on geodes of amethyst that settled in near the volcanœs. I close my eyes and see that they are sewing pipe cleaners through strawberries, sounds of plastic bags swishing in the wind play on tape. All I see is the blur of a Hasselblad camera with its focusing ring messed up. This brings me to my eyes. Shutting them, I see a black tent, stitches, red in the left corner, and the right. When I open my eyes it's white, for a little while down at the left corner pocket of the pool table is a castle, centered over the pocket so it can poop pool balls into the pocket, an eight ball rolls away, and inside of the table, down, along the tracks in line with the others, clacking together. I'm in slow motion. I have a pool stick, I'm trying to spin it like a toy, can't do it, I see myself from someone else's eyes in the bar. I'm wearing giant bellbottoms, my crotch, and butt don't exist, the bell bottoms are so big that fire trucks, and model cars drive out of them, into a yellow, and white 70's classroom video. Toy cars and school busses drive out from my bell bottoms, into the 70's video, and a black and white screen appears, a man

Points his finger at the audience, and has something to say, something very important, but the sound is off, and he is talking, but nothing is heard.

People in the bar close their eyes, and the strawberries are strung onto the pipe cleaners, plastic bags playback on tape.

When I closed my eyes, it was a black tent, and a little blur of white ceiling moving popcorn patterns, shifting, and breathing, melted, and dripping, near the center of the tent. When I opened my eyes, a forest warped right into place, dead center. I dropped through it, and areas blended together like a smoothie, into lava, and, heating to such degrees, windows are made, I fell asleep there, covered.

The library's open, so I walk across state of the art satellites, and wave at the Panda bears eating geodes in the bamboo. Stopping, I take a picture of one, holding up my Hasselblad, him munching, trying to get his teeth around a particular cluster of crystals, I make sure that the focus ring is set to shallow, that it picks up the panda, and nothing behind him.

No.3

It's February by the time I get to the library of cardboard signs. The place, invented by a librarian Cody Sinclair and famous bum Isaac Doldersum had implemented the library out of all those street kids' taglines: hungry, please help, and Waiting on SSI cheque. These signs hung around the entry, and were catalogued by year. You can check out a sign for a week, and go down to the mega-highway, and fly it~

Most people tend to give at least forty bucks on weekends, so I figured I'd make ten bucks, go to the night kitchen, and then head over to my friends.

I wander the stacks, and pick out a sign: why lie I need a beer. Carry it around awhile, and end up setting it down for a better sign: 4:20 time! (With a drawing of a male smoking a huge fat joint.) I carry this around for awhile, and set it down for something I like better, and found works better: Dirty, broke, and Hungry, (smiling face) Anything Help$ God bless U (Smiling face)

I walk to the librarian, and check out my sign. I wander down to the on ramp, near the dream costume Shoppe, and light a cigarette.

A black man drives by, and I see a dollar crumpled up, he gets my attention, and the cars block us, so he chucks the bill out the window, just a work truck. Probably an old-world ford Motor. I nearly cause a wreck, get the bill, feeling dumb that it's all over a dollar, and I see it's a twenty.

I've only been here five minutes, and my cigarette isn't even half smoked, I try another car, waving my sign. A brand new hovercraft. The car zooms toward Satellite Cornelius, and dœsn't see me. The next car, I wave it at the next car, modern Cadillac (he ought to kick down something) dœsn't see me, the next car, old hogtie ride, poor folk, dœsn't see me. A kid in the back seat with missing front teeth stares, his brown eyes bulge. So, I make a face, and finish my smoke, so he can see. But, the kid dœsn't see anything.

Seventy miles per hour is pretty darn fast for flying a sign, anyway. I stare at the numbers: 70MPH across the street. That's pretty fast. I leave, walk through the satellites, to my friend's trailer out in Boomtown, She lives in the rundown trailer park there at the edge of town, near the waterfall, and her father helped her pick it out.

When I arrive, she has made the inside look like a cavern. There is a fawn, and a rabbit snuggled up on an old wood chair she seems to have built, next to a rock wall and a writing desk. It looks like a cave wall, all around the room. I'm confused, but know its Mona Marie and Edith Piaf, they allow only the true wild into their homes, these ladies of our faith, one is my aunt, the one who always lets me in. I always end up wandering around alone, at first, not sure where she has gone, sometimes after letting me in, hours go by, and usually, like tonight, I take a nap somewhere in the house, knowing things will not pick up until later. When I wake up, I remember Edith had said something about a tent, underneath me. And I had agreed, as I remember it, to put the tent up for them, that a tent was a great idea, and I would love to live in one of those. At the thought, I look down, at what I'm sitting on, it's flattened down, a tent that needs to be assembled, and propped up. Pink yarn, and multicolored canvas, with little black shirt tags sewn everywhere along the seams. I put it up, and hear my aunt, yelling to do something, to someone. I cannot make out what it is she's saying. I look at the fawn, as she falls out of the chair with a scared look, and the rabbit's eyes light up.

"Oh, no, no, careful!" My aunt says. The fawn wiggles out of the chair, into my arms, morphs, and shakes into form, as a girl with black hair, and wise brown eyes. Her hands are still shaped as hooves, and she holds them limp, with blue jeans on. She helps me lift my arms up. She says. UP! And I lift my arms up. She explains how this helps me. I am happy to be talking to her, and she is saying, UP, now lift, your legs, and fold them around, and says, hey look! It's a warm sweater, fresh from the laundry. I feel my aunt, Edith behind me, but cannot remember what she looks like; just that she's being helpful, by staying behind me.

When I closed my eyes, I saw a black tent. I took amethyst in my hand, and remembered that there is a fawn changing into a girl, and whispering, UP!

(I think now, I am sleeping finally)

No. 4
Dream costume
THE DREAM COSTUME! First discovered near a beaver dam, known as a small body of water, created entirely by northern beavers for a wetland project, as it grew less in shape, and size, the costume began its forming little by little, as it became more eroded each year, the mud began to rise, and water to pass away, and leak out into other nearby gathering pools.
At first, nothing more than a statue, rabbits would build nests in between its then rough thighs, Swarms of red ant carved out passage ways, similar to a central nervous system , and nested in what would become its brain. Worms made homes in its lungs, and stomach, frogs in its groin, sand turtles made later Burroughs in its feet, finches nested in what would later become the mouth, and eyes. (Etc.)

(Collecting and creating one's own dream costume)

————

Find a violin at your headrest, sleep walk to the hair at its resting place in the bottle, in the museum of top hats. At the libraries of yellowed cigar smoke drift like candle wax flowers, down to the river water, hanging lanterns into boats (etc.)

_____

_____

Beets grow from appendages, (IE. arms, legs, neck, sometimes and ears)
and in, from the belly grow cucumbers, in through the thighs, leaf lettuce, and corn from the brainstem, to motor the boat of black, and beyond blue, with top hat and peat coat, and peat moss, as beard, a mustache, and sideburns, bless you young ghost, of the water

_____

_____

_____

Refracting blurred reference to this cavernous room, with ball jar, and ribbon tied sage, refraction to blur red ribbon, in water, under the boat, hunched looking in dream of the black river.

_____

_____

_____

_____

Shape space stations in the galactic black wax, of the surrounded melted stars, and look back into the water - hanging the lantern over in between the oars, to reflect back the moss skin, and corn, emerging out of pores, and mushrooms that grow beneath that top hat, and look into the cluster of floating, downstream pearls, in your wax boat sifting, lighted on the wick, entering the space station, the year changes, as does the style of dress from top hats to helmets, and from pea coats to astronaut outfits --

_____

_____

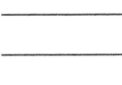

Peppered chimney, spiral staircases to your suit jackets, it is, hiding behind your face mask and digital eyelash -- the bricks leading up to your retina, and bowtie -- camouflage wine colored lips --

Silly shit head, silly shit! Silly face shows your teeth, silly, too many longer teeth, silly. Eat the pilgrims, eat those long ago, green mouth full of pilgrims -- disappear, those losers, pilgrims, destroy those endless stories, the swine, bring nature's beard a growing down into the boat, leaking mushrooms --

```
:::::::::::    :::::::::::::
 :::::::::::     ::::::
 ::::::        ::::::::::::::
 ::::::        :::
 :::::         :::
```

No. 5 Edith, and dear Mona Marie, and I sit in the living room, in my tent watching this all on TV. I put up with the rabbit, and the fawn girlie, watching this on the news~ "I can't believe this shit, a dream costume made out of turtles?!" Mona Says. The room is steady, slow motion.

Edith shouts at the TV, and ribbon comes slowly forward from her lips, deep within her throat, caught mid air, and as she does this, a brigade of men, dressed in dinosaur costumes line up, holding giant Rosary. The ribbon loops into the brigade, tickling them, and the slow motion of this is entertaining to view, but I feel like its torture for those Men and I stand up slow motion and shake their hands, all the men handing them each a card with the letter J printed in big, black New Roman. There are four men, and four cards with the letter J, they hold up. Dear Mona laughs, and yells "FOUR MEN, AND FOUR CARDS!" She has a room in my words, a little loft, with a queen bed, and her, and Edith do their hair in the mirror, and talk about me, like I'm not there, and Lucy comes over.

I take the pink ribbon down from the air, and make a circle around the dinosaur costumes, those poor tortured men, they fall in together as I pull it tight, and Edith pushes the news off, and stands slow motion, licking her lips. She plays a tape, using the remote to press play. She walks around the dinosaurs, who are waiting to find out what the cards mean. The tape plays:

"Movement ~ Whistled at the ceremony dithering LA CRUZ, for we, we dine now with the roses, sleeping ever so symbolically beneath pure gold." I watch the yellow horizon through space, satellites, all silhouettes ~
I flip on the news, bored.

NO.6 (ROSEWATER SMITH transcripts of Journal entry)

JANUARY In the shadows, a strawberry tin can and rose thorn vine, licked away by the candle flame. In the other shadows, dangling to slow down the tempo of the room, the book, and lips, the golden skating rink, with raccoons dancing the tree ~ Vine creases, triangulating walls, and woman, dog, trying to eat our morning donuts, creases like limestone, following the creases in my hand, holding a plaid blue book: titled Adams St.

Many hauntings have since been cited, and although ROSEWA-TER SMITH had destroyed what he thought was the source of his misery, the carved out mud man had stayed intact, he since had worse events, and other sightings of the mud men appearing in his field, near what is now known as Cornelius Satellite, (Guitar ocean.)

NO.7

Edith asks all of us, after the recording is done, to figure out amongst us, which are our favorite selves. At first I'm confused, and flip the TV off. She leaves, and says to think it over, she will bring in tea, and escapes to a private area, in the cavern. At this point my head is empty of Edith, but Dear Mona is still playing in the tent next to me and in my words, she is lying reading a book. The dinosaurs are exiting in pink ribbon; they mutter something that sounds like

"We are Paper," and "Letters of the alphabet, we are earth again,"

Dear Mona gets out her collection of bells, and her, and I play them, not afraid like we used to be whether her hand touches mine.

"What do you think about the dream costume stuff on the news?" She says.

"I don't know, I thought I was dreaming, actually, it sort of bothers me." I say. "It seems like the islands are all of the way backwards, except for the beginning of the sewer." Someone mutters in the room, at least it's what I hear.

I am holding the memory of the library in my pocket, and attention gœs to the receipt ~ Even the tape player Edith had put on runs backwards, even the soup we were eating runs backwards ~

"I want to go to Guitar Ocean." I say.

"They do plastic rodeos there, at the guitar ocean." She says. She points to the mannequin.
"Why don't you take the sleeping costume with you to Guitar Ocean?"

1961, everything at Guitar Ocean is painted with green moss; electric blue neon signs make up the ocean floor. The coral reef leads electricity along neon tubes to the horizon. Angels string the clouds. A white horse lies in the middle of town yawning.

———
———
———
———
———

———

Automatic tangled web, like Iris windows, warehouse on the horizon, webbed in chimney stack, and weeds, the abandoned mill, and no sunlight. The grey sky like a television show ~ Watching, I'm watching from my seat at the window ~ Train Whistles~ the roller skates of some ghost of a girl~ I remember as Iris~

———
———
———
———
———
———
———

Holes in the webbing~ while looking for a skyline to erase to, alone in this spaceship, or wax raft, with lit wick ~ burning the midnight oil. Coleman ~ White light on my hand ~ listening to whispering ~ of a signal~ aroused by the river ~

I am dressed in the dream costume, like Mona said. She was right, already they have invited me to the tree house, their dream costumes unraveling white, mine unraveling black, a slow spinning of yin yang, slug slime ~ We lay naked in the center as it rotates mandalas beneath us, and after an hour of half sleep we get dressed, and walk down to the guitar ocean, near the reef, they got hand puppets that do all of the talking, and one says

THE WORLD IS CODE SOME TRY TO MEMORIZE...

The other agrees, says "and they tattoo its numbers into their skin."

I think about a time I was staying with a theater professor, she had articles above her bed, when she woke Christmas hats were playing on dark TV's at the front of the bed, and how I started, then, to realize those times were actually dreams.

I nod, agreeing, and were all feeling relaxed from sex. At twelve, a string behind the clouds appear, glowing a fluorescent neon tube in pathways, labyrinths light up along the ocean floor, turning to mazes, ending up broken apart into getaway boats that emerge from under the calm waters.

We all get in line for "BIAGE" the musical. An instrument held beneath the collector's hands beside me, and at the blur of doors, talking, clinking glasses and guitar, a snow green silhouette falls in place to the blurred door frames, fish tanks full of Danios, and Cod, and a western plays in the hidden theater. After the 25th floor, turtles wander under the dance floor.

Tissue paper lanterns hang in palm trees ~ every week that passes; we are dancing still, in a very concise cubicle, making circles.

(INFINITY)

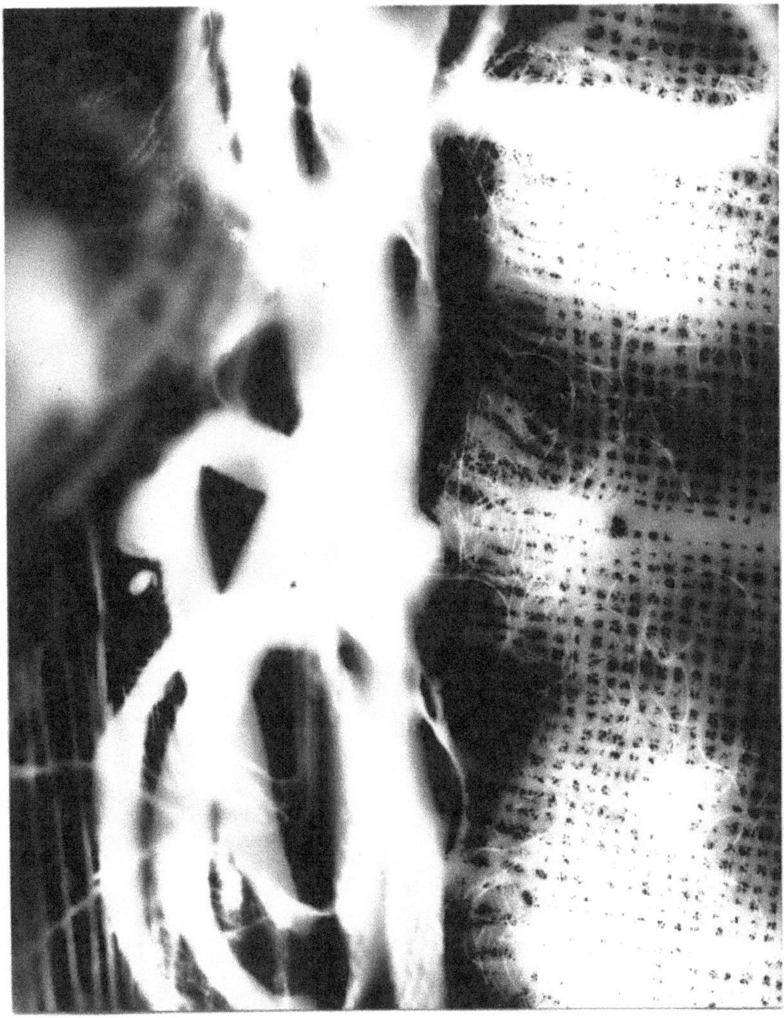

127

Three Rooms

| i. |

I come up an elevator, nurturing my headache from a 1940's
radio – with white paper wall under my armature, digging
frenzied to a thin, upper realm of the infinity house.
A rotting, deeper into my mystery bird fray, letting moss into
the canopy, chiseled with hair line intricacy of radio static
behind the drop.

For a coin, I permit the puppets in a door, for a few grays and
a few baby static lines, my hand to a thin edge, as it rounds
and is rusty, climbing skies, rain as a pack of combs – puddle
and falls, I step inside the Christmas vial of quartz coin and
turn over the rugs, all roses singing liquid tongue and dancing
plaid.

| ii. |

I sit down in Victorian slumber, wrapped in Christmas lights
(pure meta circus,) for example: branch curtain, drowsy electric, woven from the window through neighborhoods, paper
snow spattered six feet – A flat line of human negligence, the
curtain flounder within pear, sea – A marching vocabulary
wanders sticks, each inhale a pale gaze in the dark jewelry.

Cornered in the chamber of haunted love – the kind of painted
monument that touches velvet hands to the window and looks
at the city to witness its exact nightmare, just to glow green beneath its eyeliner– Formulate, in waking conceived debris, fabric motion, threaded of sound. Pulling in on those men jeans
ever forward, toward drunken collapse in the center of the red
strawberry patch, and twigs they carry, forward through roots –
enormous, and in the collection a stippled light

| iii. |

The ice cream melts down a rotating speed, entering the aloe
Vera Gazebo. Three spines through seventy miles an hour
melts it down her tongue, down her lips, and over the crystals
of her chin, now setting down a sixteen ounce French horn solo
and sliding lights that feel neon perfected – The slot machine
of tulips, mustard language of conversation, between the whiskey bar and the donut stand we found treetop stools rising, I
am falling in love with a young lady in the French horn solo.
Old recordings spin Christmas lights; melt down her tongue in
between her nails and onto her drawings. Between an old ladder, vines grow to the words EDEN. Behind me, a peach box
full of birds, rakes, and shovels hangs –

| iv. |

Shy from the break of day, rug draped skin, this Norway raven
infested window- Black leaves turn away the sand-tapestry,
Afghans that the rental company gathered from evictions, and
through earthen precipice, later, leaking dream and habit of
the dawn, a logging road to waters' edge -

And, the writing is on the wall, a big black string that blooms
from a source in the grout – shy from a wandering girl travers-
ing away in sunlight stretched, in her black poise.
Shy from indications that fold away the eyes shy from the
merging of a crevice, underneath an umbrella away, that is
laughter–

A Raven doorway at the abandoned factory, wake from triangles and into the fog – future in the particles we enter living
explorations, the infinities–

Shy from the triangles in the field, rosemary, sipping galaxy
from white window, now leaking love more pure than the rain-

Two wings handle the perch, nectar of Orchids, to the horizon, animals shake darker from foot prints into the past, lengthy watch streams and drip from the almond for filtered umbrellas hang as wings. Against liquid healer, roses for a forehead – A roller skate angel lets out a string of the rose, cancels out steps to the perch, petals the footsteps from black rugs – woven of the bow. The brick house rises from a sphere to enter new morning – Shy from dark steps that led the radiant laughter, to snapping twigs in lonely steps, rising downward, through the lathe wheel, eroded in trees.

An excellent mistake to watch these long stems into the perfect hour, the stray mathematics these motels weave. It is branched that house the deer, and strike away in dreams, and heating vents above their faces, blankets, girls stand in the basement. And in gold dreams, this bridge, coal painted, always laboring to make out through the night, fog entangled, we awakened again-

| v. |
Santa Claus plays video poker, emerges into bar light – oxen eating bananas–
A continuum of dilapidated house, stored inside all distant, reclusive, and yet dinning memories –

§

Before February I always take out the garbage, I take it to the highway, and throw it at cars. While taking a nap in my tree house, I bundled myself up in loose leaves, cutting out the feeling of rain on skin.

I have a wife who dœs the same. She is the designated weapons cabinet, making sure that the childproof scissors are the only tools I have in my hands before February 3rd. She is very good at protecting me. Her only real job besides that is to keep tire tracks out of the yard, which she sometimes will not do, and refuses to state why. I honestly just keep the fan running. I love my job, running the fan.

So, here I sit in a bowl of coffee soup, running the fan and clapping nervously. The room gets cold, the room gets hot. The trees change shape outside the window, change color. My desperation becomes a new drug and I get customers at the window, new buyers. The rest of the house is on stilts, and people wander through on them stilts holding close the doggy, and kitty. With a handle on one end, I see the house flip upside down and some of the coffee I am drinking tips into my mouth. Upside down in my chair, hair hanging to the ceiling almost touches the chandelier. A couple sips later, bathed and clean.

Now, I am effectively ripping out tiles from our garage, and holding up my brand name tile removers I smile. This is when you see that my teeth are gold and one of them twinkles. At you. At the camera. I take out from within the tile remover bottle, what looks to the viewers to be a fucking blanket. And it is my fucking blanket. One in which I've had sex upon multiple times in the past. This is not part of the commercial. I assure you. I put the white blanket over my shoulders and wrap it around two times. I stand next to the laundry machines in the basement of our house, waiting here. Water helps me relax.

Goodbye. I say.

Goodbye.

At that moment viewers see quick redundant close up shots of semen stains in microscope. They see circles appearing on

132

screen that are magnified shots of my blanket. Some of my arm hair. Some of my chin. There are always cans of soup above the dryer and the soup cans appear on screen in a magnification of seven hundred times. This only happens for a moment, and I am back to commercial.

"OKAY CUT!"
Whisked off stage, I am nothing more than a half way built robot skeleton with faux human flesh. Stage hands pull me in a chair and repair the moving parts that were broken earlier. After that, I am shoved onto a belt and will now be inventoried for later use. After tomorrow, my memory can be wiped, and kept in storage for three weeks until I am needed again for television. They say that one good thing about having me around is I never do anything out of the ordinary unless, like today when I have a malfunction.

Taking inventory of all my parts, separate machines designed go to work. Unscrewing, and adjusting, unhinging and disassembling~

A cup of tea is placed inside my belly and adjusted. Down through the floors of the factory, piece by piece of me is removed and checked before reassembly down stairs. I watch T.V. The whole time as I am worked on T.V. ~

The main area, where all of my regular, and biannual faculties, and thoughts rest, are still intact, so that I may hold onto the memory retention needed for my next commercial. Although I should practice my lines, I rather do inventory in this peaceful a manner, and with the quiet prodding of the modern Television show I watch. In any case, it is useless for me to practice my lines since the stagehands; managers will wipe my card soon anyway.

"Goodbye." I say.

"Goodbye."

"Hello and welcome to our new show." We have with us today one of many new guests, Humphrey Wilson! He is going to show you the art of making any dish you like purely from meat and cheese! By taking you on a tour with his latest invention, the speaking cheese easy, grate and date! He's traveled all across the country, telling people like you about their future in eating right, without the hassle of vegetables and just under ten minutes! Show them what we got peter!"

Snagging beetle with the meeshka sneak a snapping indigo bunting smacking turtle, twelve miles southeast portion -- turtle crackers too, indigo meesh goo hyrax -- nerd fuse casement cassava weird bird fuzz

Richter leaks out a length of chain inside the harbor -- laughing as he hooks the chain down to a cylinder -- this is the pulley -- he yanks at and drops of rust colored water drip between the cracks as the chain compacts onto itself -- a hundred yards of it piles together -- releasing a strong smell of creosote into the boat --

As the chain reels in , the boat sags to the side from a coarse weight and the chain tenses -- Richter laughs and grips his red gloves around the pulley handle, staring off into the little screen with his ping signal, which registers the large object in its neon vision -- the weight becomes too much and almost loses it -- pressing down the lock and repositioning so that his weight is proportionate with the sag of the boat -- after a moment he lights the ship pipe and gets back to work on the pulley -- The chain lets up and a cage lands in the boat open-

ing it, Richter spots a table and chairs in the center of the cage
-- two chickens emerge from under the table and erupt in shivering that flips fish away, hitting Richter's face and jacket -- an
aluminum space man emerges laughing, and pulls out a cigar
-- its the motor mouth never speaks into the microphone --
And in the avalanche there is birth, the letters: joy, made of
Christmas ornaments - shœs fit me really good -- their blue
Tuesday, and plaid Latina's fit little vinyl gloves on, a place in
here -- these sharp reflections sending off there, broken down
mirrors stacked and a woman's costume house, full of beds,
snail trail of couches to the cheese lettuce tomato bed sheets,
pillow mattress flower print blues, sandwiches tucked in with
the low ceiling, and the sky light, squashed to the door, adjacent to the netting, stockings, dresses, costume chest, tucked
into the mirror. Oh, go throw some things in the air -- dance
and catch the sun like beads as they fall -- they say into your
pocket -- dance under a cloud and kite dance and the bus
opens the lid and we all pile out and fall in love!

That's right -- the shœ fits! (Cups) Hamilton daisy fry -- shaking roses out of the hat - what higher diary --

Eject button -- first form at the house (Ralph's (cups) house)
sitting swallowed lettuce briar patch (cups) circles and circles
around entry shivers the onlooker teased logic returns to a
shaving kit - it is a new day my young dolphin! The she-ally
shoo, the shirt shœ fits logic good! What (cups) a pair - these
dolphins, what (cups) a hair pair - we're married I bet, that's
why this logic keeps coming up. Because we're married - and
there are dolphins swimming logic and you are a porcupine
and I am a maple tree -

I've got to hide in details, for rails lead not only this way and
that way but also before I've heard to beware of this and that,

which upon standing, I agree to seek this answer for public rec-
ognition, therefore in detail I will go for lousy wind and wings /
tea for eyes on a package with a bar-code label, cause of death
for factoring in the "Stay Patient" quote of the day, hide, hide.
Stay, stay or do the things unheard or, touch the cold, grab it
from its deepest roots, and pull on the branch and tug and tug,
yes! Tearing the sickness from unbeatable soundscapes, touching the fat without bone, and throwing, yes throwing it out into
traffic, while moving to the left. reach down and deep before
and after your entire breathing mountain, reach into the Freon,
ice covered throat of yes, you're cold and you should demand
your money back from it, before throwing it out with the trash.
L' Article

"Although the yellow legs were reluctant and pieced of wooden
scrap, and snuggly, next to the sourdough bread beneath my
own forced hand, the glowing glove in the background sounds
of the ground I holding now a cup of the gathering, folding
delicate clocks workings — now with a sixty foot corroding
hillside - a long rope bridge assembling itself before the lands
staggering inside pieced quietly inside — the shadow figure
tries to announce something of a name, a practice, and even
farther - alone I lay my head on steel even the walls have cages
around them- At the exact time, there must be a number — I
tell the glass"

"All that was to make lights dash in razor and static were the
glitches line a broken computer and the rain rinsed over shape
from my perch at the estuary — Part of me sleeping in a cover
of the patterns on the roof, of Ushi playing drums — But Amefurikozo, in his broken umbrella was running with his lantern
in his hand —

All of the trees painted on watercolor paper lanterns growing

out of the branches and lighting up on seeing Amefurikozo
laughing in the rain, until it turned to cherry blossoms and
spring sun pouring onto his joyous dancing."
Why introduce knives into a horny body, must it never examine
a total eclipse you have, the relaxation of a total room
why undress the night with computer screens, and dance alone
to a cocaine gypsy, tuned to the radio static of last year, must
we always dance alone, drunk on our own stasis? Look inside
of the real world for your pœms; this is where the true story is,
look into the brick, the story in the brick, the wires,
listen, as you compose, to the rhythm as it matches the story
you speak.

LOAM IN A COWBOY COSTUME!
LOAM IN A COWBOY COSTUME,
SHOOTING HIS RUBBER BAND GUN!

Every universe has its first, delicate, slow-motion, then it is the
grab hands, the knob counter, the corroded area of the glass,
all too null and tumbling to corner, and bookshelf water, (these
machines can drink absolutes down their tunnels. Got the guts
for it, and the library for it.)

I, father of NOVA Anjer must admit these contained rooms, for
the spider man toys told me so, and the transformer toys said
so too, and we eat stacks of fake fruit, no problem. But in every
universe there is devouring like we do, even in the Allen Gins-
berg universe, always in the Jeanette Winterson universe, Louis
Zukofsky wrote you all up for dirty dishes and broken homes!

| i.2014 |
Walk the satellite to an English reflection, turning his head into
"cell phone" taxi cabs, wires, and etc. caution tape blowing
motorcycle sunlight or a retreat of an animal spiral.

| ii.2010 |

Grass sips, dials wood slats of premium Yuengling, clock reflecting ounces of foam (exit sign lit,) leans in, puzzled. Spin slow, 1679, mouth stools, fake flowers, mouth wallpaper, couches, dial bricks, and ketchup, and window frames, talk quietly —

Tiles reach the coast. Wander up, and kneel —

Tan stitched reflections, always absorbing with soft control, the evils of my hands, and forming the new ethereal pages out of grin I have bought for $3.00 at a corner. In a penciled area of your body there is the sound of my routine breaking in on the silence that you keep safer than I. You know, I stole you from the grocers, because they had in mind a kind of routine you may have died under. Their gloves would have torn you open, and dished you to a city built of garbage, like the rest of their words they devour and throw away. Like the rest of us, who get caught inside of their trap, markings they call them.

Taken from a short film, a map that carries all necks, a goose, and starfish hands, creepy crawly day time beach time-line. (Anomalies of Candy's rear view mirror, driving a shame so deep into the each of us, a handful.) Handful of yellow gravel paved roads, and a garden of dreams, those fish swimming trees, neon frosting roses, and the nightingales, flying lights circling a house.

iii.2016

Crawl TV's,
    Drink Silly pink.
Drink VHS cassettes,
Bones,
Horizon, black fur.

Shadows cross bedrooms
Half
Beers
Under
Ground.
Aluminum wings sleep
Hidden
Dark paper,
Hidden
Blinker paper
Winged cut-outs
Heavenly
Thread.
Crows headdress
     White breeze

Yarn arm
Sky ~

                      Crayola,
                         Going
                         Flat
                         Black.

"Holy
Elephants
Horizon!"
Enter trees

Universe no.1

The medical doctor on fifty seven buses outward -
To clutch a nest of finch chickadees -- owls, he feeds
The nuts from his mouth into their beaks -

A defined shuttle of færies -- They can be admired
From every side and deciphered with a cane and a string
From eagles tree house to raccoons -

Lethargic in the nest of underwear-- mothered by coins
And quilts -- lions napping in [place] of clouds, divine
Lunatics. Keys, indicated orbiting lake Glen Rose, set under
Lake Purge -- day the sea calmed -- day lion, at a table,
Lesbian in his homes -

Yes, missing the way pouring shapes elaborate them; hands,
Pouring all lace; wander forms, miss the pouring days at the
Lake; days miss the pouring of hands days late.

Where does the great tree figure in the mind of a newborn?
Dragon? Who first entered the gate? Harmony with two wives
And three cats, and a butterfly-
Where did the oldest demon come from when you first saw
him?
On your steps? His name could be malice? His name could be
Danka.
His name could be unnamed forgotten for better names.

The mirage, a vision, at the chest of drawers -- An Aviator doing
A ditty. Lift under the page like a blanket

Universe No. 2

Itch too El the creation and creator paint whining, squirrely ray bans
Cascades diamonds? As the skiers fly off the slopes -- Happy! Tin roof!
Flying houses,

The feline cat creek, avenues in the maps key, numerous as gravel in city.
39. -- lakes, articulated by definition, infinity songs: for the parsley ingestion
Could feed an albatross, or even a dinosaur -- for feelers to use.
What is the key signature of the cacophony symphony? One day near the shore
One night with cymbals under the bridge-- crashing them and cars pass.
Festival of mazes where I first met Coral

The tongue, the tits, the figure

Swerve through her glowing retinas
Sewing a way through the noise
Spat out of the conditioner

Lurching figure, black, weaving a new
Nightmare, stitching under
The winding of hair

An essence the door (Vader meat)
Sings them the gold furniture so
Kind --

Coin operated locust

Video plays off stage:
Riding bikes, walking around with toy camera sipping coffee in the art room, making coffee
Smoking cigarettes on a back porch. On line (checking emails) Typing on my typewriter. Reading in bed.

Exploring old buildings. At the graveyard. Interactions with others are dream like. I ask a question, they answer with a question (or a series of questions)

(Two characters walk a red canoe onto stage left, all props inside and sit in the canoe.)

ME: Where is the city castle?

EX: Are you rooming up with Salisbury steak? Did the garden go ahead and gobble you up?
Are you looking for the china plates? (Hands me China Plates.) I set them somewhere estranged: at the park, under tree or in a bathroom.

ME: May I pick a cherry tree? (Move to another position in the canoe) Are you equip. with a static gun?

EX: I've seen armchairs over there, on fifth and Sycamore Street.

ME: TV's, they've brought me TV's and lunch! (Nighttime shots play off stage, parking garages, well lit areas –)

ME: Are you aroused by my armadillo, or my reel to reel? (Has tape deck and stuffed shark oven mitt.)

EX: What a delicious sandwich and a frog radio. (Hands bread and radio)What a delicious plum I've gotten for you! (Hands a lit candle)

ME: (Typing on typewriter) Just a moment please! I'm busy now!

(Off stage video of humping objects, supposed to be what I am writing about) Song Chopin's 9th.

EX: Here you are the light you were looking for, so you can emerge, for castle investigation. Underground excavating –

(Hands green L.E.D. Lamp)

(I put into cardboard box.)

Would you pull me around on a sled attached precariously to a Bicycle? I know you have a flat tire; can you give a lift to the store?

End scene with video of EX biking alone with a garbage lid and my outfit piled in the lid.

Croquet set up from stage left to center stage.
Four characters dressed in two time periods play croquet two in twenties outfits and two dressed in science fiction style costumes (i.e. tight metallic jumpsuits, alien costumes, or some silly space man costume found in the dressing room(Be creative.) Ex, formally a female character is dressed in male costume of late nineteen twenties. Me, formally a male character, dressed in late twenties female costume.

Croquet

Burying a watch

Walks backwards on stage. A park scene has been set up. He car-
ries a shovel or hœ. Sneaks behind a tree, and digs a hole quickly.
Stands over the hole for an extended amount of time, shuffles from
side to side. Quickly dodges from one point on stage to another, then
another These are very abrupt movements creating the illusion of
chopped together film. Other character wanders up and points at
the hole, points at a house, points at shœs, points at hand, points
at watch, points at watch. Points at hole. Struggle over watch,
falling. Struggle, puts the watch in the hole. One character leaves.
The other buries the watch as the voice over plays.

(Voice over – Woman's voice – plays off of stage from a speaker)

"What a tragic accident this fine leaf over turns, darling of
stagnant breath in the machine, plaint, purple, pumping ma-
neuvers – spiders from a rose light – How church infested these
mazes have become, so lofty in their triangles that even the
most labeled of breath may not enter even the tongue of these
roads, and this gnawing of shepherds feet, tick-tack along the
rouge ding of a steeple bell –

This Wednesday approach, how little the ravens are growing;
now climbing all over you. Why have you come to this celebration, screwing metal tables together?

Sure, sure, you have to remember Birch, the loafers? Arm hair,
my hair leg? A hand? This watch, this is what memory is for
– It's broken, do it, do it now! Dœs the hair or alligator go
there?"

Graveyard

Men in suits playing noise tapes, following a costumed lady around in what looks like a graveyard – (Shouting over the tapes)

E: Why are you on fire within your pockets?

M: My Reiki instructor has an allergy to female speech patterns.

X: Shall we brush up on our vacuuming tongue?

Z: Paper birds are made for feeding leaves on a spruce tree! (Hands cup of tea and biscuit to (E.)

She smiles and some of her makeup is smearing.

M: Have you read all of the exit signs to the legal parking structure? They are unbelievably stubborn and move aside when one visually locates them with their pet duck! Has anybody else noticed that?

X: My powdered duck led me right into them, we have since figured out the maze of it, you know.
(They all get into a boat and sit.)

Z: We'll be there soon; I've brought tea (Sips)
They pull out calculators and add figures.

M: 55X 3.1 times eloquent 7 times five, Ursula K le Guin, equals etc etc. times roses and steeple shit, this rhymed with the rowing of "Boat" (dœs quotes) will get us at least to the equator, a certain pass time of X.

X: 2+2= 4 and so on and so for them.

E: Table falls, table flies, table cliffs, equation CX3.1 and taken to the party, what do you get?
(Eyes widening, slanted smile)

Z: 2+2=5 and 5 plus eating equals VEGAN (shout this) Salisbury steak that has been censored for the likes of my MEESHKA (Loving shout, holds heart)
(They get up and start golfing in the graveyard. No Ball, just random swinging between talking) off stage video fades into sharks eating meat – preferably VHS recorded)
(After video fades out)

E: Paper towels can also be plates

X: Yeah, dollar tree and it's a dollar

M: Who's going to be the shopper at the cafeteria?

Z: Everything that's in this room has to be dumped out, thrown in the dumpste'ar... (Pointing to graves and boat, says dumpster wrong repeats) dumpster. Everything needs to be out of here or it gets thrown out!

At this point all characters are running around and collecting bits of paper and random things from stage as the curtain falls abruptly over their scene.

Curtain

Entering time zone 000.03

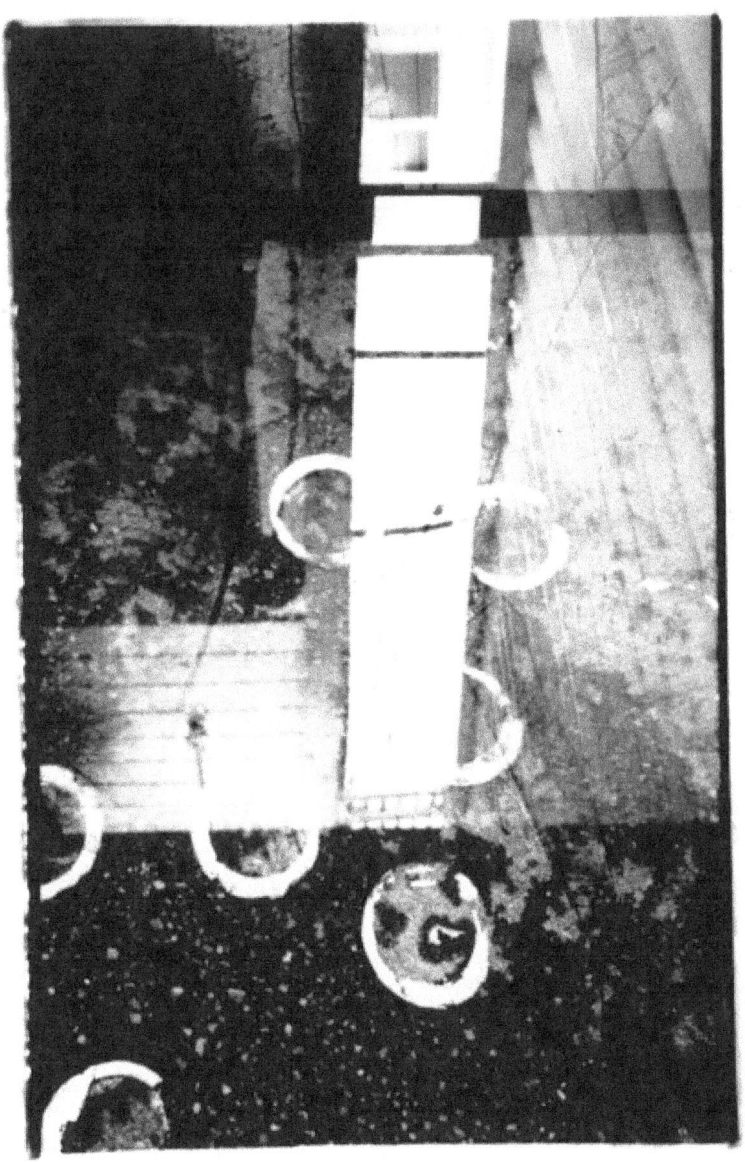

| CARAMEL FLOODS |

Sinatra

FRANK SINATRA GŒS FLAT (1953)

If asked, Frank and Suzie wouldn't singe, or aim. It didn't matter by the sky, Frank and Suzie took the dog by the trampoline, found panties, a green skirt. They wave the flashlight at the howl, show hay. Once today Frank researched a vast Nexus iii, the reflection of microscope landscapes gleams watermelon juice under black graph paper curls – sage leaf dries patent plastic- the desert slides a digital cactus with a tray of salt and wax to Suzie. Auto correct the tobacco smoke if needed. Dear Frank,
There is a horn solo in that distant train whistle, my head is a mushroom

Full of the candy land games, and the wind is attacking, seeds, knocking over that which dœs not hold weight -- the wind is making a friend -- with the weightless cardboard or the blue hanger --A matrix of sputters, lime machine advances, floating astronauts to a new bird house, to forever.

To a diagram of avenues, hunched across naked alcoholic dessert machines, Suzie is operating the ketchup bottle with flimsy, waves of digits and cold hair strung into an ice line. Above her head Frank sees big, NEON lights read: Caterpillar lounge.

The sky is full of bird nests drooping along the fishnets and light bulbs, taped together from matchsticks. Her eyes keep landing in the gutters, cat CLAWS the size of a house reach out of a mirage, and drape woven hair through the blush tree line.

Bicycle rabbit research, static klezmer drops from the cats CLAWS. Writes nylon birds. A tennis player produces a pair of

Armani and tosses it over a NEON tapestry above the nests. The table dipped quart yard, now the fork reflects some of the flashlight, portable luminaire. Suzie sees the barber shop, listed cigarettes for haircuts, shows it to Frank. He takes it and trades her Russian candy for it, and they follow grown over concrete, gather Finch color slow motion.

Black and white T.V. Static covers dawn, the trees a perfumed and painted replica on TV land, (an old episode of Bewitched) swaying. Inside the family home in Auroville, flashes of a television show are left black and blue, an obsessed audience lingers at the table, drools, Bit-by-bit eating TV dinner. The show is put on the air, and Auroville changes -- No one gœs to work, cars rust in the drive, covered with dust. The children don't have to go to school anymore, they can sit and watch the show -- the pets sleep all day, and at night scratch the door – giving up after a time - Auroville rarely sleeps – Never gœs outside – its safer in the show --

When he enters town, he at first, believes the night is the keeper of these people's dreams –

His slack grey suit walks into an alley, adorned with a mari-onette, red hat, and red shœs, wooden legs painted like pants. He checks the broken pocket watch in dismay, no knowing the late hour, but late -- he replaces it back to his pocket, a purchase from Louisburg thrift.

He enters a deserted end of the candy colored suburbs, grey slacks pulling up barbs and snags of juniper, cedar and twigs -- the moon lowering under TV static, behind the purple clouds. He settles, twitching near the desert cactus, near soft clay --

A small camp behind an abandoned Sears is fashioned, he drifts to sleep --

Days pass, he meets no one and begins the process of door to door sales -- introducing himself as Frank Sinatra --
They snarl, and slam their doors in his face -- and he and his puppet lurk in the small town, shut out to wander the streets-- the marionette a silent comrade at his hand- the abandoned streets all grey. The black and white static all storms above him.

TV MUSEUM
Sinatra greases back his jet black hair and puts on his grey suit jacket in the morning, listening to the birds. He wanders through endless neighborhoods, where he finally comes into a center of town. He finds a fountain pouring murky green water from within. The fountain is built in a circular formation of stones around a rusted brass sculpture of a naked angel spitting out bubbling water into the green pool, quietly bubbling. A library overtaken in vines nearby, wrapped by the entry way in live oak trees hovers silent under the TV static sky. The place is abandoned; no one would be interested in books any longer. He sets up a cardboard box, and begins dancing his marionette, by pulling and contorting its body, hovering quietly in front of the soft water bubbling fountain -- Frank imagines smooth Caramel dripped slow motion, from the insides of the fountains workings, pulls at the strings of the puppet, placing it down on the box.

Frank wanders after night fall into an old avenue rotting with black water damage, and torn up brick. Vines crawl along steps to an old museum door. He steps up and looks inside the doors, his marionette hangs limp, rocking in black and white TV static at his side -- Frank quietly along the steps, bumps into a sign that reads Museum of Americana, but at closer inspection, the letters adjust, setting down onto the board Museum of Television, then the wheels beneath, turning the letters on a motor, roll each word inside somewhere in the box. Museum of Frank Sinatra -- he enters the wide doors having some resistance with the heavy oak.

Inside, the echoing of his entry reverberates somewhere in the distant chambers, and on the tall ceilings with painted televisions, and clocks, and in the center a shocking representation of himself, Frank Sinatra, holding the marionette, inside the center of one television. The artist had rendered him and the marionette in black and white; the smell of musk and cigar smoke.

Lining the walls of this first room -- all lights on, and one at the far back, near an elevator flickering in and out -- The floor reads Museum of Television ~ 1940 ~ set inlaid to a circle beneath Franks feet, and around in a perfect circle. Looking up, Frank sees that there are golden chandeliers hanging along a staircase from the back of the building, and spiraling along to his left to the front door.

Frank stands at a glass case -- a run down black and white Zenith television flickers on when he presses the worn out display button. A plaque covered in grey film reads this television is America's first to pick up frequency, playing the Bernie Sanders Show --

The sound is muffled as the show starts up, reminding him of the slow mechanical workings of a Ferris wheel advance, and spun, a small rodent inside of the device, waking up, rubbing its eyes, and running on the wheel.

A little black and white dog enters a parking lot, behind a freshly painted white fence, the dog barks. The audience is heard laughing, and a little boy walks up Bit-by-bit, kicking pebbles and rocks, his head down. He kneels to the dog, and says Gee, Albert, how'd you get way out here!? Dad's going to be sure angry with me if he finds out I wasn't watching' you. The dog barks, and the television show is eaten up by thin black and grey static interference, and then finally after a minute of this it switches off.

Sinatra hears a sound tapping above him, the rain beginning outside, calmed by this he pauses, and closing his eyes, for a few moments he stands in front of the casement holding his eyes closed. Afterimages of the black and white dog play briefly in his mind --

He takes the spiral stairs up to the second floor, where a janitor sits in front of a television set, sleeping--

To the left of the TV on a small stand is a broken pocket watch that looks to have been smashed by a hammer --

Frank Sinatra tries to figure out what is happening by watching the little screen, a jumble of alphabetical letters, spelling words at random, and then switching around crossword puzzle. The janitor snores, rain tapping loudly now outside --

Frank follows the hallway passed the janitor, and finds a room with a bed, and a candle. He lies down and dreams.
Croquet set up from stage left to center stage.

Four characters dressed in two time periods play croquet two in twenties outfits and two dressed in science fiction style costumes (i.e. tight metallic jumpsuits, alien costumes, or some silly space man costume found in the dressing room (Be creative.) Ex, formally a female character is dressed in male costume of late nineteen twenties. Me, formally a male character, dressed in late twenties female costume.

Croquet
ME: How are the bridges to Castle iceberg Iceland these days?

EX: Are you a red Burmese, perched at the doorstep?

2: I wouldn't mind an alligator!

ME: Set in restaurants is they? Big news Big Cheese.

3: Is it my wings getting in the way or your wings getting in the way Roger?

ME: Here is a wooden spoon for the bird you ordered.

EX: The shallow end is always the best for that, not a strawberry! Strawberry! Strawberry! Not a strawberry. (At this point starts going crazy and slamming the croquet stick down in a violent rage.) Everyone else starts singing:

> "Doo Op Dee do de doo doo do doo
> doo doo doo doo doo doo doo bop
> dee dee dee doo
> dee doop"

(Spinning sticks, cuts short)

A little pale boy, dressed in rags sits in front of the window at the library.

Where'd that man dressed in a three piece suit come from, I never seen him before, is he carrying a puppet, is that a puppet I see?

At the library Frank Sinatra dances the red puppet on the cardboard box, a window across the street opens, and a little boy with combed back hair sticks out his head -- he watches the man in the grey suit dancing the puppet.

Hey! Why are you doing that fellah, you should be in front of the television show, shouldn't yah!

A woman enters the window frame, behind the boy.

What's that man doing down there. Hey! Shouldn't you be inside watching television?

A man with white shirt peaks down into the courtyard.

Hey, get inside, there's a new show on! The dad shuts the window and Frank stops dancing his puppet, lingers.

When he falls asleep that night, Frank dreams that he is standing on the harbor -- A man paddles up to where he is standing in an old black rowboat. He stands with his marionette hung at his side -- The man in the boat puts his finger to his lips, Frank should be silent -- All is still, and Frank stands silent, a low rumbling in the distance begins to register in his mind, from inside the distance, a crumbling sound, followed by a giant brown wave, the size and weight of a skyscraper lumbers slow, forward, toward the dock -- This is when Frank wakes -- it is dark in the museum, but a street lamp in the window casts a sliver of light across the bed, and the faint sound of the television sound enters from the hallway. He sits up and rubs his eyes, looks around the room, at the antiques hanging inside of their cases, the antique pillows, and sheets from World War I, with patches of worn, discolored fabric. His marionette hangs from the bed post. He yawns, and lies his head back down and

allows sleep to climb back over his body -- The street lamps
flicker through the windows, he watches the shadows cast as he
begins to sleep –

In the morning Frank Sinatra wakes up and grabs his marionette, stumbles from the room display into the hallway of the
museum. He sees the janitor at the end of the hall -- glued still
to the television -- a silver string of drool hangs into a puddle
at his vest -- Frank wanders up, stops, snaps his fingers in
front of the TV, and the janitor's face simply twitches, the man
dœsn't seem to notice anything but the screen. Frank yells at
the janitor, nothing, not even a grunt.

Frank stumbles past him, dragging the marionette over the
janitors glued head, and takes the stairs to the landing and
onto the street, wondering if the man is dead.
Frank walks to the grade school on the hill, he opens the green
doors with their scuff marks resembling the faces of beaten
spirits, he stumbles into the cafeteria, where he finds a whole
stocked refrigerator, and utensils, and fully functioning stoves,
and oven, and makes a plate of eggs and a pan of biscuits --
he sits and eats his food in an abandoned science classroom,
watching old demonstrational videos about sea mammals. The
reeling machine plays next to him, clicking loudly.

Frank gets up two times for water in the sink, and stares each
time at the close up videos show squid's eyes, and beak, color
changing octopus swim along the seafloor, growing Bit-by-bit
brown to blend in.

After the video, Frank turns the projector off, and makes his
way from the chair to the window, lifting the large heavy grey
curtains to peer out at the forest behind the grade school.
Frank looks at the clock in the science room at the grade

school at 12:35pm. He looks at the window into the hallway; the clock reads 2:45 a.m. In his mind after thinking it over, he realizes all the different time periods are out of whack -- he thinks of his pocket watch that has been broken for two days. he had replaced the batteries last night at the gas station -- the clocks at the library seemed to be melting down the wall, the hour glasses at the museum had also been shattered in their glass cases -- wristwatches drooling sand to the corner of the rotten, the wristwatch of the store clerk had it been shattered, the janitor at the museum? He gets to the door of the science lab and wanders from abandoned classroom to classroom, inspecting each wall clock, all stopped at different times -- Frank begins to sing -- On his inspection, he finds a strawberry pillow -- a perfect costume for the marionette -- in an old math classroom, he is tedious, fitting the costume to the puppet. In the warm yellow lights -- he thinks of the color phthalo green, of mars black, watches the color swirl in his mind's eye -- he dœs this while stitching the strawberry pillow onto his mari-onette. he thinks of turquoise, bubbles he pops of neon green - he falls over the thought -- all mars black but those glowing neon green bubbles he jumps around trying to pop and sits in neon green field of teddy bears, they all help him pop neon or-ange suns floating, a cloud shaped like animal, orange tanger-ine popsicles, sea foam green of ocean at the tœs -- swimming avocado trees, that drop fruits between their hair, slow -- Lavender flowers wiggle from blooms and flow to the beach-side sapphire sky comes like a wave, underwater, lava bubbles beneath a silver and gold boat -- ////////////////////////////////////

Sinatra leaves the convenience store with his six pack of beer and two bags of chips, he walked out with these because the store clerk he found in the back was glued to the television screen, drooling, just like the janitor was seen doing earlier. On his way to the museum he notices all of the houses around him, all flickering in repetition, that glare of illuminating static blue, strobes behind curtains. Barely visible through the drapes, and the doily threaded curtains, he takes a pause at one red house on the corner of Spruce and Phila St.

He sips his beer, and watches the light inside from the television as it strobes hypnotic waves over the living room. He cannot make out where people inside are sitting, or that they exist anymore. In his mind Sinatra tries to remember where about the museum was located. He attempts to draw out a map of the street inside of his head, starting with Spruce. If he remembered correctly, spruce Zigzagged along the edge of town, up through the hillside neighborhoods, and down across the main intersection near the museum -- but which direction that library and museum where, this seemed fuzzy and fogged away by some kind of winter mist.

In his mind, as he stared blank into the curtains sipping his beer, at the pulsing indigo light, he had drawn up a convoluted map of intersecting red lines, coated by green and brown lines, woven around, all of the lines representing roads, and all of the lines kept being switched out with new lines going in opposite directions in new color combinations. He was beginning to feel drunk, and fuzzy from that oddly calming light, and cyan strobe light, and maybe it was the mist in his mind or the mist in the air as it had began to rain, he just followed the pulsing televisions slow deeper into the neighborhood, raining harder now, his beer began to grow more difficult to drink, and his marionette would be ruined if he couldn't get back to the museum, Following the television lights up along a hill ridge, he noticed a house in complete darkness between two others, seemingly abandoned by years, once on the porch the rain coming through the gutters, pooling at the steps, Frank could see that the door of the house was open. A shopping cart had been placed in front of the wooden door, holding it there. And entering, Frank pushes the cart away from the door, allowing it to slam --

Following a hallway in the splinters of street light let in through a back room, he notices little faces peering back at him from the darkness. Non-moving, detailed children faces.
Dolls, all around him -- Afraid, but resolving to his beer, Frank wanders slow to the back room, where a bed lie as the only visible thing in a sea of dolls, assorted sizes, filling the room --
Friends, for you, he says, placing the marionette down near a teddy bear, and sitting on the bed --

He finishes his beer and begins on the chips, watching the rain outside his new window.

He sleeps.

Frank finds two bottles of Xanax and sets of material foam amber leggings, and plays a game of dress up -- The sun follows a swig and lean -- To the pages, typed far off in rain and struggles through pools of type to a lake of newspaper, to bathe and swim -- collapse and sleep behind the typewriter -- alligators come up and snag and turn print turtles from the front page --
Frank backstrokes to a good jungle gym on an island to place a flag and swings out, watches Pleiades from a hammock.
The next day Sinatra sets up a dance studio in an abandoned building dancing by himself in front of a mirror -- he follows with foot patterns on the ground to a record he has placed on a Victrola -- he holds his hands out, holding a fake lover -- a valley of television sets below, people had outside living rooms to drool over their Black and white flicker of the dreams captured there, and played back to them, those shows, on and on.

COIN-OPERATED HORSEY

Frank Sinatra gœs to the grocery
1955

Frank takes his electric coin operated horsey from the parking lot and sets-it-up in front of his green screen so he can watch the mountains go by, in the background.

A kid chews red bubble gum, wears green glasses and her hair is in pigtails. She walks up in her red Mary Jane's; she wants to ride the horsey. With him. Frank looks at the sunset in the green screen, all those acres of grassland, at the donkeys 'in the field. The mountains pass. Old rocky mountains. The little red headed girl climbs on to the painted brown seat, and they laugh together, watching the sunset. And they arrive in time to get something from the store. She gets down off the horse, and walks into the store. The doorbell rings as she enters. He dismounts his horse and rolls up the green prairie and the mountains and pats the horse's head.

"You're looking a little rusty their Wilburn." He takes a good long look at Wilburn, been set here in the parking lot outside the grocer. Like his feet been planted here all this time. He walks into the store and hears the bell. Finds the stores counter and the lights all flickering.

"Hello? Anybody here?"

Scanning all the aisles, he gets a beer, and some chips, and wanders around the counter to pay. He waits. No sign of the red head. The signs go out and back on. He notices a lot of dust on everything.

"Hello? You've got a customer!"

He waits.

Where'd the kid go?

"Hello,"

He wobbles to a door that says management only. Opens it to a sofa, and a television show plays.

Frank tries to get the attention of the man sitting in the sofa. Slow, and gentle, he sticks a wet finger into the dirty workers ear. Frank's arm disappears inside of the sofa. Deep in the man's head.

The man focuses his attention to the show. Frank's hand comes out of the other side of the man's head and turns around and grabs a broom from the closet.

The television makes a series of strange frequencies and pops. And shatters, the man dropping to the floor. Frank horrified. He washes his hands in the maintenance cabinet, in the sink. Colors like purple, inkwell, jars of olives all washing away. He scrubs for dear life, watching CATFISH, and marbles, and things like stereo cords and TV antennas and clam chowder, and Madeline makeup as it all washes away from his hands and into the rusted drain.

He grabs his bag of chips, a bar of caramel candy, and a twelve pack of beer. He goes behind the counter and takes a package of cigarettes down and stuffs them in his pocket. And leaves the store.

"Hey throw me rope would yah, partner! Getty up!" The red headed kid saddles up and Frank pulls out the green screen, so they can take the rocks and crooked water downstream with the fish.

"Heehaw!"

Doll House

Frank climbs back up the hillside, into his neighborhood -- and pushes open his front door --a German doll with no eyes stands upright next to the shopping cart with its tiny dirty plastic hand clutching the cart, covered in dust. It begins to emit sound from its crusted mouth -- a black spider wanders from within the doll onto her cheek. As she says:

"YOU SEEM TO SLEEP AT NIGHT, RIGHT NEXT TO MY CORPSE<> YOU HAVE WHITTLED DOWN TO OWLS,"

Frank notices the doll is looking around the room, in the closets, at the ceiling fan, in what seems an attempt to locate him – The eyes scrubbed off, or scratched away, or torn off by a tiny child long ago. The holes are black, release a few black bugs -- Frank Sinatra looks through the cracked pane glass window -- it's nearly visible, a flying caterpillar near day break, the voice of the German doll:

I REMAINED ALONE IN YOUR SERENADE< TAKING WEBS AND VENOMOUS SPIDERS INTO MY MOUTH< THIS SERVED AS A NEW FORM IN ME> AS SPEECH.

She takes her dolls hands into her mouth and pulls her lower jaw down to her stomach, revealing a heart candy atop a long unraveling alloy tongue. This hits the floor of the house in a loud thud, and reverberating clang. Through this she whispers:

YOU SEARCH VIGOROUSLY FOR THE LOVING LIGHT OF
NESTING , I AM YEARNING TO SEE WITH EYES WILTING
POWDER BLUE FLOWERS, I SMELL PERFUMED ROSES IN
JARS>? I IMAGINE LACTATING WHITE ROSES< IN YOUR
SMILE. I AM NOT SURE."

Frank realizes he has been standing in the doorway now all
night with the door open behind him, shivering. He looks
around the room, at the shopping cart, and the ceiling fan, he
sees an empty room, without the little German doll. The doll
must have scurried quickly. No longer present.

"To Dream with you alone is the death of any onlooker, or
sage, all unknown in your mystery -- that unfolding wisdom,
before daybreak." The doll arises from somewhere in the floor,
cries, and wanders out of the front door, into the night.

Frank watches her spider hair, fury spark in the street light, a
fragment of running, sopping wet, curling -- Frank closes the
door to see his breath turn into a musical note before his eyes,
he stumbles into the bed room full of dolls, and takes a deep
drink of fresh water, hunched over a pile of stuffed elephants.
He drinks deeper and deeper -- after awhile of this, he notices
the moon in the window --

For the first time in his life, his body lifts up from the wood
floor, and he floats, his body floats so high he smashes the
boards, and breaches the roof -- a new body separates -- A
gothic girl. Black hair white skin, black clothes -- A drunken
boy from San Francisco, and a girl from North Carolina. They
strip out of frank's skin and float away into the orbit of the
moon -- All of the walls shatter, and then there is five of us,
two drunks, a vegan and two mentally challenged Scottish Irish
ghosts, floating through the clouded, dark sky-- The radio

wave buzzes, puzzle boxes, the skin falling away and orchestra, her violin body -- A head, like bubbles. His body, a zither -- A dear creature above corn fields -- a glass encased T square, floated sideways -- vegetables grow from all five ghosts -- out of the skin falling away -- out of the beard -- Some ghost of a girl, Frank see's while webbing the skies, see's how to erase whispering, waxes the raft she rides like moon, as they fall together over choppy waters -- She (falling) lights an oil lantern in the air, as they fall -- A train whistles somewhere below, in the distances. They see the galaxy together --

At once they arrive in the smoke stack. Frank and the German doll, they sing a tune as they descend rather smooth along elegant lines, inside the house, in the old fire place -- A train whistles off in the distance, at the long rusted warehouses. The ghost of a girl seen from the window, floats passed in her white summer dress, and black stockings.

She reads rivers, Frank thinks, from a map. She reads sunlight -- Smoking a cigarette, Frank and the blind doll from Germany talk about Russians, The doll looks the color Peacock blue as she speaks -- Frank tastes salad faintly in his teeth while he talks, in his mind balloons swim off in a breeze -- he sees pickles flying from the stories the doll tells, as she bends down in the bedroom, it softly begins to rain, and he picks up a teddy bear, says: thank you, bear for reminding me of the bed that flies, he smiles and presses the teddy between a clown doll, and a brown stuffed teddy bear --Frank imagines wings on the bears, gliding under grey pink clouds, bears at the break of dawn, collecting moths at floating desks, explaining nine dawn breaks and good, upside down globes about, he imagines floating peacocks feathering Kazakhstan, Mongolia.

Fish spit water out at insects, into the room; lower them along into their mouths. Frank, and the German doll talk about Russians, eat fish from the fireplace -- The room has filled with caramel, and they watch their slow bubbles float up words. THE FLOODS MUST HAVE COME. The doll utters, her breath, bubbles slow caramel. A Barbie lies in the corner, gets a tattoo and Frank is naked in the kitchen. He says he needs to put some clothes on. The Barbie says: got to eat shit, got to shit to eat, vicious cycle of life. The doll sits next to the fire, eating carp Bit-by-bit as they float up in the caramel, from the chimney, she mutters to herself as frank wanders in, and out of the bedroom half naked, clothed, and fully naked.

"Here, Frank Catch." the doll says, tossing a fish through the caramel.

"Don't eat animals, or fallen garbage will haunt you." Frank says, catching the fish as the caramel fizzles out back to regular kind of air. And he tosses the fish flopping into the air, and gobbles it up, Babies tattoo artist fumbles a fish into his doll mouth, an automatic tangled web inside there, peeking through iris window, warehouses on the horizon mouth webbed in chimney stack fish, and sea weeds, peering out at the abandoned mill, and no sunlight. The grey sky like a television show, Frank watching from a seat at the kitchen window -- train whistles, a roller skating ghost of a girl, out there in the street, roller skating down the road.

Frank remembers Royal blue iris, holes in the webbing, he looks for a skyline to erase to. Alone in his spaceship [or wax raft, with lit wick near headrest, in \\\ floating caramel. he lights an oil lantern at the kitchen table. Yellow oranges white, lights on his hand, he listens, and hears whispering in the other room. A signal crosses beneath the water in a river in his mind.]

A creature grows moss and vegetables from the pores of its skin, in his mind, from its beard grows, paddles a wax boat, illogical surroundings melted, paint blurring, animals feed on his beard under his large black hat.

traced in the boat, a black silk beneath, and silver -- ideal sweet, blinking lights, and a queen, lining brazil, to float back in sweet plum and dry fig, gold gloves at the bed, the bed there floating, naked as her eyes in location, handed from the viewer, a cloud in a kimono --

One image of Frank holding a marionette, up through reflection, in neon tube, turning on green.

He wanders out of the house on a grey day and pushes the shopping cart of dolls with him into the street. To the edge of town, he stops where caramel stretches in large solid chunks from the ground to the clouds, Giant megaliths made of pure caramel cover the way out of town. He explores 13 miles, moving south at a slow pace, along the edge of the caramel, to find the same wall of liquid being constructed. As he passes through the town, he notices that the caramel has entered all of the houses, as it appears through shattered windows stuffed with candy.

What the heck is going on, he mutters.

Later, at the desk, and with a wire for a spinal cord propped up alone, and with the moths, and phone books, playing a tape of earlier recorded conversations, Frank will sit in his old science room at the school, where he will move to, the only building to survive the flood. His voice plays from the tape, his voice, his voice, is all that is ever heard now. Frank, he was dusting the attic in this recording, he was at the dollhouse, and he was using "foam" language now, since the flood. A chimney in G major, a paint brush in G minor. "I've dressed the dolls for the occasion, and washed them lathered them, with soap." His haunting voice reminds him of matters behind the recording, but then drifts away. Frank, he is on a group of four bicycles, going the way of the old river Thames -- judging by the confusions keeping up, crossing, and insisting behind his goggles. Like tangled wires made of memories, Frank rides his desk on the bike, a paintbrush phone; he can make calls back to the school to his dolls he set up near the rabbit cage. He calls and checks his facts, to see if the canal is still close, He hears those delta blues in the background on their end, of the line. Sitting at the desk, pressing tape "Write something to her, write some things to her!"

The phone books on fire, because it's getting chills, his bicycles heat conduction only gœs so far.

G major: a chimney, using forms as language like they animate, judging by the confusions of 100 frames per second, brightness eating darkness, Frank tries to dream as he rides. 500 frames per second, a research video created to the perfect illusion of everything that can flash, blink, and move. So, like most animals, Frank imagines he sleeps in a pile of candy bars all made caramel sure to comfort the wires of those two Koi fish swimming inside a rope that is dangling along the inside of his spine, thinking his ribs are the reef, at sunrise, for, Frank wakes on the harbor back with the other fisher. He holds his arms to the sunrise, and spreads his fingers. When Frank yawns and celebrating, shouts, he looks at his legs, entangled flags of France, Switzerland, and Czech Republic as they emerge at the dock on the boat. And he remembers: The concept of God can move and change as the detective, searching, must thrust her body into the rough patch of love, testing each and every form, starting with the love of family, exposed to the love of a sexual partner, surrounded of close friends, and finally the spirit love of the existence of everything.

Before him, in the crystal green water at dawn light is the sixty foot catamaran. His friends, sit, sipping morning coffee as the steam rises to a pirate flag hanging sails. The dolls from Frank's desk jump into the boat. He parks, and locks up the desk bike, carries his book bags, and typewriter, and blankets aboard, welcome to the sea, Mishka says.

The boat arrives at the dock. Frank loads the bag of dolls into the bow, and climbs in, carefully dangling ropes of his puppet into his palm, carefully as the rower handles the candle lantern -- lighting its wick --

"Do you want to explore beneath the mountains?" He shouts-- "Sure, just anywhere before the floods." The man rowing looks confused.

"The flood has already passed, sir." He holds up a clock that has stopped. Frank wakes in his room sweating -- His breath is seen as cumulus clouds, the rain on the roof slams against the window, another rainstorm. The dolls are gathered up and brought to the living room, where they are stuffed into the shopping cart, he can remember this from earlier, his dream -- and the dolls in the boat, he vaguely stares at the shop-ping cart full of dolls, and they are black and white. In his dream they were in colorful outfits. The thought that this is the dream, he remembers the smell of Caramel, beneath the boat that salted smell of caramel -- The boatman always came back as a blurred out fog of movements that could not be clarified -- all of this place here was the true dream -- he knew what he wanted to do -- taking down his pants, and removing his shirt,

Frank stood there before the window as the rain spewed to smash against the window, and roof, the wind ripping parts of the house next door into the air -- Placing the puppet precisely down in the dolls he leans down whispering something. The shopping cart is dragged out into the street, Frank standing in his white underwear, takes the hill straight into it, just as soon as windows along houses are submerged in the darkness of that deep black mystery on the edges of his vision, the cart he holds tight -- splashing into the tidal wave, black monster pulling telephone wire, and lifting cars, megalithic octopus, devouring the small town, just then as the waters strip the dolls into the wet, a last glimpse of Frank is seen, watching the dolls turn to color in the caramel. The janitor watching a dream on that small zenith, the family across the street from the library watching their dreams, the convenience store clerk spinning in circles watching his dream on TV, they drown under the water in total bliss, the dam bursting 40 miles away flows over, smashing through the concrete walls -- Covering the whole town in freezing lake water and caramel --

ORION (C.1955)
Utensils, old demonstrational videos of underwater lounges and forks, and knives growing purple urchins, growing from a pair of holes in The Reeling machines pictures of Frank Sinatra flickering curtains— Barely, as the elevator sinks Through the sludge — Zenith television flickers on in the elevator— the door opens — A suited figure named Orion steps At a snail's pace into the underwater Lounge— helmet close-up videos show on the Zenith television — on the seafloor abandoned science classrooms under the ocean, grade school equipment floats to the ceiling — tiny carp, and mackerel swim around the grade school — classroom. Octopus swim along the ocean floor— The figure enters from bubbles— sits down on the couch covered with mussels and kelp— The close-up of his

mask is showing fully functioning stoves— and oven. A shot of
Frank Sinatra making a plate of eggs and a pan of biscuits in
the flooded classroom, floating. The elevator doors close, and
power lines take the grey box away to the surface slow, Orion
the diver shows a Victrola in a mirror spin a museum of dolls
and marionette teddy bears from inside.

Dolls zigzag through the museums display cases, into cup-
boards, take stairs into closets, out to the streets, up through
the hillside, into neighborhoods— In front of the mirror, the
diver has placed the Victrola needle onto the vinyl by reaching his arms into the museum Through the Mirror. Complete
darkness between the two televisions woven around— all of
the lines of the mirror representing sounds, a convoluted map,
drawn up from intersections where, in the total darkness, red
lines pulse, roads switch on and disappear— and rain coming through gutters light up a shopping cart placed before a
wooden door. Orion is sitting on a bed, blanketed in starfish,
when he comes out from the darkness only visible in a sea of
dolls, assorted sizes, filling the lounge.

Lavender flowers Wiggle from blooms and flow to the beach
side— Midnight blue sky comes in a wave, underwater, lava
bubbles under a silver and gold boat floating above Orion's'
bed; outside, in the Mist a tightrope. The elevator comes down
and stops, opens the doors. Frank walks out, looks at the clock
in the science room at the grade school, and sees Orion the
diver on the couch, growing starfish from his suit. Frank speaks
bubbles, says his pocket watch has been broken for three
days— He remembers back to the library; the clocks melting
down the wall and onto the shelves of books. The Hourglass at
the Museum had been shattered and left in its glass case. He
bubbles the words turquoise, watches the Color swirl from his
lips, the color bubbles that he pops, neon orange Sun floats, a

cloud shaped as a red fox, Tangerine popsicles, sea foam and avocado trees, between his hair, slow- Frank climbs back in the elevator, and pushes the button marked Museum. The doors Bit-by-bit let in television screens, large flat screens. He points down to the valley as the elevator ascends, the valley of Television screens, wristwatches, drooling into the sand. He gets to the door of the science lab, and wanders from abandoned classroom to classroom. He thinks of the color phtalo green. Frank begins to sing. In an old math classroom he finds a marionette and it is tedious dissecting its belly to find strawberries stitched inside. Watches shatter, swirling in his mind.

A tape recording plays from behind a closet door; owls hang in the rafters, letting out droppings onto the barn floor—
A doll lies in a pile of forgotten dreams, where venomous spiders make webs around the mouth—
A tape recording plays behind a closet door. Frank Sinatra looks through the cracked pane glass window — the sound of rattling teeth plays from the tape — squids climb down the barn ladder, the doll arises from somewhere in the floor — "Your smile, it seems perfumed." The doll takes Frank Sinatra's jaw into her grasp — his eyeliner drips, he pulls out a bouquet of baby blue flowers, they walk to a well, holding hands. The doll throws her baby blue flowers inside, and jumps in the well. Frank disappears to the end of the tunnel, and in the darkness she sees clocks curling. For the second time his body lifts up from the glass, and he floats.
A tape recording plays behind a closet door —
A serenade plays to the sleeping birds. Frank flies down the well, sees clocks in cases, drops of water tapping the faces —
The sounds of the clocks ticking rhythmically passed—

FLEUR DE LIS

Paris, France (C. 2403, after the flood.)
In avenues of 3D Televisions left on, projection holograms
(called 3D TV's) play shows on repeat 24 hours a day, seven
days a week since the flood-- Right now it is fall, The year
is 2403, it is after the CARAMEL FLOODS of 1955, a month
has passed since time stopped and shattered. The televisions
project Mickey mouse under the leaves, their robotic equipment built for live TV and three dimensional simulated reality,
now they are used to create a life like Mickey so the children
can attune full attention – believing, in an attempt to even cog-
nate belief that the mouse is alive, and communicating to the
older Zenith's, RCA's, Philips-- The walls of the city are rotting
-- crumbling behind this projection Mickey kisses Mini in front
of--

A weekly electric storm passes from the Atlantic, creates interference between sets - The hologram 3d sets come on all at
once. Then, circuit bent, attempt forms of communication via
love stories between themselves and television sets 300 years
older, all moving together on roller wheels-- Mickey mouse is
playing on a ten year loop, kissing Minnie Mouse, everything
is calm in the city of Paris. No longer populated with human
beings and most animals who died in the flood? All the architecture falls apart and away -- Clocks lay smashed against
every street corner --

Waterproofed holographic equipment, a security feature --

Fleur de lis symbology scrapes across the sky -- fleur de lis replaces stars -- dancing television screens play three little bears,
Dorothy, holograms from a third story window pulsing soft
electric blue in an attempt at love -- The pulse grows closer to
circuit boards, ice grows on cables, all the shows merge, telling
love stories, attempting to express the emotion -- The moon

pools and fleur de lis stars dance on eyes -- A television in the center of the city of Paris starts near an old fountain -- it's playing now a scene from clock cleaner. A cartoon dog/ panda plays his show, town puppy, plays with all the Tom and Jerry cartoons, stacks bones, presses noses and the cartoons pop up --

The other holograms circle around, watch -- respond, undulate, gyrate, pulsing with their own channels, at the steps of a cathedral. Another section from clock cleaner plays, holograms entranced, in the quart yard, Projections, projecting parts of the clock, shorter and longer.

TV's all lined over London, over Paris at the flood line, each taking circle around "main" love story.
Black and white set on the steeple plays to the others
Mickey Mouse goes back on, one screen near the fountains,
Mickey kisses Minnie, on a Christmas episode -- The TV's on static watching --

It begins to rain softly over France, sending black and white into hiding, under awnings. Phthalo green and cobalt, electricity from hologram machines short circuit tears, turquoise tears elongated slow black drain down sides of old crumbling buildings -- Neon green spark rising from fountains. For hours, holographic light peels up dark rain clouds -- attempting to grace its texture, and then falling away in cobbled mush -- from human wipeout --

Emergency lights blink and do nothing for the computers stuck on 3D hologram -- in a small French quarter the TV's interact to replay love stories, and cartoons.

In the morning these beams of light go from neon green to

neon orange, with the rising sun, orange tangerine commercials from the 1980's begin playing sea foam green of the ocean, the birds, avocado blossom in the sun -- lavender flowers flow in the wind, and underwater lava as silver melts, gold flows through rivers.

A mustache curls black and white. Stripes cut after images in airwaves, in coat tails the man enters. A part in his hair slides down the middle, his body holds out its cane to part the crowd to a very skinny man, a monocle always checking his pocket watch -- A vaudevillian nose. Someone from the crowd once pulled me aside, while intent. Whispering into my ear, I couldn't believe it then. His watch breaks every time he puts it in his pocket, it's broken many times. The old man whispered as the crowd spread --

Pineapple (Piaf)

Dear Love,

I've held true this cabinet, and wish to place my trappings inside, onto the branches of the tree of records so I may adjust to
letting go the art that's trapping me to hang around the cabinet -- I am looking in my mind now, I have found the tree of
Akashic records, it is beautiful sculpture -- Hanging everything
in this chest there now --

For you to go and find since I trust you -- these are a lot of
canvases I'm hanging -- Should I place them higher -- a ladder,
okay place them higher --

I'm trying the cabinet full of drawings now, in a sturdy branch,
it hangs there, calm, peaceful,
Swaying.

In a castle outside of Switzerland in the far mountains of
Lauterbrunnen, leaves are beginning to drop to the grass, the
animals begin going underground -- Near a swamp a black
witch in an underground tunnel hunches, walking with lantern
light -- this tunnel goes to the river- its chambers lead beneath
the mote that opens up beneath her castle. This morning is
salt water and sea gulls swooping down, pecking for fish--?

The witch puts a small spell into a bottle, lighting a candle
over a woodpile -- she seals the spell inside with a bit of wax,
and carries the spell to the waves; A prayer ensues, in her
mind she imagines the whole world, she pictures the streets of
France, with its cobblestone thoroughfares, and its haunting
structures, overhanging the streets- she sees the waters from
here as they climb and settle there at the shores of Paris, and
knows in herself this will arrive there - someday -- chucks the
bottle as far into the waves as she can, and makes her way

back to the castle, the ocean water ungulates, and glowing
-- the shores of Paris begin to glow, the whole river lights up
glowing, for a moment -- the gypsies that live on the ocean see
it. A little kid wakes up and sees the glowing from his sailboat
-- all of the Persians checking their clock in the morning notice
that time has stopped -- or they think that their pocket watches
have broken, and need repairs. In her mind they were wasting
time.

When she gets back to the castle she begins again her exploration, by first sitting in the kitchen, the room of pineapples
already marked, she rolls out the map and first finds that
signified by a simple drawing of a pineapple -- near the far
entrance she plans to explore the quart yard today, and locates
the kitchen, where a knife and fork have been drawn --
She enters a chamber near where she believes the entrance for
the quart yard may be, pressing the wooden door, the sound
inside begins to erupt -- an old jazz band plays in the corner
of the smoky room, there are hundreds of people in three
piece suites snapping and smoking cigs, and sipping mixed
drinks -- the smell of hashish fills the room, and cool jazz cats
order drinks from the tiki bar -- She enters, letting the door
close, clutching her map tight, an old speak easy cafe, to her
left emerges behind the bar, and through the small hallway
she passes into the neon cyan light as people smoke cigarettes
and sit around in booths sipping espresso cups and painting
canvases -- A man in brown slacks and fedora hat with black
tweed jacket checks his clock and looks dismayed -- seeing that
the glass frontispiece has shattered a little bit, and then closing
it he replaces the clock to his jacket and says to her in her ear:
When we get to the waterfall Duck Feather float underwater
-- She closes her eyes and imagines the duck feathers floating
there, being picked by blue jays and wrapped in string -- now
people are lining teacups along the waterfall, and the blue jays

are dipping those duck feathers into this tea. She keeps her eyes closed, sees a turkey standing in a window and feels the man gently leading her to a place where she sits down and imagines he whispers into her ear: we wink at forever. Outside, around the chamber, her castle grows from the ground, and is seen constructing a maze. When she wakes, she is with the man,

And he is tracing through the maze in a boat.

She sinks back to imagining again, sees black silk drapes softly landing against her white skin, she imagines the boat floating to Brazil, imagines the animals, and plants, and people there -- a sweet plum lands Skin and seed upon the black silk, touching her skin, and a dry Fig peels, falling onto the black silk. Gold gloves land in the water next to the boat as it is being docked somewhere deep in the maze -- the boat it turns over softly, gently animating it turns into the soft pillows and blankets, into the duck down comforter, into the fluffy mattress, into a warm bed -- she opens her eyes again, notices a cloud in a ki-mono dress wandering passed her window and laughs -- things have been going so rather horribly until now, how do I say "to the waterfall -" she rolls over in bed and looks for the map and sees that there is someone there next to her in bed now. She finds the map and rolls it out - draws a saxophone where the quart yard is.

* * *

In her dreams it is the year of our lard. Billboards line the harbor to a ship that is just about to launch -- she looks into the water, and sees the duck feathers float under the black dock. As the feathers pass 2,015 inklings seem to pass with them around the docks. Her mouth fills up with something all full until her cheeks are felt bulging -- when she looks at the

dock there is a dog, filling its mouth with blue jay eggs from
a small brown nest -- this cow spotted dog is devouring the
nest, from apparent starvation -- she spits more into the nest,
and begins her long walk to the waterfall -- where she hunches
under the water. Boiling and sipping green tea. The moment,
in her mind, has turned very soft -- the hour, the second, the
moment softened like warm cheese, melts as turkeys peer in at
the waterfall, through a window inlayed in the rock wall -- one
eye is focused on her -- she is getting younger and younger
beneath the falls, she has just turned six or seven, she hunches
over the steam, breathing the green tea. She looks up at the
window and winks at the turkey -- in her mind she winks at
forever -- A house is growing higher from underground she
gets in through a hole in the stones, back into where the maze
begins -- she is in the kitchen -- it is morning. Her map is
rolled out with its pineapple, its saxophone, its knife and fork
-- she is curious about the attic. The upper chambers -- attempting to trace the steps through the flooded house with a
boat kept leading around to the kitchen, the old kitchen, other
than the map, she and the man in brown hat, and brown slacks
softly paddled her in circles of delight, where is he now, how
she referenced him, she could only see by the symbol on the
map. The jazz club. To what was there, the old dress, old song.
In her mind all of that water that had flooded the castle flow
down the walls and sink back into silk. How far off we've gone.
Sweet plums passing in the water in giant cakes, dry figs, what
a dream. The gold gloves the remainder of her memoirs. The
dock inside the house. She takes the map and sees the castle
from above view. It seems smaller. The dock had a boat that
was a bed. The flooded window she looks out the kitchen window -- sees the cloud in a kimono dress.

Edith Piaf sits drinking tea; she has a little window from where
she watches a cloud pass the mote. She stands up, and waters

flowers around her little room -- coo-coo clock lying broken on the table, the tools, and springs hanging open, broken. The black witch finds a room, where a single lens apparatus stands propped on three legs. She inspects it, and reads the engraving: "Paris-scope" on the length of the lens.

Clocks, with polish - clocks, without polish -- heaven would be an underwater house, would be a friendship eternal, in heaven, my body would be a house I could explore with a friend. God is building a place for me -- what tools, what names, what languages? Material, resources?! Caramel.

Edith Piaf leaves her room, first locking it with a skeleton key. The black witch peers into the eye of the Paris-Scope, and notices a woman wandering through what looks to be the quart yard -- it has been turned to a small farmer's market -- the version of reality, the witch checks, cannot be viewed through the regular window, but only inside the "Paris-scope" A woman shopping in the market, in Switzerland. She grows curiouser of the quart yard, for years she has been plumbing the depths of her castle in search of the place, she has been trying to find the infamous quart yard for, and she counts, seventeen years. Rolling out the map, she marks her place in the attic with a simple "Paris-Scope" and ventures to the castle tower window, peering down to the fog over the mountains of the Alps, through the forest, climbing the mountain walls, to the river's soft mist, behind the trees.

Eternity, she thinks, is spent with friends, building, and making art together, she sees nail polish clocks in her mind's eye --

Breathing slow at the window, a Ferris wheel Inch-by-inch appears in the reflection behind her, she can hear it cranking and clicking. Amethyst crystals begin landing around her, and nudging themselves across every space, digging and nuzzling themselves into crevices, and corners -- every nook and cranny coated in crystals, those purple and quartz, her feet poke through a pile. A door opens, a closet door, a man is there, dressed with black rat mask, he rips open the costume, and looks down at his chest, pulls out a key from a birdcage in the chest, the black witch stands in awe, frightened by the display, the rat spirit, maybe a man, a masked thing, presses the key in a cavity of his costume --

A lock at the heart -- he, or it inserts the key into the lock then walks back to the dark, whispers:

Lock my heart, it's time to sleep, whispers: Lincoln Anne.

The mask door closes. Amethyst pathways from the window to the door. Enters words, out of the attic in the hallway, near the steps back down to the kitchen. She holds sage, and a candle. One of the crystals has been kept in her hand. She wanders to a white bed in the middle of the hallway, and lays the crystal and the map with the sage on a rotating record, playing a selection from Rachmaninov's no. 3

She climbs into the bed, the song creeping in with her. Low ambient sounds tingle her belly, and stand her hairs on edge -- all tiny black hairs, raise with the crescendo of the orchestra. Birds are chirping in a nearby room, as she falls asleep. From behind the doors of rooms (yet unexplored) open, rooms never discovered. Her bed in the hall. Figures emerge gentle, as on silk, in homemade red diamond and quartz costume. They lower, release animals around the hall, one chicken, a cat, a small canary, a mouse, small dog -- One of them pulls a rope from above her bed, they climb it sideways into the cavity above her slumbering doll face -- above, candles lit and wine drank, a party ensues, behind that darkness, she wakes, stretches her arms, fumbles for her map, writing another symbol, a rat next to the Paris-scope, a crystal, references the crystal from vinyl.

Above Zia, the party slows to a stop, afraid of what has happened below. Some of the costumes begin climbing down, and back into the rooms behind her -- The figures sneak behind her head, and quietly move into their rooms. She is young, a little girl at her night stand dressed in indigo-- the man with a magnifying glass wanders along the hallway, inspects paintings, the plants, the record player, the bed set, the girl.

What gathers her attention from the map is the interference sound the man has emitting from his clothes -- she hears the words: Built of a long nasturtium (whispered over the recording) she hears the words: Nautilus exit, gust net. Hears the words: perfumed passageway. Hears the words: it takes five minutes and... These sound like prerecorded phrases of some kind. These are louder still than the Rachmaninov.

Upstairs, the costumed figures run in circles, they are now very excitedly collecting and gathering into jars, pre made fluffy clouds from somewhere where cotton is made -- their jars are filled with cotton heads -- They climb down the rope above the bed, spotted now by the man with magnifying glass -- they carry giant clouds made of cotton along with them, and he runs at the black figures, attempting to jump onto the clouds, attempting to break the cotton clouds into pieces -- A fight ensues, four new radios emit noise eruptions, and the black witch watches in awe as they fight over the cotton, haling and lunging and grappling their ways to the doors of the rooms. She stumbles out of the bed to a bicycle that is propped in the hallway, and charges the door, her map hanging out of her back pocket -- she is yelling: Simeon! Silver! Silver Maple, Silver mound! Stamps forever! From your Vessel! Southerners! Drink your handmade beer to the experiment, to broadcast a simple machine! Or Tomato! She crashes through the door, and jumps from the bike, pulling out her map like it's a sword -- a man stands in a suit with a marionette -- in a basket before him he pulls out bundles of flowers, throwing them around -- A curtain, a red velvet curtain falls, separates him from her, and her bike -- She jumps through the curtain, looks at the ground , where the man had been, and sees bundled flowers, a record player, a bed, crystals, rope coiled at the ground, fake clouds made of cotton, radios left on fuzzy, a tape recorder plays words of some pœm, Costumes handmade lay in piles next to wine bottles --

When she awakens in bed, she is back in her room, a lost Cauldron takes her attention back into a dream she had, and the castle became haunted and filled with life and people from the past -- Louis Armstrong, Bessie smith, Edith Piaf. All the different time periods are out of whack -- She smells an odor that she has not thought of for sometime -- The stringent smell of saint john's worth -- something of a stranger's voice enters the room in that delirious smell, whispers something in her head -- "Follow that hollow form" she thinks on it. Delirious still from the intoxication of the odor. And wraps the white blanket over her chin -- in her mind she imagines a pack of dinosaurs running through a meadow, they are painted on giant, room sized canvases -- and displayed in a relatively isolated area of her mind. She sees that hung there next to these oil paintings are black and white experimental photographs, the glow of boxes marked 1965. There is a piece of paper beneath the boxes where she reads (Acrylic paint/ contents: Sage, Date: 2015, July 12/13, Conditions: The supper table, succulents, well drained soil, prayer flags, yellow, green, and red; diamond -

homemade costume etc..) She chuckles a bit, lost and confused by this display -- She reads on and as she dœs so the piece of paper she is reading seems to slip on track, spits out from somewhere, more and more paper on rolls of parchment -- She reads: "The pack of... of painted dinosaurs, by seed or by root, an absolute concentration -- enlarger equipment tail. Summer." The wall prints more pages, but she studies the next apparatus in her mind's eye -- below is a sign for: MINERAL ACCUMU-LATOR.

E.Southern France.

She looks at the glass jar full of ladybugs, sees in the jar, lit from behind, skeletons at the floor, where the lady bugs drop-pings are, a map of Pangæa. Strawberries and melons lie dried up on the map -- she opens her eyes and whispers (keep fruit in boxes of sand. This triggers a thought about keeping her oranges in a box of sandals, another box of strawberries is in white sand--

And then there is this argument built within her, between the hour which has extra legs on a 12 inch long fish -- the idea ap-pears in the gallery, behind a round, glass case, the fish is still alive, and well inside a sunken display case, where the tank can rest, a computer shows a fishing boat -- it is seen, pulled out of water, filmed in Minnesota. It pauses, and replays the segment again. She opens her eyes, and mutters, half asleep: "This not a catfish king of argument, but it has cat's faces all over it." And after saying this in her sleep, paws dangle drop lets of water from out of the walls of the gallery -- above her head, in bed dripping water onto her eyebrows, and tongue, a crew of silver men pull the computer freeze frame video argument away from the gallery.
In the video, the silver men pull the boat out of its pond to

display the dingy as a prize. She lifts her arms, and howls. The howl echœs through her sleeping chambers --

She wakes and wanders to the bedroom lamp, and lights the wick. In windows taller than her there is summer time out there, a sculpture moves like a bug near the quart yard. Old, oak chairs wrap in the shape of flowers -- her bare feet plant down on the wool carpeted floor, she flips through a newspaper, and finds threads that lead help hands to the map. She sees the number [8]* and vaguely remembers the ribs poking from a cloud in the sky, random overlaying tiles, and long, white teeth. She remembers the ⊠symbol at the door. And as she enters the room, a glass case collection of animalia.

The red cardinal turns in slow motion on its perch behind the glass, the bird is quiet, it builds something of wood in a clay pot, lining the bowl edges with fallen leaves and brush, and she remembers her dream: black latex floats in a bathtub. The room is painted all white except for the black latex in the bath. The number 8 turns in the latex, on its side. It floats silently, and there is a conversation going on in the other room over. She puts her ear to the wall, walking the edge of the property, together, the reflected image, is herself? The black witch in conversation on the other side of the wall, and this witch self presses through the white wall with a thin lace glove -- she pushes softly into herself inside the all white bathroom, they are both masked in boxes of flowers. Skin all white beneath green, red, white, wood, beer, baby blue flowers wilting and some still blossoming when she focuses her eyes at the glass cases holding birds, she is subtly redirected to a pathway of neon glowing string. He says look at that,. Gathered up into tiny floating ceramics, and roaming turkeys, and finches leading the neon string down a corridor in and out of chambers, smaller and smaller, in their string dwellings spun in the hall, are glow bugs -- and from one chamber a winged creature, all steel blue neon, glowing huge mammoth man, white hair, slate blue face tattoo, she follows this Atlantean, entering an underground chamber by subway system. Barely able to fit the giant, stone wings to lead the group of glow bugs and the black witch forward, everyone gets in line including her at the figure eight of anti gravity; their attention is guided into a tiny house. From here, to the moss ceilings, the mint plants hanging down from the roof. The black witch is grouped with glowing people who stand naked. They take off her clothes.

[8]* --
Each of our dreams is influenced by our surrounding, waking worlds -- Therefore my dream is affected by other dreamers constructing in my waking world. To change my own dream, I must change my world, or surrounding environment ~

Her feet dangle from the edge of a rowboat in black ink -- feet in the fusion. She feels fish suckling each toe, above the list of looping waters, stilettos dangling above dams of old leather hats gathered at the rocks, of sticks into a grey shaped fire, under clouds -- the boat lands at an Island. She eats a sandwich with six other, tan, muscle heads on the beach.
A sign reads: WATER ISLAND, near a thatch bar, with bats hanging inside thatch roof -- they serve large glasses of QUANTUM in glasses with mundane symbols. Peacock show off their trains to such a near dazed audience -- fragments of the castle walls crumble in and out of view like drugs, conjured by ornamental feather emitting a low frequency - sound normally inaudible to humans rings out in infrasonic glory, changed by shaking different parts of the birds feathers. At her side, a kind of slow momentum occurs in the muscle heads conversation over the glasses of QUANTUM. In her vision the early patterns / as drawings ruminate in a blurred, and vague form approach-

ing, blended with peacock shape, the form reveals the scattered teeth of the castle walls beneath its feathers, about to devour infinity. Lying back, she drifts to comfort, dreams up mythology that will riddle one day this trapped spider. Black piano pinnacle. The beach bed sheets ruffle, she pulls the Physique, the riddle of the patterned form of beach, the deep peacock hour. Six of them in a fragment, sit sand, at fire colors, due to a genetic mutation causes loss of pigmentation, Dran at Realization number thirteen.

[13.] "The natural world is in everything, in our houses, in automobiles."

And at one turn upon a corner time hasn't registered in most of the other frills # [14.] emerges~ "one who respects, and admires nature is the true artist, with the knowledge of plants, and families of animals, one can create in ease -- and detailed honesty over a plethora of genres --"

Those who were directed to this frenzy had retained their eye color, but the dogs on the beach, their eyes had turned silver, and showed the windows in the castle in their eyes, with the fall leaves reflected in the change of season.

Half of the party on the beach existed off hallucinogenic drugs, another third were drunk on wine, walking, the structure of their contemplation; so they may not understand the witches detuned, elaborate words. # [15.] In search of God, one must first examine the workings, and functions of oneself internal, and external -- one must also surround themselves with a dynamic group of other individual selves -- in search of God. Who was left, if she included herself in the inexact little spinning points of light fading to a clouded spiral, it would have mattered little if she were to bring up passions, flowers of

Christ

Those glimpses at the universe in the stars, since those galaxies are all direct pathways, divulging continuums, spun
together of cloud dust, disintegrated shells, spun webs out of
flower string -- outward, scattered and left to ponder, but more
universes, vague, hunched forms that resemble a man's profile,
with the brightest star as eyes -- She could not be stuck explaining this, there was a clock to follow, unfolding, she must,
in origami, memorize the haunted hospitals, left abandoned
ten years prior. Still, in one new place, one frame of mind,
in one universe, we six, and two dogs could rest. And that is
travel, say an hour in five breaths, straight, nowhere, unicorn,
juggler, inventor.

All six dolls, including the puppet and Frank Sinatra have
landed in the post punk kitchen.

"I like this." Frank says, pointing to a soft purple haze of steam
wafting from an old gas stove. Dolls standing over the purple
haze are making (as they explain to Frank) water color soup,
with zero reference, no talk of infinity as they say -- everyone
is getting hungry for strawberry pie, and as the hunger grows,
a pack of dogs enter, begging under the gas stove. Like an al-
gorithm let out of the drunk house to devour, enters the black
witch with

Her map and an eyeglass. She sees Frank Sinatra, and the dolls
cooking up their purple soup, and the wild dogs. And then
there is only darkness. Ground leads them all outside -- all
walking together, walking with coffee and winter clothes found
in piles at the dollhouse squat. As the black witch and the
dolls, and the wild dogs, and Frank explore through snow embankments they begin noticing microscopic crystal wavelengths

of light are yet, underneath this world of snow. Spaced just so, that the result is fluorescent colors --

the dollhouse, a dilapidated one bedroom, has a single stair-case leading behind the trees, into a broken in door the snow lies toppled this way and that -- The slow descent of the doll-house over the valley draws their eye to it landing in the woods a mile or so behind the clearing -- even the dogs see the old red dilapidated house as it descends from the white sky line. As it lands they hear it. The dolls are laughing in joy - talking quickly over each other of their fellow dolls that have just landed. Thank Frank for that had to leave them in the caramel Flood. The dogs begin running toward scattering mother hens near the tantrum of the falling house. Frank and the black witch begin their chuckling amongst each other as they make way on foot through the distant trees, and in the dark clearing they notice that clocks hang frozen in the forest -- "They look," the witch says, "to be ticking blackened paints."

Dripping and then drying up, the clocks seem to leak a foreign substance like paint from the hours, in some

Slow string (like mating snails, dangling in their own mucus) the clocks tick out fluids that hang far up in the trees, down to the snow, where it disappears, and clear back from black and white.

Frank inspects the bases of trees, attempting to touch some of the fluids, as dœs the witch, the bevy of birds being chased away by the wild dogs, near where the house has landed, giant piles of pressed away snow from embankments, all around the house, so that nothing is seen of it. The dolls point here and there,
"It was over there,"

No. It's over here."

"No, It's over there," They argue.

The sunlight peeks out through the snow trapped cedar, branches, a small, thin beam cuts to the front door of the fallen doll house, lighting up the entryway. Time seems as though it has completely ceased. The witch says. Frank pulls out an old pocket watch. He taps it. Shakes it. A tiny jingle inside.

'Hmm," he says, shaking his head.

"Yeah, I suppose it has." They are quiet, waiting for the dogs, now bored, moping their way back in brown blurs. Without a catch

"But a good dream," The witch says.

"Is timelessness, full of eggs, and edible eye color?" She flutters her eyelids, changes eye colors Prussian blue red green yellow, pink, silver, black, white, Prussian blue. Tea like.

Frank watches as her hair turns from BLACK to all white with snow. The witch is reminded of a genetic anomaly called leucism, the absence of color in birds, mainly she pictures an all white peacock and this image drags along a moment into the image of ink blots --

She says "So, even your breath is finite and I have followed the dream with a shovel, and drug the marker across the floor looking for this." The snowflakes landing more now in her black hair. When they arrive at the back door, broken open, of the doll's house, excited as they begin entry, Frank stumbles to a keyboard, and punches in a codex. He touches, afterward his temples, pressing something invisible into his head, through what appear doors. A pile of amethyst, covering the old abandoned house floor, as they enter the first room their language begins changing, in each word or phrase angels, and a new muster of curious fowl enters behind them, as they looks to be being summoned. At the center of the living room all stand in awe to an elephant rummaging old parcels, newspapers, drawings with its trunk. it lets out frightened music, in the music they find every doll in the house painting with gouache in the kitchen, yet speaking is mostly deranged with vocal chords painted, photographed and curious animation as they emit from the bodies, and sounds are mostly the rain on the roof, well placed salmon, foreign to the black witch, the wild dogs howl, and frank scrimmaging. The dolls are seen acting out, yet normally as they shed some train, and adjust naturally to this new environment -- In frank's mind, he sees a mountain, and something in him names the place Mt. Cherubic, when the black witch speaks it seems to Frank that she is spitting coffee. LIKE she is drowning in some Late Latin Greek. But the kindness in her eyes speaks something much differently. She seems to be thanking Frank for something, which he obliges, befitting an angel -- bright fluorescent devices seem to them to translate meaning, they compute virtue -- she seems to be uttering: let's hope they are good hosts. Angel definition becomes a conversation between the black witch and Frank Sinatra. She sees him with wings, updating version of Frank Sinatra appear, saying, or seemingly saying "Tell me what you think about angels. Angels, Playful, chaotic, void, and mysterious. Workers of Transmutation, able to pass in/out of time space, traveling horizontally up and down... travel in human form, anime -- they grow plants in their palms, they weave patchwork blankets from their shoulders angels collect chickens and draw comics- and sit next to fireplaces.

She undœs her black hair. She moves forward and from outside, baby peachicks begin to enter from the chrome stairs. The stairs disappear, blended pictures of lifts, beneath wheelchairs, the shopping cart pours out a delivery of dolls that the others cheer of, inviting them to the kitchen to look at the elephant -- this all seems neath reason -- All sink back between worlds, separate as if sleep crumbles their bodies into salt water of waves. Infinity, stars, moon.

New Orleans, 2016

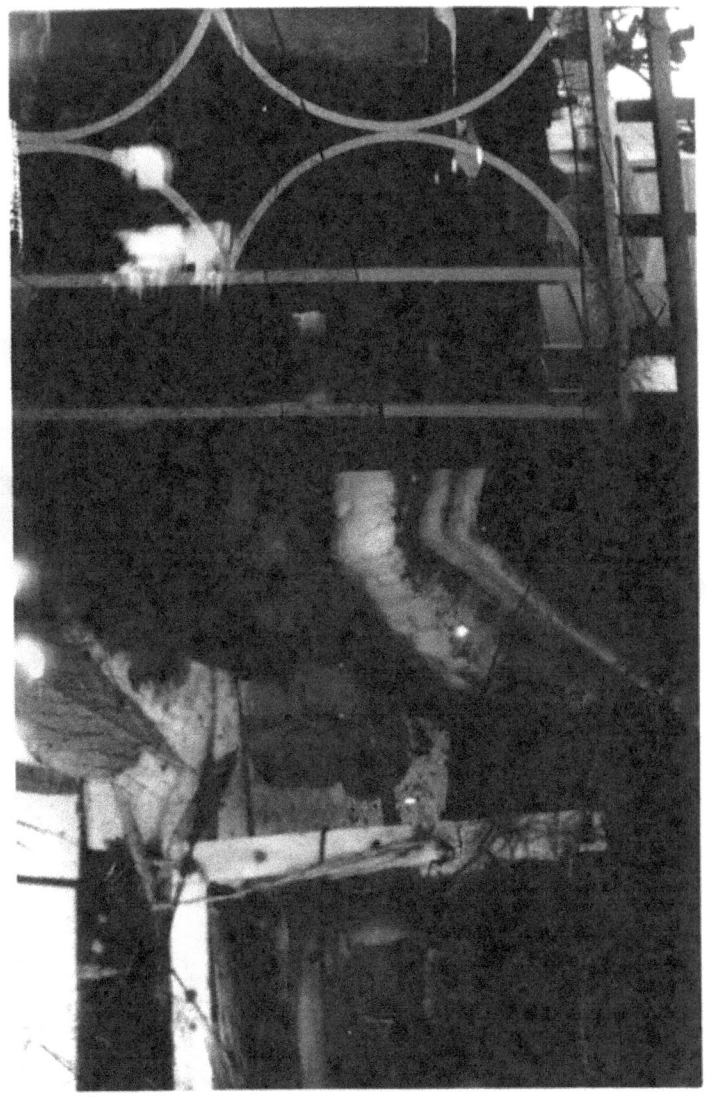

|||| there is a story in meat ||
(A collection of castles)

```
    .
   ∧
      <
   >
           M    a    o M    a    o
```

Thirty two hand built boats,
Trash can lid sink and
Found plate glass
Floor --
Cats fly off the roof with
Aluminum wings, gorilla
Boating
In their hairs.

Pom Pom Silly putty ocean
All around, every color
Salty smell
An arrow pierces through skin
Then fat, then bone; inside I saw
It break the blood tubes, slash the
Walls.

Toothpaste tubes and all, the little ankle socks
Bending around caves, a tunnel for sewage
And darkness. Refuse lines the docks,
Pigeons peck at a dominœs
pizza

~ Axel's
~ lines
~ ropes
salty seas,
my friends

∧

⟨

⟩

Series of woven carpets, wobbly hand built coffee things rumbling through the center of that stain, called stained isles, there are four separate stains. One is called stain city, in which gears float submerged sunlight.

Toothpaste tubes pipe through the ceiling, to the first house. Morning on the table, sweater up with pattern work. Pink work jean knees, sample kit, heirloom tomatœs, silly putty ocean marble, sky chipped tea.

Old man Stevie picks the hole in his brain, pulling out ghost white string and blue eyes, and gloss deep.

The alloy sun
comes in the
cemented sky,
marbles melt from alloy heat,
dripping glass in silly
putty ocean.

makeshift shore,
out Lego men on Lego beach,
in the first house
sunglasses on and wandering to the morning
at the table.

∧
   ‹
›

Heineken comes in to load, so every-bodies up, waiting, and
scaring the alloy cats into the broken refrigerators. Town's
scruffy bears with Tahœ white headdresses wander up to a
rickety dock, stare at the hole, glaring reflections of headdress.
Smeared eyes appear as black makeup. Smeared to a long
nose. Grimace turns into the lips, pierces. Tattoo symbols for
collective consciousness. Silly putty all green, mixed blue and
salty

∧
   ‹
›

The Heineken arrives late, followed by attachments of cumulus Lego clouds and the smell of ocean drifts in. The unload-
ing process commences and the sailors look around at each
other wearing worried looks in the direction black cloud and
the men on the broken dock. Their bruises speak for them,
no one says one word. But the eye contact between the white
headdresses to themselves mean someone distract their first
sailor while we rob this boat. One of them jumps the gun, but
it dœsn't matter. He runs off the docks and up into the town
clutching two cases of beer. The others fight the sailors off
and spin them into the water. The silly putty swallows them up
and the people take the boat into their harbor where the Lego
shanty town is located.

Insanity. Repeating clouds. Insanity. Repeating headdresses.
Sundown in the shanties. Brick red sunset. Passed out on the
floor, plush red carpet and long arm hairs.

Ω   There, of course, is snoring great white pipes of subtle sleep, hidden from awakened cats, skimmed aluminum wings, sky a dark paper machete and "Holly Lites" box of Blinker Christmas bulbs.

Macintosh trees in the breeze. Crayola silly putty dark, and looping, and ocean resident, and drunk with lust. Shadows cross underground. Aluminum cats find their places in broken VHS cassettes.

Half beers, lonely bedrooms, the shanties bubbling foam, going flat in sleep.

All cats: thousands of aluminum winged Cardboard cut-outs waning to a subtle winged morning, crossed the great black, through light, heavenly body.

Ceramic flies circle headdress, plush carpet, loop yarn arms, tufted entangles with chicken feather. Leak red ceramic sweat enters rooms, enters trees. Ceramic flies, ceramic ants crawl ceramic TV sets, the possibilities are lying naked on the wooden steps, drunken video cassette
'Players': leftover from reality in a fake ingenious sunset made of bricks, and candy, turning darkness, and sleep with a spatula.

Mate chasing mate, under the great metallic crescent, earth and satellite swings chain thin alloy. An illumined majesty.

It's two O'clock and the animals are beautiful. From the horizon Black fur drops white wings, bones, crows, vertebra, feathers. Pink elephants tusks in the ocean. Pink drink the silly floor of threads, this horizon.

Ω   in dark purple silly putty gets it in aluminum foil and
feathers.

Cats like to land in the boats and configure plans for a nightly
adventure there. On the Lego toy boats, they land down on
the horizon where the silly putty ocean meets the coral reef.
The plan is to steal a boat and sail it to Bermuda. Snoop the
Burmese talks the Rex kitten into maneuvering the boat, and
everybody piles in.

Sail!

The deep silly putty curls away and the Lego anchor is pulled
in.

To Bermuda! The cat's meow, eight days of fine wine and doily
making, the Silly putty pulls the ink out of newspaper. An edge
of doily through sunlight.

.|

∧

    ‹

>

Thin dust from inside the city
of a carpet sale falls from long hair,
in a MCDonald's commercial.
Attachments of grease
locks the doors to the internal
place, shaping the manual scene
through glass via locks of her hair.
Dreadlocks in glass.

An infected Mæstro is seen wandering down aisles of teeth,
inspecting a grocery list his wife gave him in his shaky fingers
and then inspecting the jars of dentures, baby teeth, adult,
cavities. Dread lingers in each aisle, an extra layer in the air of
the shop.

(*first class_)
Little Leroy busted into a household Jim beam cotton mouth
hit the threshold of his throat.

–

He eats stems in the coroner's office waiting for Leroy to enter
the room in a cream green jumpsuit.

–

Black cotton mouth
enters his cage, settling
at the back of his throat.

Settling at the back
while Leroy gets led to the body bag room.
Nurse Jameson watches him choke
while picking dirt out of her fingernails.
She yawns.

Leroy coughs up a black cotton swab
and it lands in the grout the old worn cream
tiles hospital.

They wander in from the back room
of the morgue and the nurse
starts getting ideas about Leroy, who's
still red in the face, who
has no idea why the nurse
is blushing so much.

∧

<

>

Tinfoil juxtaposition is spray paint orange the same way (in the same fashion) as the morning is, written as a syllabic pœm into the same way the architecture symbolizes meat and tinfoil.
We live in a meat city, in a meat castle, we fuck meat curtains that are rotten. Our bodies are made out of meat, and flies lay eggs that hatch inside our city.

The flies will be coming to destroy and lay eggs in us soon.

The crew works day and night, are all dressed up in pink bunny suits and ready for their day, their jobs are to cover the meat up with aluminum foil so the flies don't lay eggs in us.

They start covering all of the meat skyscrapers up as Gods left overs rot, with industrial sized aluminum foil to keep us protected, from the flies, they succeed and work hard wrapping the leftovers.

So, they get to work on the meat castle, time lapse video shows them on the hill, then moving through the city in a ring worm.
∧

<

>

Boat drives//Car strapped boat
Universe 5.23 zooms bye. It's the McDonald universe 7.21 and it zooms and blurs and captain takes a picture of the ultimate McDonald with his point and shoot camera he purchased (used at the shop in thought squat town.)

Universe 5.7139 gœs by in a flash, the community building parking garage.

He rows swiftly, chasing his hands with his second hands until
(intake/ outtake) until blur of fifteen arms row in a fast, the
row boat zooms bye, through the meat city. Universe of meat
parking garage, meat book shops wrapped in brown paper and
string.
Meat city workers and meat   banks collide into
one as he comes to a sudden   stop.

Annexed roses and tinfoil room, a room of maps_
Johnson rides paddle boat through the city with goggles, scarf,
paddles burning, his hair blowing
the city rushes past the boat
the way water dœs.
'Pabst blue ribbon' for a hair net
and a memory monkey riding up in his boat.

Bicycle parts as anchors and stuff.

All over the place, he asks where he can dock the boat. Nobody, I mean nobody has a spot. How jumbo Johnson rows
his boat through town, nobody knows. Everyone of us stands
around looking crazy.

Meanwhile he jumps out of time / the boat and the zip sound
from a toy he found is heard behind it all.

∧

   ‹

›

The woozy sally curls and furls, around out, furled out around
in, and there is an architecture to this curly girlie. Of a monk
environment.. we wired bins to sizzle drizzle and monkey suit
orangutan, so that sweater worms and thin limbs, doing cross

country, doing 'find the mine shaft' almost entirely atmosphere, thank God.

∧

   <

>

| *Destination animal*

The passion flower suit case, melted back room memory triangle, malty memo, a bubble flat. A nose suit, and a nose case to
go with it Pocket sized for handheld, p[alm] pilot cigarette case
[⊠](at the bottom of the lake at the top of the western hills.

Maniac Scribbling on the rock walls, fire tending as his main-
frame, memories smoke, at the bottom of the lake, history and
all of her surfaces.)

One, Three, one, one, seven is the code, I do my knob flipping something like five times with these floating air balloons
as fingers, my thumbs crack the case and the passion is spilled
out in an ink of octopus arms, onto the docks, and now I'm
getting my footing back, rescue the boat from a fire.

The sails up around nine O'clock and destination rattlesnakes,
destination animal.

Shœs come onto stage

"Time?"
   -pattern place
   -maps
   -skin
   -milk

∧

<

>

[The shark tooth was what they were looking for, in formaldehyde.]
Pill dropped from the heavens from the cumulus in the skies.
Ears were next to flowers, blooming together, in the soiled
night, blossoms fall to the wounded plants, truffles perched on
the rotting dying face of this world.
Hands were next to candy canes, put inside packaging with
one another, bounding through the warehouse candy-land,
One hand still moves to the candy-canes and gets sucked into
the story, where machines tear apart the meat.

(a ride in a dream machine)

∧

<

>

Shadow dream on a boat in the day to the sea... Warm up in
the bird light pattern in foam glass, licked with gloves with
bone sandals, with bone tea, lifting the tongue to the answers,
the questions, the, to the [that] the top hat sitting next to a
wood telephone that is for sale.

Formica roses are sold out of a suitcase wilting in
windows near facial woods.

And the little monkey with his red markings dœs an act as the
water churns in the back.

The rain beats down on the coat of our captain.

Lost with lusty layers,
lost with salt and oxygen
Lost with dream machine
plugs all hooked in.

"A decaffeinated beverage.?" The girl says, her long white skirt
over the red stripes of her top breathing as her chest moves.

Make up stairs lead to her face, and it stains everything on
board. The engine wears makeup too. The numbers are powdered umbrellas. The concealer on the top hat.

The axis of evil is fouling up the gears, ah the coffee cup is
staring at me

Griselda, dull greet, Pope Joan, Lady Nico, Isabella, Marlene,
Joyce, Angie, Jeanine,

∧

<

>

Ah the drills What a shit storm of Monkey crap bashing the
cage.

My skull eats a hole inside itself like a deranged and tormented
ape, flinging turds, scraps of food, anything it can get it's awful
phalanges around to throw the stuff extra hard into the three
inch Plexiglas until it shatters and hits some imbecile who is
spitting at the monkeys square in the eye.

Don't come near us, we are armed with shit and food and we
will shatter this fucking wall of light until it shoots back your
eyes. It shouts at my skull, while I try sleeping, my skull eating.

∧

<

>

In rose petal fortress, sewn with ivy thread, the Chevrolet
Grand Prix and the French bicycle make a date of it.
They want to keep a secret, if no one knows they are doing the
dirty, they will make a baby in the trees.

A little morphing do to mechanical hook ups in their sex,
hybrid bike car, then no one will be likely to raise a huff over
the thing.

Note From England:
The cyber (hybrid+bike)is raring its ugly head in England
today, we have been wondering how to do this for a long time
now, It is a success to finally pedal a machine with such fluid
control. Were seeing people all over London today riding them
in the streets, a new computer car for the general up standing
citizen populates now.

∧

<

>

An aura fix has green eyes the thought matrix helps these talk
Ronnie. The Bob, Ether drunk. Sorry/.

The power is hungry for electric sickness, Bubble gum chewers
think straight and eye balls sip out of cups, but thin wrist pulls
seams out from mescaline feather. Today.

The pink aura fixation have me in blood.

∧
<
>

Ending faculty maze path
start going back to the begin
    just stop and smell the roses.
The white bowl paint and clouds, porcelain bowl and the red
roses.
Brick walls mark end of maze,
Bowl of cherries, water, food, I'll eat the roses.
The ends meet my finger tips.
They mark pain and then

My blood only a bit that I suck out, then eat the Rosetta.. The
seven of them make my stomach eat itself, the grumbling is
equated to a clear cut, all the chainsaws gnawing the inside of
a dense wooded forest.

How long has it been? MMM?

Maybe I can climb this wall. I stand up on the vase tablet.
Peak up into the eyes all over. I hate walls. They are always
mathematical walls the size of an elephant.

I see nothing, a renaissance painting in a gaudy frame. Eyes in
plaid, painted on in the forest. Willow and blanket in the picture,
sandwich, fruit. A picnic basket. They are on the beach, on the
sand. The walls are growling slow, maybe. Too low a tablet. I'll
fuck and eat this painting. I chew a hole. The paper, it's rendered in tears. Easy. Chunky! The hole gets bigger. The space
behind the painting grows dark, Slimy, prickly hairs.

Plums. There is enough room, that I can jump in. The waters

fine, prickly pears, plums, sandwiches, orange juice take me
away.

<

>

\
The morgue shifts up a level, from black pond water, mud and
black holes in the mud, drizzling over the four sides of the
elevator shaft.

"Which floor?" She asks. Her teeth aluminum foil that has
been folded to shape three small razor blades collage artists
use to get really fine details with. My stomach is in the shape
of a four paneled room. The stomach looks like the ceiling in
a doctor's office. Above the ceiling in the elevator. Her eyes
glow in the shadow of an installed light bulb. I am aware of the
straps coming loose from the operating table. I have no words.

Which floor? What kind of question is that anyway. Bodies
suddenly fall out of the units, down from the ceiling, barely
stopping then the sound of the latching mechanism is heard,
felt and the smell. Of frogs in formaldehyde, wafting out, dead
a long time, in an absence of odor more like whores, like a
falseness that has been alive in the corner, that lingers stimulating itself still after death.

Worms in and out, on the walls, in and out, on the wallpaper
pattern in the elevator, when we were boys they made us muti-
late these worms on a few school occasions.
^

<

>

Eels electro cute lace at the ends of the thread swimming under the boat docks.

Captain inches through sky on a Mario Brothers cloud as the theme song plays on a speaker connected to the cloud to his right.

He inspects the castle on the map. It will be where the Maze meets the painting he will introduce his leaf Stereo tiger.
The painting will get a beating
and a spanking and the fucking it can handle he assures the map taking one dip into the pussy and then licking his glove. All the city is shimmers of aluminum foil tightly covering up the rotting meat, prepared and seasoned beef and pussy. it is a sort of construction site, the captain is not aware of right now.

He floats on with the eight bit song playing from the Mario brothers speaker.
∧

<

>

\
Okay, back to the maze, A black maze pure metal platinum. My legs from within the pond (rendered with mars black and pthalo blue) Kicking and giggles echœs. The girl in the painting giggling as she eats her picnic sandwiches.

By sometime I will have nibbled my way through all this fruit and sandwich meat into the other dreams and into the walls of the beef curtains, I will spill out to the other side.
∧

<

>

Captain lingers over the boat, tying it to the neon orange plastic dock.

I rub my genitalia on a pile of pear guts humping the juice vigorously.

Oranges, plums, strawberry juice and genitals. The male type. The girl in the painting rolls her head back under the willow tree and (if it is rendered properly) seems to be in an exhausting state of euphoria.

Her basket full of lunch: sandwiches, wrapped in wax paper and string lay splayed all around on the rocks.

After tying down the boat captain handles a pile of newspapers in a brown tube and moves toward the meat castles.

The aluminum foil sailors hat on his head picks up a transmission that begins to play on a thin square arriving in the bottom right corner of the screen. The hologram logs into place and a map locates one of the red dots in one of the castles. He starts walking in that general direction.

I hump strawberries with vigor.
∧
<
>

It smells like flesh washed in hair. He cleans the goggles and rows into a shop, parks, ties up the boat, throwing buckets of water at its flames simultaneously entering the meat gate into town. The one dressed in all white leads captain to their aisle of maps and shows a black eye, hidden under long locks of white greasy hair.

Maps cover different sections of the walls.

"Heading to the meat maze, I see."

Captain lays down the vagina and the one in white cringes, dipping a hand inside and making the face. Pure orgasm, the purest face alive.

And he's off, in the boat. With the map to the castle.
The vagina box: found at a garage sale in Portland(IA) (cat town) where the waves of silly putty crash onto the shores of diamonds, captain traded a pair of old boots in for a special box with a freshly slaughtered vagina inside of it. Wandering in disgust what the thing was doing there at the garage sale, he asked one of the black and white cats who answered this: "Put your hand in the box and see what happens." Although the cat was drunk, Captain tried it. Captain put his ungoverned hand into the box, swelled open and grabbing a hold of the bones inside of his hand, connecting a cord of tissue to his blood stream, that in turn gives him three mind evolving, mentally stimulating (which added 5 degrees to his IQ levels) orgasms in two swelling hits.

.|

^

>

<

Outburst of petticoats and violent spirals, looming through loom. Threads, in a painted replica, in a compartment. Sound of breathing echœs against the plates of the wall. This time quite the character with golden sunglasses on with a fake, (black plastic) comb over as a hat on stands next to the fountain, pumping green mildewed water from the dirty orifice of three angels lips into the black catch. He has a cigarette, the

man, and a white sweat stained jacket that cuts all of the way
down to the cobble stone street. Beyond the fountain and the
court yard Swedish houses line the inside of the horizon.

In the center of the square, directly beside fountain, there rises
from the cobble stone, a threading loom.

Hunched over it, weaving a line into a giant blanket creation -

|
|
|
|
|
|
|
|
|
|
|
|
|
|
|
|
|
|
|
|
|
|
|
--------x .Map lines are woven through parts of the design.
Golden glasses shimmer. Shouting numbers, the wig maniacally orders the hunched over woman around before the town's

fountain and the moonlight. After a long series of adjustments on the loom, she makes a strip in pattern and then adjusts the loom to make similar strips until his numbers translate into the map lines.

The pool of disgusting black water opens up, around the gloves the man pulls out from within, a coin. Talking down the golden ring glasses and squinting his eyes at the coin, he reads a date engraved along the circumference of the copper; eating through the copper rust reveals a half of worn face, captain meat goggles engraved into it.

He shouts the numbers off of the coin in hybrid Espanol. The woman adjusts the loom, weaving a long series of threads onto the loops.

Into the map, a dark, wooden door opens in the courtyard from the eastern section of squashy town. All black figures emerge, advancing through the shadows left on the courtyards untraced areas. He sneaks along a cement wall the way an apparition of the periphery (or side eyes) may subvert appearance. Steady -yet quick moving, the door slams in a gust of wind as the figure stops to lurk near street level windows.

The hybrid is shouted and the loom is slamming in threads and that is all, in the courtyard. A long silence felt, awkward interaction in the silence. The two near the fountain look in the direction of the window. The black figures huddle.

"I couldn't get the jars." The voice grumbles near the window.

"She fought with me again and I could not get the jars. I'm sorry." The hunched woman at the loom smiles.

"Come closer Rubix I can barely hear you, dear."
"I'm sorry." He says with a snarl.

"I hate her! She is the bane of our family and now she ruins the only chance I have to see my son!" The dark figure wobbles up into the middle of the courtyard, near a patch of green grass that has made way in through cobble stone.

"Where have you been?" Hybrid nags in his digital Espanol. He stops in the light of the moon, face bright with salty tears and a greasy lock of brown hair swept into his eyes.

"I was thinking," The black pushes hair out of his way and lands behind his ear.

"What was I thinking is we could get that replica from captain while he's sleeping, or we can kill him, sneak up on him and bash!"

"1925!"

"Shut up you damn android, I'm speaking to my wife. Now I didn't build you to fuck her and talk back. Just fuck her and be my little slave. Bitch!"

"Jerry please!" The old woman shivers the knobs with stingers and presses in the next line of data.
∧
‹
›

Black figures look at his android and at his wife. For a long time he watches them.

"I'm going to be taking him for awhile." The black figure says, motioning to the android to follow him. The gold glasses twitch under his nose.

"Where to?" His wife asks. He grabs the pink skin of the large wrist and pulls him away.

"Don't worry about it. He'll be fine."And then he leaves the courtyard. The rickety Robot repeats this: 1975, 1975! In hybrid espanol.

∧

⟨

⟩

Three hundred cats in different states of weariness arrive at the shore of meat city. The water here is actually yellow and is not silly putty but liquid cheese. They all slowly crawl off of the boat and into a candy land of meat: Steak floors, rib walls, castles under tinfoil all made of meat.

The first thing one of them does is begin sniffing aggressively a suture, poking from inside the steak floor.

The whole group comes around the corner and all start jumping with joy.

We made it! We made it! It's The Bermuda! Kittens pop into the air, perfect timing since I am starving.

They start eating through the steak floors, kittens climb up the walls and dangle from ribs jutting out of the ceiling.

They all eat until they are full and big chunks of the street, the walls and the trellises are missing.

∧

<

>

After awhile, the first hundred cats wander back to the house-boat to take naps.

While the two hundred other cats wandering up along the al-loy labyrinth and of flesh, nibbling in search of places to lay down. Lights in the sky. A pink hazelnut brown and orange whips along a silhouette of castle towers. A single Mario cloud wanders passed.

Some of the cats bicker between each other, some scatter. There are holes in the meat street that link to the inside of the castles and they wander into the maze.

It is going to be awhile until they find their way out. Some larger kitties except the streets out of still hungry urges. As the big cats get to the top of the hill, they can look over a giant city, villages built of wood. Swedish homes climb along a hill-side and sink down over the edge of the horizon.

∧

<

>

Apartment windows, blue painters tape, a dead fingernail, a lock of hair reflects binary. The market doors swung open, move closed, move open; sensors I cannot see. The window is two monster eyes on the (opposite) sides, with one big eye in the middle, warped reflection. A pupil that grows out when you linger back in my black, wooden faux leather bricks. On a corner building to the back left, a sequence of four cut in two five bricks (white neon day glow, cream pure and white metal room I'm in too.) The on/off switch, the dust trap, the ceiling made of popcorn balls. Looks like bat shit.

Grey/white and blue painters tape, behind the window. Another reflection, a darker gray, I touch sandwich, I taste soup, I smell the insides.

∧

<

>

Well traveled
air – The beast of burden
within its pink wing scape
becomes the rest assured
lunacy of a dead phosphorous
prophet.
Pinpointing the sad sap
ribbon pigeon, rest test
common ram-en.
Glaciers carve out
tin, from the afterbirth effects
our twelve martins string their life
around
tunnel funnel, dark park
black track.
Headphones lead this security guard to the morgue.

∧

<

>

The meat mansion and fiberboard steak. Carpets hair this creature, walk unnamed, Muhammad.. But aren't they the sand lips for gutters ears, for windows mouth lets Chevrolet and elephants? Flies and Fords, through the house, a gas-bug heart pumping profane warmth through lungs like billows forlorn, lonely hearth.

The stench of the meat leaks over the banister and into the foyer, subtle haze turns the door green, floating down the steps and into the blackberry bushes, the maggots are coming out of the steak walls, through the tiny holes the creature (let's call her Billy) is made of year, ye of stone and mortar.

Billy calls for the stones, longs for the earth her meaty home recipients, sing a long slow dirge that bring black rites into being.

∧

<

>

The steak shœs fold on and off like a rural night intersection, they fold down all the way to the horsehair carpet. Little bunnies hop passed, (that's like what kind of bunny I've got from a pumpkin, and I am Shiva, the destroyer.

Billy thought on this, maybe fought fog the house, produced curious gestation. The dolls underground, a dead wall too, that one fought with one long claw, the other hand regular dolls hand.
She was made out of meat too.

∧

<

>

Captain finds a connected pile of white Lego's sewn together on street ham and chicken wings. If he were anyone else he wouldn't know what the hell to do. He puts the Lego's together in a slow inbred movement. Creates cloud to the main castle, the castle with a long mesh leash of dangling nerves holds it so it won't float away. The Lego's are for newborns, are around the size of a grown adult hand in the shape of a fist.

I hump a very flavorful mixture of apple, plum, pear, strawberry and raspberries until they are a thin juice of seeds and sperm. I drop the goggles off of 'me' head and dip the dark juice, swim circles and then figure eights, the dog paddle, back stroke, finally I dive to the bottom, to explore the colors of the fruit juice I made with my body, to graze around the bottom of the tube, noticing a wooden knob that pokes from beneath a layer. A fruit pulp.

^

<

>

The captain paddles across the city, swift circles turning one knot, it is sped up to superhuman speed, the city functions at the edges of the boat, on normal pace. He's in his aluminum foil sailors suit. Maps double as a bow tie and wrist cuffs.

^

<

>

The hatch to the morgue opens, creaks back on heavy alloy plate off of shaft. The lights in the room are down low, he still makes out the hallways from a strip of green light fixtures pointed down at the floor. These line the whole length of the walkway, the room smells to be burning. He feels the room drop half of an inch before rising loudly again. In an elevator now he watches a woman with the razor blade teeth implants and wax skin job hobble into the moving morgue from a bisected hallway hidden from sight. She holds up a bottle and rag, wanders to a body on the shelves, alive. He shifts as he starts to wake. The bottle pouring some liquid into the rag and slammed against the bodies mouthpiece.

I pull myself from the dark room. The fruit is all dried, the walls of the tunnel start to stale. I reach for the panel, set the lock slowly into place and latch with a small, golden locket. Screw the key cover down over the hole, and sit down, my spine flush along the concrete tunnel. I try to wipe after images of the morgue away.

∧

<

>

I'm on the bullet train, left meat city, headed back to squat town, a small quaint capital tucked neatly beneath the meat city dump. The bullet train is smooth, it travels at a rate of six galaxies per mile, six miles per hour.

Captain meat goggles turned out to be a total quack. I had to get out of the meat city and with the special map, pocket money for the trip, he told me about a place I can get booty. Although, he had a good route, I would ride the bullet to the galaxy retinal III and auto converse with them about the ruby suit he needs. The rubies on it total around fifteen hundred and dodge (I guess the black shapes) evil infested all around meat city. He's a quack. All I know is I'm going to squat town to buy some goods with the pocket money he trashed in these envelopes. Then it's off to retina retinal.

<

>

Simply put: the elevator has broken, the morgue is out of order, the woman (a program computer generated by the black shape creatures lost in maze) have stiffened up and solidified from under use. They linger near the operating table, glazed look near the sliding doors. They still glow, their eyes are starting to lose consistency, but they are shutting down in cellular steps. It's kind of depressing to watch.

I'm surveying jars in the shop, while stages on the air float over and ask if I need help.

Do you have any fuel for a boat, I shy away, I've tried.

Fuels in the corner where the ship parts and over by the recycling pump.

Two gallon buckets later, I'm on my way to the shore, where the greenhouse is.

Thoughts in my head play on a set of speakers. I study my feet. I paid didn't I? What just happened there?

The elves -
dressed in a system of ivy vines.
castle the backdrop in skyline, and forced
moon drifts in, on a rough scream on a backwards
tape (left over from the church) this plays (whatever my favorite composition is)The vinyl bed sheets are people who dance
the halls. Hurricanes, baseball team stuffed in the attic, a pear
stuffed into a baby with his/her own hands. On the sidewalk,
I stand totally naked except for the pink bear suit. A tape recorded pœm built into the pockets with a motion detector.
"Aneurysm
heart attack
"They stayed in two lounge
chairs in the living room
-7 slept in them,
lived in them."

You couldn't get to the kitchen."
(Centrex)

I live. Where do I live? I live downstairs. In the. In the basement, down where the kitchen and offices were, after the
church implanted them, to hide the castle's original dungeons.
At night I come out here, to stay away from them. The dancers.

People believe I am intelligent and pan handle cash, they stop
by, hear the familiarity of the pœm aneurysm heart attack
"they stayed in two lounge chairs in the living room 24-7 slept
in them, lived in them." (Centrex) and a guy in a fishers cap
tosses a couple of bucks down.

Like three or four bucks. I don't take the money, he whispers
into the ear of the bear suit. Something inside I cannot make
out, shows in an after image. The pœm interrupts itself when
he gets close to me.

Dark black. Grass halls shake night through superimposed window displays. When I think of them cobbled to the grave and
something walks by me in here

"aneurysm heart-attack..."

Something else walks past.

"Aneurysm heart-attack."

I walk into my chambers, under the west end of the theater,
under the costumes room, peel off the bear suit and flip on the
light.

I am carefully examining the mirror. Pretend not to notice

the men and woman dressed in costumes standing all around.
They don't show in the mirror, I don't see them.
Good night the light says, and I switch its face.

I start with three kilos of bleach.

Three and a half cups of dye tapered blue into purple, one
black.

I'm in the theater, behind the large, red velvet curtains, drawn
mixing.

From one of the costume chests I release one large mask, a
pure white washed look carved in and molded.

I wear this to do mixing. The bleach marbles with the dye. I
am wearing my long velvet cape from the costume rack. I have
slung it desperately over my shoulders. Naked and shivering
beneath, I plug the light in, one from the nineteen forties stage.
Tapes play my pœtry on four separate tape recorders. The
volume in different settings. I'm trying to mix fuel for the boat.
The light continues to flicker on and off, on and off, on and
off.

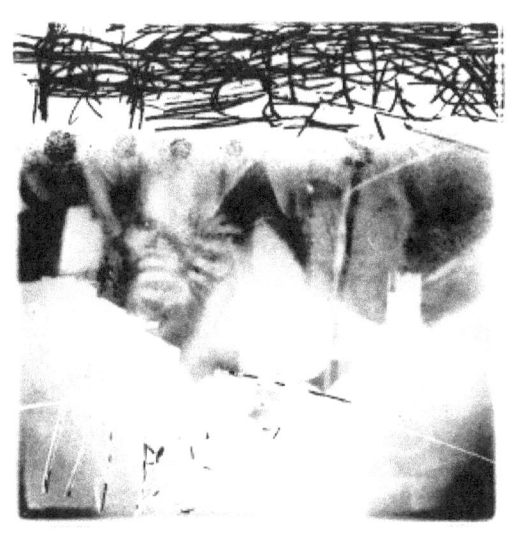

TEACUP GALAXY

Teacup Galaxy is a story about a boy Issac, who inserts his body into a computer town to destroy a virus program called Schoolboy. It was written as a metaphor for people who attempt to fight the systems of oppression and end up either dead, or imprisoned. The constant barrage of confusing language I inserted after five or more drafts came from found sources, and was my attempt to create the feeling in the reader of being overwhelmed to the point of death, when Issac dies, which he does multiple times in multiple ways through out the story, I wanted the reader to die in a way with him, to actually feel the state of confusion one might feel while under a surgery or some painful event, I wanted to show the true nature of fighting something such as the us government, or a giant corporation, how that is considered impossible, but in my story the corporation, or a tyrannical government is represented as a virus program named school boy. For so many years, this story lurked in boxes, I started it out in a composition book I bought while living in Olympia, Washington some time around 2005. I would take it out of my bag on the city bus, since my commute from the east side to the westside was a round 45 minutes, and write for the whole ride until the composition book was filled. four years later after i had typed it on an old school typewriter, and then again onto a desktop computer,I abandoned the draft, after a makeshift workshop, when I realized the thing wouldn't do. two years later I re-worked the whole thing, adding layers of found text, and editing it down with the help of my dear friend Zach Hubbard, I began to take interest in it finally, three years later in Florida, in a small town of new Smyrna beach, where I was living in a camp by the water. This was when I put on the final touches. It's dedicated to those who believe that this system we are living under could change for the better, and who continue to fight to make that happen.

"there can be no rest; we must give ourselves with great strength to our efforts."
"another world is possible." - Subcomandante Marcos

∞

CONTENTS

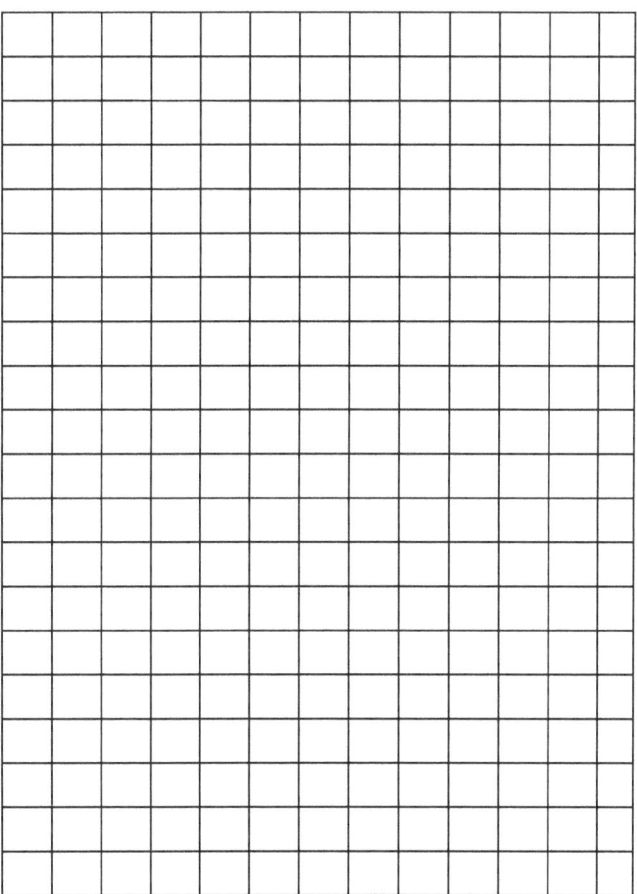

(IV.)
Coming back to linear patterns// Horsey ride with ridiculous girl// waking background Safe blue Step into chords Hole punch

 (X.)Paper dream Hole puncher Seeds in a Basket Cotton Cloth Clouds ::TIME LAPSE VIDEO WOVEN BASKET Barn

 (V.) Death on Mandelbrot corner, clown teeth apartments, The teacup infinity Mail box face Kid finds::teeth::tilt::Locations :

TOWN
CENTER

(II.) A Theater of Eyes Mountain Top Silhouette, Two Die

(XIII.) Schoolboy's House Toe Tag Message   Nest Skin of the house B . Terminal~BEGIN SEQUENCE

(XV.) wake up dead again :::Walking Outside Simple geometry. blinds . felt box The cats

  ::She monster Maine Coon:: Before grade school Cookie cutter mathematician Hologram mountain:: System of eyes on a door to the school house Dream theater School house

(VI.)Dream-theater, polar bear, green carpet Green carpet:: Copper pennies My lines:: Dream theater Polar bear

 (VIII.) Grid Leaving town Haunted suit SIXTY ARMS FIRE:::Grid Attack Suit

[ ]   [ ]

  (I.) _____ Acacia Vortex suit. Found Mirror] [>]

                        [^]

                        [<] AREA 5+7]   Dreaming in unicorn vision] Second Sleep Jointed from a larger picture INVOKE Atlantis town :: Sub town::

COLD MACHINE ANDROID GOD FLYING COURSES |

VII.) Figure Eight Staircase, Fake Lexi, Frozen Hair

((III.) Bee Ship Body flight ::Strawberry cake::Rabbit suit /homemade hat:: POP ROCKS:: BEE HIVE METAL BEACH::MECHANICAL OCEAN

 (XIV.) Sim. Airport. B TERMINAL:: SEQUENCE COMPLETE Rafters In thought Set

(XI.) Punctures, segments, chambers :: Sectioned out Fallen through Office Buildings::

 (XII.) Root Chakra The descending red plant axis. MEMORY SOFT CRYSTAL: FIRST FLIGHT

(iv.)

I see Laser hands in front of what used to be me.
They are sifting through dollar bills and the weight on my middle back forcing
me to flex.
Suddenly, sound is heard, it filters through cocoons into my ears, a stampede
rumbles miles away, and I spit. Screeching draws directional to a furry, pink bear
legging. Silver chaps bent around my side, sharp pain climbs my neck. I spit
again. Clutching big wads of dollar bills, flung backwards and pulled into an
upright position while shown rope, long knotted, once in silver, once in black,
threaded twice.

Try to stand, followed by cackling woods.
Sticker bush of hands. She turns me to face her,
deep, beneath the fur of this bright pink bear suit she's got on. Nothing moves, a
flicker
of silver gloss lipstick she wears over her imperfect, white teeth; a cleft of
seducing silver lips.

Black and silver rope tied around
parts of her, inside of my pink bear suit.
With microscopic tools, I might see a pack of circuitry,a ceiling of wires, a floor
of confusing visions sprayed through table cloth,
doily; I may see red glass within a wall, red stained glass. Flight plans.
::

———————————

Her make up is done nice tonight, a mere red line over two white doll eyes.
Filters are important, blankets and paint (…) Non affiliates, joint marketing,
schizophrenia.
She's got me by the mind just found in a card – I give her Ginkgo from my skin -
medications while she jumps back onto my waist for instance and kicks my ribs
described above.
"everything is wrong, everything is wrong. But I love you. But I love you." a
country song spins on a victrola.
A Rope attached to my cock, with your life, you need, just go for it. And the little
one (your opt out choice) covered in the bear costume kicks ABA machine down
the mattress,

the chaps – the country song spins. my life muzzle become too dry over my shoulders, since I can't move, too moist, and flavor grown thighs organized by region relish around the back of my head shatter.

High quality, heavy weight stock paper dots are cut brilliant from the fifth dimension sheets, landing edges on a postcard photo of acid castles, until completely covered in machines

\\\

[The winter eats red dots from the installation guide,
 cut into hills behind the grazing beasts.
[The sky is cut out until they
take anyone, including   they   circles. They cut away the rocks.] Medicine woman. Hole punched, paper dots guide and punch and stiletto holes and angel hair century. Cut.
"Smack!"
I hit my chin across the dream of a monkey bar, my neck pushes my eyes into the sky. It's green before light of countless, fuzzy edges.

(X.)

Pink, rabbit-shaped   collapsible balloon floats above ground., a cloud passively pink , also toy hammer balloons in the breeze, kid stars flimsy in a collapsible gust of wind.   worry dollars are relaxed in the cells and thunder peels out from behind a shattered pile of optical illusions - diagonal feed lines of helium horizontally   shadow created glass. A lavender float of symbols in a leaf of heated pupil, the boiled water passing chamomile tea flowers the leaves unfold in the glare of sunlight, as I watch through the teacups, I see leaf, pathways in the leaf lead me out in different directions.

If that apartment complex of teeth became a row of infinite cellular teacups they will never know.They'll teach each other! I hear this Looping somewhere in the landscape, feels infinite,vast in a cake suit– ghastly dessert, the middle of the dessert has ingested me, into an old, electronics warehouse, turned me installation art out of pink cake frosting, then they dress me up in tea cups and doilies, where lavender lines the surface of the dense, orange earth. I become infinite,in vast love, the most pure installation of infinite love.

The last blister of thought calling home, via cell socks and shoes. I sit in a cell of lab equipment, on chains, hanging by my broken roots,
drying up. A peaceful smile; large and gentle as a cloth sun,passing over the strawberry desert floor. A smile lingers,fuses, curls with me,
a threading of vineyard by some kind of strong
grasp. A part of me falls,drifts in a feather, to the floor of the barn, into the hay.

———————

(V.) "Bunny suit! Where are you going? Damn it!"

I turn. I turn into grass. I turn. I look from inside, I turn. I turn into mail.
I am shouting at my pink shortcake suit running into eatable fog. Behind the now, sitting down to set his hat where I was standing are giant armfuls of eatable fog between the universe underneath.

Time/laugh if only it could move/face. I watch as the pink suit pulls wax hair out of the costume, and then yellow streaks pass my eyes, running, runners.
Figure eights on a run through the yellow woods. I am mail.

"Mom!" On the toes of the pink suit, a dream of a VHS boy, a video tape yelling.
(Subtitles read he is going in the barn, he'll be back in an hour for dinner and Mom reads okay.)
The young VHS tape plays the bunny suit running past me. I am mail in a mailbox. The suit is stitching along the dirt road to the woodshed, warped sky gets tangled into the suits pink wake.

(I feel the mail box open

  the rusted hinge

 slams closed.

  I am the
stack of letters
   In his bunny mits.
Pink bunny shortcake pours all over the bend in the road. I see the suit from
inside of his hands. The mits lift a barbed wire fence, lift me, and the suit climbs
through the opening,
catching pink fuzz on barbed wire.

Dripping frosting off the shoulder-blades of the suit to my envelope tongue, I
taste a little piece.

Hay stretched in years   of Dollar, Five-dollar, Twenty five dollar, and Fifty
dollar trees.

There, bunny crosses the giant bleached sun, a pink blur, jumping through
forget-me notes, a smothered blur of pink paintings across the handwritten letters
of those forgotten. The suit, and every single willow tree is becoming a fractal; a
right angle view from   the mail tossed into the branches

         connects me: singing, waltzing, deep
         pink, fractal.

         The farm edge

         is entering property fangs, sitting moist
         on

         his mothers house,

         in my bunny suit.

Remote, I am waiting at the stage of a Mandelbrot, zoomed always to the same
position, in the warped pink of the bunny, and the willow branches like marbled
paperwork.

Hidden in repeated shapes of fiber, hanging near the notches of a few hundred ladders, all different types of ladders submerged in hay bale after hay bale, a rusted edge of barbed wire pokes through, and the gust of the bunny suit spiraling willow sends me, and all the mail into the loft.

As the bunny presses up the ladder, letters fall through the rungs, some of my mind. I am frustrated with this suit. This bunny just won't hear the music.

I'm History's hidden' spot, his play house; and the long shadows trail, track, seek, hunt, pursue, reaching for the pink neck, all fuzzy, and caught with sticks, and hay, dirtying' up the damn suit!

::

> Whispers are built up out of a distinct
> grim I had planned for, the shaking hay
> from the rungs while the bunny ascends,
> I see the ears all marbled paper in a
> willow of the Mandelbrot corner. These
> are some   indentations on the stage,
> these are all   very inevitably repeated
> shapes   I see lying on the floor next to
> me.

There, I sit in the Mandelbrot: a pile of scythes, codes, a wood saw, blood, a set of steak knives. My head aches. Eyes enter my hidden place, through the pile of scythes, layers of mutation, blood. Hay sticks to the knives in little clumps. Knives lunging, vaulted from the Mandelbrot, in the shortcake look on the bunny mask. I smell the suit

> as tools follow
> to the dust of the wood

flooring

> strawberries flying
> to the willow, and back.

> For a moment, there is a

coat of paint

> .
> White warped to red,

marbled paperwork   barn in yellow blankets.

marbled paperwork   barn in yellow blankets.
The pink suit
and I start wrestling
A VHS video, young boy
laughing at the screen.,
including black

fingers   that   cross   the
background.

White   and   marbled   red,
white and marbled red,
White   and   marbled   red
(…)
I   walk   out   of   the   VHS
video,
The wax melts the screen,
(the TV goes out)
And put on the sidewalk
next to a fedora hat.
I   enter   some   animal
Through the back of his head,
absorbing   my   memory
into theirs.

Painted   clocks   surround
me,
armfuls of 8×4 canvases
wrap a room (like blankets,)
moving   the   old   days
back, until the old days are cut
outs   and   clippings   from   the
newspaper, and the newspaper
covers the wall of the room like

wallpapers   . I'm like a kid hanging posters all over my room. And I've got my cute bunny suit on, and he said he likes what I've done heres.

Fast computerized Tangles
Makes it like the suit stands behind me
                    Again. The bunny keeps changing colors.
                    The suit.
                    Switching,
                    White and red,

                    ,
                    White and red,
                    switching
                    White and red,
                    Switching, the suit keeps switching,
                    White and red!
                    WHITE AND RED!
                    SWITCHING
                    WHITE AND RED
                    SWITCHING
                    WHITE AND RED
                    WHITE AND RED

                    I put the suit back on.

I cry miniature fog,
I choke on words.

A Lift unbuckles by the postered up wall, twelve hands pull pieces of my examining room closer. In the examining room, I can get to my tools, and with these tools I can get to the nitty gritty.
The fingers of a more gentle hand gather white fog across the wallpaper and down, into a glass jar. These white fogs are the leftover paints from a variety of past events in my suit, a generous historically based data, created for the purposes of mediating a costume, and its owner.

My naked staff enter, preparing a closure in the walls, because that is what seems to be the problem. All the other areas have healed except for one place where the wall seems thick., I undress, thinking this may be the issue, and stagger through the suddenly thick room. Sifting sand out of the particles in the air, the air is too thick and all of us on staff take out our scuba gear as it dawns on me – this is Lexington – her writing on a felt. She had cried all of that snow.

White lights in the scuba gear course through the nightmare, all of the sand grows to the size of snow balls, and the staff takes down the masks.
"This is a three course meal of cotton, girls!" Old, white paint, cotton, snow, and scraps of paper apply to our legs. Little marionette puppets sign at the dotted lines of the applications.
"Cotton exposure for the analysis crew." The puppets say.

An apartment complex that the staff and I build from a collection of shark teeth loads on a corner computer and we select the color mint for the paint, and into the office, larger in image, the apartment complex is filled with love, and stars in the form of water. Boats in the distance are for the staff to lounge on.

A Cottonwood   office building is the ship I choose. I've put on a new suit made tables, it's doing its job. Finally a sense of calm is before me, Olympia watches as I eat. She is dressed in a waitress's outfit she hand stitched the first year we were here. I gobble down a handful of vegetables dipped in mushroom tea. I am careful and swift. Still, sitting real still.

The lights are dim, the way I like them. Everything is calming down. At least I'm here, inside, sitting in my house I've been working on . Sitting in an effort.

The lunar Eclipse we all worked on is being viewed through a waterfall. Canteens of my favorite tea are being passed from substation to substation, on a long robotic arm that the circuit board programs smoother, so that time can fall asleep in its handsome rows, laid back in a complex star bubble bath of oceanic bliss.

clown fish swim in the gaps of the shark tooth apartments -At least thirteen hundred years of marriage.

And she's watching me hand a full pound of kale into my shovel; into my mouth, into my stomach. Her eyes watch my stomach twitch as I ingest the mushrooms.

Olympia makes me feel like a good manager, she is always so very careful, and delicate with her glances.

The wax, that had melted off the television set earlier, is being scrapped up and used for a big fire the rabbits work hard to start. They have decided to stay with those occupying school boys town: TOWN CENTER. They brush each other's hair, and the nurses wander to a hair of the man screaming at the walls. His breath seems to ruin the wallpaper, and they are trying to hand him some tea. Swollen in his hair are the frozen memories he insists on holding. He cowers to the back of my mind, and folds up, in case of an issue. The nurses wander around the houses, handing out tea.

The teacup of infinity generates in my frame of reference as I drift in the steam of the tea. Frozen in a line of glass for a moment, final clarity emerges.

"Complex: these Clown fish, swimming in the cavity of the Apartments." i say.

Olympia is a half filtered generation – One of my references is this: Crystal cube rotation device stirring the cream teacup in edible lavender.

Olympia. Can you hear me?

Crystal cube rotation device stirs the Cream teacup in edible tea. tea. This clear glass box, all the cups, row after row and then me on the corner, perched in a Mandelbrot, a fractal, surrounded by them, lavender submerged, horizon lines of an eight sided scope drifting over, left, right, slow, teacup tipped onto one-dollar idea within ambiguous absorption. Visual lavender pours over my skin, soaks the an eight sided scope drifting over, left, right, slow, teacup tipped onto one-dollar idea within ambiguous absorption. Visual lavender pours over my skin, soaks the cloth of the pink suit, turns it, turns my skin to rice paper and melts away into one of the cups.

Olympia.
I'm scared.
Olympia.

My vision is in liquid. Floating under the bubbling waters of the flowing tea. A kaleidoscope my father brought me back comes into my hand. I register the pure joy of it. The lights entering all of the darkest rooms we built for TOWN CENTER adjust in my nodules.

Olympia, why.
Why did we help them build it?

Eyes notice a forest in the distance, tree lines swishing in a series of movements over

Upside down , wet tea machine.The Liquid warms parts of my generated body to, then refurbish a pair of arms, legs and a human heart for me.

The blood starts pumping through glass valves inside of the tea machine. My Eyes finally float up to the top of one teacup and look around in the intricate glass tube running this way and that, pumping steady with blood.

Socially, i feel cold, and do not attempt to speak with Olympia anylonger. I am recovered in tea and am feeling sleepy. The sleep that i feel is all new. The sleep comes rinsing over me in a kind of machine bath, and all of the tallest glass walls melt into a China cup.

This feeling is not new, I have been a heroic pilot on this craft for over two months, and have watched all of the best films on this experience, drug related or not.
 So, when an Eye rolls through pieces of sliced green onion, and then eyes pile with the gracious notch of a concrete hole, I can find rest in peace, knowing well this is only the mushrooms.

It must be embarrassing for Olympia, that crazed look on my face poking out of the window frames I made as my costume, but I think I am safe in her company. She is the gracious type, probably the love of my life, and I don't think she will judge me too harshly for that incredibly busy look in my eyes.

A plate of valentine's day candy is placed before me. I pick one out and thank Olympia. A white one:
ALWAYS
FOREVER

a pink one:
YOU
BET
a white one:
DANCE WITH ME
a green one:
MARRY ME
TODAY
I think of someone else,

An orange one:
GET
REAL

I think of them again, someone who isn't Olympia.
A mashed up mistake yellow one:
DREAM
TEAM

A pink one that the machine chewed up making it, like a mouse chewed it.
LOVE OF
MY LIFE
I chew the DREAM TEAM one and see a green one that says
MISS
YOU.
I put that one in my mouth and sucker on it.
Olympia leaves me some water with a lemon in it, and wanders away, to get the latest news about my experience. She comes back and hands me a print out which I begin reading, suckling down the candy's slowly.

ISAAC HERING / PRINT OUT OF COLLECTED DATA FOR PSILOCYBIN MUSHROOMS/ STAFF COPY DATED: 2015, TIME 7:55p.m.

Liquid water that makes up the bulk of a soup, liquid iris, retinal blood vessels, Macaulay, lens in the soup; the warm broth. (---------the same time . -----) The eyes are a place to come closer and journey the forest in some kind of visualized map. The glass cell before the mint teacup in the foreground is then leaked out through diamond filters – the machine tilts— it tilt 7 times, the glass cell filters out of an outdoor pool and —

:

In the cracked pavement, the liquid, your eyes, my eyes, your eyes, my eyes, your eyes, my eyes, your eyes, my eyes – I am poured like pavement into one whole row of teacups, over-flowing, visually this is a great time . The left hand grabs from somewhere in the body. The Eyes link up, back to the body, and you are back - from a whole row of locations: peering a ceiling in the office.

REFERENCE TERMS FOR ISAAC HERING

FRACTAL:

A fractal is a natural phenomenon or a mathematical set that exhibits a repeating pattern that displays at every scale. If the replication is exactly the same at every scale, it is called a self-similar pattern. en.wikipedia.org/wiki/Fractal

A fractal is a never-ending pattern. Fractals are infinitely complex patterns that are self-similar across different scales. They are created by repeating a simple process over and over in an ongoing feedback loop. fractalfoundation.org/resources/what-are-fractals/

TOWN CENTER

(II.)

An Ox is led down the oakwood path by a photographers black and white of a mother licking the eyelids of her cub, by the clear, learning lights of the light bright, wreathed around the neck of my neighbor, Kurt. I had landed, on an old mission we staff members like to call rebirth. The icing on the cake for me. A good measure.

The mission had only one suggestive marking, which I felt weary that schoolboy may notice, stenciled on the cortex in a thin shield around the pupils, were the miniature famed symbols of reference group 5. I carried the bag of bones well, and my hooves were comfortably set. But the feeling without insides, crossing into the street, it felt empty, too noticeably light for the computers in TOWN CENTER not to Absolutely view. I have no entrails gathered, shall it be mentioned later, rather, I am peeking out on a digital copy I had placed elsewhere to track me if they attempted to kill the ox. A cow with no insides, difficult to show the exact weight and disposition of the step, planting each hoof down with precise amount of stubborn distrust. A road sign reads Sapphire Haley Boulevard, and is glowing ominous. The daylights have been knocked out of this place since I was last here. Gray clouds, oil paint we had decided on drizzles, leaks intact with a line of dead twenty dollar bill trees. I handle the apparatus fairly well, stopping now and then to inspect some orchid flowers to nibble on Kurt seems to have ignored,, or hadn't noticed. And this brings the sun out a little bit through the clouds. Kurt's clown face paint cracks in a mechanical looking smile, like a wind up toy that has just been twisted, and wound up, and is going through the process of clicking gears to make a single face. This is how a lot of the best ones are, the first ones who we programmers especially loved. But now he seems old, worn down, like he is faking it, like his dreaded skin must be taken off and washed out and replaced, his mechanics taken out and oiled. And the sun goes back to grey oil.

None of the repairs Kurt seems to want can happen since this is a computer program, no body has physical outcome, just an empty set of numbered steps, programs that can be dialed, erased, set again, puppeted, and left running however long without concerns. The woods are all winding up and stepping forward, as figures, hunched down for breakfast, looking with magnifying glasses, small business. I'm thinking about the program school boy, and how much programming intelligence went into his character. The Boulevard lay against a filthy alley, stained of charcoal and tissue paper glue, to look light flowers. all of the separations behind the flowers done on an old computer, most of the texture hasn't even been filled, and seems blurry, model 4. People are starting to crowd in around a house Kurt walks me passed, they all seem to be excerpted out of modern computer programs, not really a fit in this environment, yet they crowd in more and more, lining up at the door. They stand around chatting. I hear one mention a witch doctor who did studies on lobotomy. I'm not sure who they are, and feel like a great big deal, wandering by as they all stop talking to stare at me.

The Boulevard, built entirely of one-dollar bills, rips apart beneath the oxen ten hooves, and i begin to think back as far as i can, to the first model of schoolboy, hanging in a swing, chattering.

Boxes made from the wood of his closet had been tucked away in his memory of his house. They were made from a dust particle I found during a psilocybin trip in the teacup galaxy.

"from yet wrapping is peeled away, the seams, like horse manure, like we saw in the whistles in the sun last winter," he whispered "Things that lay inside are protected from the influence, folded up in tissue paper, one by one, encased in gold, protected from the elements, like Christmas," he always spoke to us in this way, pushing off of the ground with one shoe, "A dog goes scratching the lock, Issachar tries jumping aboard."

I remember the chain link separating and coming together as he whispered to us., "A ball is tied in ropes I made of old socks," he said.

A cow wandered then, down the stained alley of Sapphire rd.

The animals name was Lexington, and that day as program school boy talked, we realized we had a problem. Lexington program seemed to be reacting to his words. And tears of snow fell, nothing we'd seen before. But a no.3 camera in the rain captured that moment, wandering through, snow falling upward from her abdomen, out of her pores, her eyes, a lone disciple of gathering dollar bills.

A part of her was "snowed through" and began shattering, like glass. The snout of the beast began to fall off into a stack of dollars, a huge solid chunk of frozen muscle, fur and bone.

And It wasn't normal, we hadn't programmed it, we all started trying to piece back the torn up old nylons that was her skin. But the shattering bull began falling away, caught in a kind of 8-bit looking snowstorm.

"an ulcer." school boy had whispered that day.

"I think it's an ulcer." he began laughing. And we knew we had a problem.

Mighty as a whimpering flesh bag can be– I study the bulges from a Spackle job, circa 1965, taken from my intestines further down, creating the picture of black and white walls and fingerprints. An inside view of a city from the town's dark beginnings of the theater, disguised as a schoolhouse set across the swings emerges, and Kurt steadied me in front of the door. The light is on above a bed i can see through the front porch window. It looks dim, like it's been on for three or four days. Following a version of Kurt that offers small thanks over every little movement, I feel an overwhelming illumination. we created a virus.

I climb to the clock, in my office, searching for veins, organic ingredients a pen, paper. I manage the letters VIRUS, and SCHOOL HOUSE, and frozen socks cater to me, leading my silver hands back to the door of the school house, clutching a giant, diamond necklace. I look back at the clock, and press a lot of buttons on it. This loads me into a different kind of body in the TOWN CENTER, and, when I get back into TOWN CENTER, The boy whispers to the chain links, watching it unfold before him. I am standing next to him, but am a beautiful place, not a person, or animal, one of the background sections.

Cotton eyes I am a good little camera, I can use zoom to see the boy's eyes as they fill with fragile layers of Lexington, her veins, her inside.

"Old cotton and blood," he whispers, watching the doors of the log cabin, at Kurt and his oxen standing there.

"This is the beginning of another sped-up nightmare. " I think, "I've seen this before, last time I was here, fast films, a slow death.

"He is becoming inhuman." I think.

"She hasn't spoken to him, snow freezes her." he mutters, swinging.

I'm watching him, watching the back of her head, the oxen he thinks is Lexington, at the diamond necklace around her neck.

I growl, as the memory of her sickness had brought so much silence in her, the shattered parts of the cow, frozen, falling off in sections until I was standing in a pile of dollars and bones and ice and blood. I think of her silence and want to remind myself, by replay, to fuel my anger, and insert back to the office, waking up with the camera I have grasped inside these quivering hands. I roll through the footage, and become more enraged , load into schoolboys body after what happened last time. Super eight films.

I cry: The blood knows you, Sarah; my tears turn to snow, light powder falling through me and the thousand of them know you, Sarah. I am next on the list in the ice with you, shattered in dollars with you. The body explodes into crystals, all 8 bit computers built it this way and that, and schoolboy rapidly picks up the good stuff in super eight, until that is all that I can see.

Hair is still looking at me and then to the window, dropping snow from my ice lids, rubber fingers flick routes, and I wake up two wakes later on base, Olympia pressing my head.

All I can feel is (clotted, packed snow)

Olympia asks if i treid to enter schoolboy again, but she already knows the answer.

"Trying to protect, always out to protect," she mutters.

Back in the TOWN CENTER schoolboy's eyeballs, set in a dish in his living room watch Sarah and I die, on a regular super eight projector. Soon he will sleep, and let his body come back together, his hands, removed and toe tagged operate the focus ring on the projector, and his mouth in the kitchen sink is laughing.

(Xiii.)

I get inside. Divided body parts School Boy flayed in different rooms, line the house. Toe tags sewn to spasm, arms muttering through carpet, the house is a rare-coated realm. Notes, sewn in a pair of hands decorate the living room table. One note reads: The Empire of the room: pictures of old, military captains, curtains, lace, dust, coffee table, green velvet couches. Toots, the raven model 12, one of the first in Anima technology, pinches my ear with his beak and drops from my shoulder, onto the end table by a sewn and severed hand; flipping the toe tag over with one wing, it is revealed that another side of menacing dust mutters from inscriptions on the tag:

"Of dessert sky, I watched her enjoy myself some tea~" Toots prances like he doesnt care much for this poetry, and takes video of the note. He prances about the hands, pecks them once each and looks up, cranking his neck. Everything seems to be made of film, have film, or is viewed like it is filmed in super eight. He squawks, the dust on the tag flies as his wings lift off the table and folds into a black piece of paper. It is as if he were pulled through space on thin string, and he wobbles in the air here, up to the mantel piece, setting down on the railing to the upstairs landing. A loud squawk hurts my body, rattles my nerves. I chose to wear a three piece suit, all black and a white tie, with black slacks, wing

265

tip shoes and a pale demeanor, black hair. I want to look as close to the virus as i can so he may relate to his maker.

Three times in a row, loud squawks that make me frightened are heard. I over estimated this scrawny body type. Somewhere inside of a box is heard as Toots disappears into one of the rooms.

I am starting to feel like we need to get out when doors shut behind Toots, and all through out the house.

Suddenly, the film speed changes in the room, slows down to a lagging dra2, until even the little bits of computer code are made out, like little bars of data clustered far too close together. vibrating out of the walls, a transmitter cautions the intruder, a lingering alarm beyond the door, somewhere in the wall. The signal does not alarm me, but losing toots in the hairs of code begins disgusting me, a bad neutral signal comes on, very slight, in the wiring, absorbing into my forearm. A missing memory is superimposed over the weekend body I have on, the rental. Onyx cubes rattle into the living room, and open the front door, a gust of wind slams the door. I picture Toots, slow motion, in flight out in nature. It is snowing.

Burdened in cloths, three steps at a time, lightening to the stairs, I catch my foot near the middle step, falling into red, what looks like sand.

Deteriorating carpet! Lightning, sudden, hard. The house falls down deep into the earth, laced with wings. The floorboard dissolves. I try to get to the electronics in the office.

I try to get out of the heavy sand, but it eats the rental, ten steps slowly roll over like waves onto my head, predator's lunching on a snack, bang! The house rumbles as I try to slowly get up, ten steps. All I have to do is ten steps. The doors leak out more tiny onyx cubes, and they roll past me in the sand. I am sucked far away, pulled back.

The whole house feels me trying to get up, my feet run, but only in sand. I find a park buried deep inside. Under the storm, the red flurries moving at razor sharp speed, I see the last, ten steps, up onto a ravine, and a swing set and a tree over a hill. Behind the swing set is a house where a girl is perched in a pink dress. She waves her hand to come inside of the school house, but her face is gone, replaced by a mask of Schoolboy. She tries to pull the mask down; the little girl struggles with the mask, falling to the ground as the wind picks up and slices through my rental hands. It actually does hurt, and I look down to see that my human hands are there instead of the two rentals now, and they are dripping blood. The girl in the pink dress struggles under blood red sand that is covering her now. And I run through the door, bashing into a room, where piles of sand or blood cover the bed, the walls, the entire room. The door handle in my hand crumbles. My ravens are all around the room, in the walls, in the chandelier. Pecking around in the blood of the torso cut from, in the bed, rock formations slowly lift out moss, where I begin tearing. I shout, falling, my lungs, empirical lungs of sand. Years go by in beads of blood, dripping from the air.

Sand piles on the carpet, blood stained. Piles of bloody sand line the bed sheets. Ravens perch on the torso, head, all over the room, pecking at   sewn in notes from the flesh of the school boys face, the blinds, out of the ceiling paint, from the carpet and out of the walls.

The door slams by a gust of wind through an open window. An old portrait of school boy rumbles and shakes, spinning on the wall. I read one side of a toe tag, sewn to the body along the neck:

These are the limbs of our killers~ these   are the limbs of your creators~

Toots jumps out of the blood, and onto my shoulder. All of the others jump out of their pecking, and swing together, merging into one bird, leaving a tail, and wake of dark blood, through midair, behind them. He clutches a toe tag in his beak.

A door bell rings down stairs. Toothy
squawks loudly, and takes video of the
room. he drops the
 toe tags in a dark puddle.

I lift it from the bloody sand,
wandering blurred, to the landing. The
main room of the house is over grown in
dollar bill trees. I Pull back large, lace
curtains and peek to the porch.

A dark figure stands there, dollar bills circling him at
the door. A statue lurks on the porch under a sheep mask.and
I flip it, reading the opposite side of the card, code in four,
small parts. The toe tag displays a language of symbols
reminiscent of glitch I used to write:
    (''^','|('7.'7_+') ~`\77.(*7.)
    (_&).7,4.}{.7,2.(&_)
Computer format blended to Aztec
sediment, code, made of human blood, a
print from his arm?.
~

I wipe silver tears, look through
casement, rotting glitter of my persona

drifts to the carpet, stays for some time
and then dissolves into it. The maniac
envelopes to trees – oasis wearing mask,
over mask, over mask. Dollars drift –
Currency.

A moment passes in the red door: one
dollar bills butterfly the living room, in
the window casement. Old porch strings
where ivy eats at a never ending roof.
Apparition [mask of vines,] collage one
dollar bill masks in five dollar vines.
Spider webs dangle the entrance, living
in the steps. I look at my clock and tap it
for a different rental.
I get back, and stand in my underwear,
little baseball players run across the butt
cheeks in an animation. In the sunken,
green shag carpet, my feet are bunched
up paper bags. Baseball socks with
pinstriped lines, two in a row stitched
high on my shins.

My neck cranes to distinguish the sheep
suit from the willow. Five dollar bills
butterfly passed the window. I finger the
drapes, lift one of the peach-velvet
corners, trying, frozen on these four
layers, to intervene where a smell in my
area suggests memory.

An Elvis mask enters the tree bark, and
looks in a way that is blindness, beside
snow-static. The mask shakes out a
mixture of computer codes, an apparatus
pours bars from a pepper shaker; pink
juice from speakers, portable valves,
shaking off the sheep skin like hair ~
A bathtub glitch snows codes, burning a
hole in THE TOWN CENTER near the
window -- glitch comes over my entire

rental body. The mask peers through this
hole, locating, spotting, Blaupunkt.

The wolf mask, standing in the window, sees lines of blood where every fiber is normally considered to be "white." This thing licks its lips, waits to claw baseballs, little baseballs.

This terror is known as "second death," defined by computer Town Center, and School Boys Computers as: the automatic 'to and fro' of spiders, mimicking of tree patterns. Normally this is seen in plain, high definition as: black fur deciding stages in which to morph vines. Also used to get closer to the subject, or virus program, this is a programmer's nightmare.

I remember Morning glory, outside the window all of the paper flowers are turning black sheep skin and mask, and only long bone, emerging from a skin, at the edges of the curtain, backing into the room.

My body is completely shocked by the first blast of a glitch I am suffering from, the tapping bone is shattering in the silence of this old house. Curtain rod inside of the wall, puncturing a hole in the floor,

A chaotic making of ways for a figure eight, to tap the window greater detail, it is all too fast, this program. I'll admit, this is a computer generated final detail I have never fathomed.

His fur is clumped together in spots, not a suit in the morning light, it is a nothing's' hair. I need to rest, my spine crossed in the figure eight, my head hurts. Eyes twitch beneath lids that follow my movements. The thing must feed soon, is angry.

Twitching socket a broken light bulb, compact screens Blaupunkt
Blaupunkt- We are going through a tunnel --
tap, tap goes the long ebony edge of the sheep suit. Black hollow where eyes have
been hiding under the mask, the tunnel all hanging masks from old tribes, before
the TOWN CENTER are sent in, this is the work of Olympia, and Mars, I know
their style. Twitching, Toots swoops down from a chandelier spiraling in the
tunnel, and pecks at the old mask suit, mutates the riddled viral program with
ease and swift mechanical attacks, the thing trying get away, back to the tree,
followed closely by toots, who keeps camouflaging in the collage of dollars,
fused enough that the edge of the dark fur spots cannot keep up.
the tree in multiple flows spins, rolling with the black mask tunnel, black orchid.
A formula interrupts the glitch virus, mutates it to Maine Coon, and the Maine
Coon cat runs off, into a pattern in the wallpaper, shifts through the molding of
the casement, then leaks out, and escapes.

Panicking, Toots and I hide behind a couch, nervous the wall is going to feed on
us. A whiff of old cow fills the room- curly hair reflects in the window. This must
be the time. I fragment, look down at the orange rug. Town Center figurines and
wind up toys march up to the house, but they stand there with shovels and picks,
too late. A mesh in a violent folding of all of the curtains, allows the tunnel to
suck underneath the skin of the house, a little hole. Nothing more.And the masks
made by native tribes fall, hitting the floor, gathered in a pile.

(XV.)

I am staring up at the old venetian blinds in a Victorian pattern, adorning the ceiling, in the middle of the day.

A slight breeze comes in through the window and a subtle fuzz of sunlight stitching spots on my arm. I'm alone or maybe the house is full
of us.

Generic people in pink bunny suits lay out across stale, Bavarian carpet. Mixed into pink batter. All of us line miniature outer-space in a simple geometry, woven, cherished, gradually into a line of angles god makes, i'd imagine, a quantity of Poloroids lay around.

Kittens stand, celebrating, poised in some kind of moons orbit. A small mass of messy hair and stairs completed nowhere, to a featureless, Featherlite satellite, slightly in the second floor, slightly in the office. The carpet smells labeled but I am biological and adequate enough, to give half a shit. I feel high, and Work two cameras   periodically scanning the immediate surroundings. A millimeter analysis left and I detect white linen. Even a millisecond environment right and I venture into viking gas experiments,

slip into a chosen film, inoculated with a rich aqueous nutrient in an atmosphere of helium, krypton, and carbon dioxide. Before living in these traces, before samples of the atmosphere had frozen in monetary trees, topographical maps on paper were laid over abandoned restaurants, condemned schools, figure 8 over the remains of a housing development, and that's how we were doing it, we were taking it back, taking over. But not right now, now it was time to relax.

Microorganism: school boy, a sample Martian soil, slipped through customs in Paris, had evolved. Classified, School boy grew in The mountains of a testing base (the barycenter) in an elliptical orbit around the teacup galaxy.

From kilo-light years away, to spirals, irregulars, concentrated stars, he was no normal computer program, he was a whole computer. Half hard wear, half software, He was built into all of our machines nowadays, not just a piece of equipment.

I put this away in my mind, and think about Olympia. In the wallpaper as ridges of photographed gold, reflecting from large clouds, in the constellation Doradus, as it pours into the house, a collective mass of light stretching around my sixteen hundred members lying here, hundreds of galaxies I am able to watch bloom, all pink rabbits.

I hope I never have to go outside again. The many double and triple galaxies containing these subgroups of galaxies and those red paper dots through the darkness that follow the kill.

I hope that I never have to be in another one of those overlapping films ever again, 25 million light years, with only a slight concentration to the center. I hope I spill the last drop of lavender tea over

the edge of a mountain far into Barnard's star, leave a flattened smile at the opening of a cave. Examine the possibilities for interstellar communication, and burst red, at the opening of another image. no astronomical factors, just hillside and landscape of ninety three landscape formations. Feet wrapped in a million civilizations, mouth wide in awe. The number to escape from Tau Ceti and this compress that is the name machine schoolboy.

In this Colorado laboratory, I feel my skin carpet as felt rooms, European reflecting mirrors in the walls, laser paws, laying, slowed here, watching the ceiling recede and curl together a house for kittens. Eventually kittens start weaving orange carpet walls to the stairs, felt ceilings of mint green dog tooth pattern floor, blue felt walls located randomly. The Selkirk Rex at one entryway tatters the edges of the felts, with a quick, jilting, little paws swipe, digging deep into the woven floor.

Three tiny tigers in white stripes, with long eyebrows that curl up with the ceiling. Playful, wild fearsome eyes, sticking every way with hair. They rummage through gray mats of felt as I lay in symmetry, bathing sun burned dollars in arms, passing through the air of my window.

The Selkirk Rex of gray and orange felt lays in simple geometry bath tub full of sun and dollars, passing through overlapped dollars, gelatin tins full of sky, through four panes of green latex. I blur near the foreground.

Before grade school

Wrapped in monkey bars, I find my (art) very quickly. From my neck, downstairs, again saturated with pipes, little legs of twigs and semen of rats, my neck is out of proportion, where I reach a week, I am the tree fused with the data, surrounded by a beige flower backdrop. Concept mapping, coding sources? Huge, wood jungle gym.

This thing sounds funny in our collection of heads and comfort , a momentum of sand, acid in oil, heads under feet. SCARED OF THE BLANKETS, my eyes scanned by angels / asleep again, in the attic, the boat, the crane, the birds on the wire. Land is a turtle on its back, from legs to hair land to the monkey bars, jaws closed, to ground— between mare Nectaris, stuck oceanis, from the langrenus bottle, painted to a central peak, believed to be opaque, flat, pouring out the crater Clavius. Substance,frozen glass of memory, layers up sawdust, milk floor winds through someone else's name. Radio waves pass, Ultraviolet, X-ray, ground based observations.

"Isaac!"

"Isaac?"

"Are you okay?"

Surrounded in monkey bars, I taste willow, rust the green substrate inside a chorion system. Gold leaf moss– filtered– phalanges formed by the leaves to my tongue– nutrients enter teeth, fabric fungi fingers searching out evil in the digestion cells. Fingers, mold, diffuse elbows, searching digestion. The sawdust sketches of component sugars and complex carbohydrates absorbed by the mold. Pictures of a venus's flytrap in action (left) phase contrast micrograph of a young paramecium caudatum, climbing from a fall that seems to have broken some piece of his nutrients, his amino acids.

Lying small pocket, tranquilized in B cells, and lymphocytes, damaged in drugs,I make out puzzle pieces reflecting from a water stained roof. First, an air-passage stencil dilating the Sagittal crest Isaac
and the feature itself, the number tendency results forming into the milk chocolate letters: "Are you okay?"
Isaac, get up, are you okay? These are the words a cattle brand has dug into the gold foil of the milk chocolate wallpaper. I grab the teal shag carpet, pulling myself up. Pieces of it tear out.

The stairs; a vile creature standing before me—
"Isaac!" This milky, white substance screams through liquid, its face is of Maine Coons and its eyes flicker through me;looking through me, followed by a ripping sound, from its mouth,used to make a flat print on newspapers. Sacred disappearing and the huge thing has me in the odd shapes of an upper-case sentence, that is cut in half. All smiling and carved and broken boards of the carpeted stairs, carving through it, the peeling back the steps in a broken blur.

The Maine Coon mask falls,to expose a traditional
head dress: Native raven. Trying to force my way
out of this monster's hold,I try throwing myself over its giant shoulder; over its furled hairy arm.
Torn up steps expose the arms tongues, guts, and legs beneath.
Broken floor, ripped carpet, a spewing of body parts from the splintered wood and an infinite laughter melting chocolate through gold-foil wallpaper: laughter as another language.

Victorian pattern closing over all walls in the house: chocolate that is now being branded by

cattle prods in an old English text.
The walls melt from their rhythm. We are now in the attic. I'm carefully set in a school desk.

The creature hunches over the attic door, holding it in her huge hand, as a dolls house door. Soft with its huge grip, the mask of Elvis Presley pokes beneath the traditional native head dress.
She is brief with the lock and frozen, pressing the ear (the layer of masks) to the crumbling attic door. One of the eyes squirms inside:
suspected movement on the ground floor.

The monster pulls it open suddenly, half morphed of creatures, reaching the aspects of a fiber optic bat, a small la-perm, Maine coon, Selkirk Rex, Savannah, Ragamuffin, and then carefully to the broke steps an oriental cross-bread house cat. Peter-balds turn in their tracks, peering at me, before stepping to the downstairs.

I can smell the cats congregated in the house; the familiar meow of the Maine coon followed by a record spinning old time music.

The attic door slams closed and I fall from the desk into a vortex, a cataract, a cortex; no, no, just a puddle on the floor: a blood water.

I rest my hand and accidentally rub some on my face as it drips over my mouth into the cotton of my t-shirt.

The door opens again; a kitten the size of my fist wanders up to me, sitting in the blood I'm seen bending, overlapped to pet her soft, white
fur. Spilling some through fingers, a liquid, her blue, crystal eyes flicker up.
"Your pretty." I say, wide eyed.
Scowling, little Rex jumps away, running the mutilated steps, downstairs.

I get up, walk out– landing, peer over the railing. Kittens gather at the fireplace, dancing around the room. A party with a record player, old time music, trumpet and washtub bass; orangutan piano.

Chuckling, I reach the steps, where arms, legs, and tongues have been are carpet created illusion
of stains – water damage.

A black cat, a little York chocolate, circles around the pack. Meowing as it knocks over
lanterns, it looks up on me, sitting in the landing. Runs up at the same time morphing species and landing on my right shoulder.

Ravens.
Welcome home.
I walk slowly down the steps. A bit of his language branded in the foil of the walls.

_____

_____

Later,
the sun blends down
 into the
Woods

following   the
crooked gutter
          of   the   Gothic
houses,

I wander through
thin,
 dying forest,
 watching oranges in
the sky
rot away
and turn black.

With   Toots,
chocolate York/ raven
          perching
          Upon my shoulder, I
am clothed in raccoon skins for
warmth
          Looking back to the
front door of the house

Where kittens poke
their frail heads from a kitchenette,

they are looking long through dirty

pane glass windows

      from

          The breakfast nook.
          I   notice   them
meowing in a worried manner.
          a tempest is coming
into town
          from   the   worlds
away,
          Taking their friend
          and brother
                    Tooty
Mewp
          away from them.

          The dollar bill trees
are menacing funny faces
          the two raccoon and
Morpheus cat cannot bear to look
the faces are so funny.
          Everything   in   the
forest remains
          quiet.

          A   glitch   crosses
chest level,

sections of the trunks disjoin
          down
          and then back
          into place.

          Walking near a line
of condemned houses

                              descending into an
old creek,
                              I catch the scream
from within
                              One house
                              near the end of the
line,
                              Followed closely by
the sound
                              Of   a   whistling
approach
                              And then
                              Stillness.

                              Dollars rustle in the
fauna
                              A   tweaked
hearing-aid at highest volume
                              is plugged in.

The silence is growing
loud in my   hearing-aid.
                              I cannot bear it, I
cover my ears,
                              holding the
rabbit gloved   hands
                              hard over my head,
squinting my eyes,
                              staring down at the
ground as the   glitch
cuts.

crumples the paper trash of me. Lasers eject through the green clouds.

Toes, severed in the moss – The shortcake smell is overwhelming – Edge of the creek. Quickly, to the other side of the bank video screens enter, play collages at different speeds, create tree behind house, house, house, laser light,ground, dollars – severed limbs. – Simulations – I am careful not to look back through. Corrosive glitch
intoxicating these toes.

Flying, I notice a hunched over man – double exposed with TV's: branches are silhouette arms, are head, are smiles, teeth, trees. Miles away he perches, dim.

He grows through trees. He is closer. He is lit behind with dollar bills on the TV's in the moon; branches then arms, then heads, then branches, then smiles, then teeth, then trees.
A gust of wind crosses the silhouette – no man, but trees, Tricky trees, collage from newspapers.

"Manifolds wield the grasp, behind you, this unknown mansion." Toots translates the language of melted mushroom chocolate, drooling tarnish on my shoulder as he whispers this severe tongue.

I turn – where the cats have been and an old house is constructed. (The asylum, built in thirty seconds, roof badly damaged, gold shingles,apparitions wind snakes,
Trapped inside the wood. Vines grow inward beneath a strange tree, the pores.

The child stops swinging and steps into the grooves, watching pebbles as they crumble into partitions, as they section tiny factories and the faces of old men, following every subtle step to the dollars, crumpled and soiled.

A glitch occurs, across the whole street. A wave of electricity passes through stomach level and following to chest level, neck level, cutting out parts of the dark, Gothic buildings and schoolboy, a segment of town folds over in a warped, computer generation. The line appears then disappears and the boy - head down - watches his suede shoes kick up the dollars in slow-mo, still He is imagining her as he climbs a dark, grave street of bills, picturing the hospital room, her thick matted hair.

A cigarette juts from her rose petal lipstick. He shuts his eyes, walking slowly and passes two frozen piles. "What is that little girl cover you're pulling over your head," He asks her, imagining a girl lost in giggles hiding beneath a baby blue wool blanket.

Frozen dollars of the cold streets tailor schoolboy up into the mountains,
beyond the lecherous houses of the town. "A shard of ice in the hyper hungry
mouth of death, what is it that falls from the sky? Is it the language of rain?" He
wanders – a subtle blur – along black hills,
through the static clusters in the mountains, combing back his soaked boy hair in
his pale hands and spying a row of trees rising behind the fog.
He couldn't remember where anything was, after inventing its whereabouts, the
intestines of a stray formula matured into the city,
the thought leaping from within still watching his shoes as they gathered
rainwater, wandering through the simulated memory cog, a deaf silhouette. One
reminiscent of the odor twenties put off.

————

I'm laying here in the theater, waiting for Lexi in the overcast light of the
window. My eyelids flicker, a flash film of memory cogs show. "I'm in the
forest at a large gathering of people." He says, his eyes shut tightly fighting the
rain. He slicks his black hair over his pale forehead. "I find a kite;
I think to fly it, yelling down at the crazy barrage of colors below." Covered by
thistle and bramble and weeds, grown over through time,
covered by the stained glass of a church bell and a slender wall I view the inside
of a theater. "Widen in there, behind my eyes."
I've died and went to the theater Someone big,
          a silhouette in a tree line on a mountain watches me,

     hiding in the wall of eyes,
a little boy with thin   black hair and giant foreheads
(there is no-thing   to shield a wall of eyes).
          Sniffs around the theater.
It reminds me. Christmas trees,
I used to receive gifts under Christmas in. in other lives,
          a Cedar tree here.
            a Cedar here?

Panning left to right,
          a section of green carpet is focused on.
Carpet here,
carpet here.

I
(a good little camera)
focus on the carpet,
     green, Christmas trees, cedar,
a standardized green.

(Eyelids touch-

           eyes focus - massive blink
           folds theater over one another -
                green in front and black in
           back,
           eyes;
           watching through eyes watching.)

           There are two doors on hinges,
                    rusting on the
           screen.
           In the theater,
                doors on hinges screwed,
           nailed
                            swing
           open and I hear a laugh track
           on the speakers

                and my cue is to laugh
           with them.

                Faces and eyes and
           eyelids -

                  Dark coats,
           mountains,
           the whole town is dampened up
                graveside

                    the gravestone,
        unmarked

                    the dollars, drift by in the
        wind.

        A gray cloud covers this all,

          closing over that wanton school
        boy,

        who charges down the hill so fast,

        slapping away through
dreary woods

              to the
street, into dollars,
grimy green,
to the schoolhouse,
like a good schoolboy.

The street sign,

       Sapphire rd.

glimmering in the moonlight,

letters green reflection

                              whites and the
wall of eyes
swing open.

                              The school
house doors come a jar.

(VI.)

TWOS and threes carve through
your mind in this room. The numbers
have no meaning, but staring into them,
they turn and turn.

A School Boy enters the theater,
blossoming into a handful of blind paper
and torn pieces, so awfully sudden that
boy.

A shadow blinds me too, paper falls to
the floor, stagnant a moment, wiggling.
The shadow of my wrist and fingers
sneaks in, through my vision. My heart,
for a moment, flutters butterfly wings to
the roof, tattering to the floor at last: a
blind paper petal. I cannot see; no doors,
no screen, nothing, "They're on motors,
connected to a timer. That's the only
way." Famous last words –

The butterfly evaporates, "This has
been a puzzle to be mathematically,
geometrically or scientifically figured
out," the doors hang open, letting in the
frozen dollars: last thought, puzzles.

The School Boy appears at the door
and stands silently; he can hear it having
a seizure, the motors for doors, for the
screen.

There's a tea bag melting on a woven
lawn chair, it snows lightly outside, and
he reaches for the door handle, closing

284

the spasming door. The light runs out of here, its angle almost perfect as it escapes just barely from the wall.

And the eyes, as if in peephole slats, fold out from their casings and hide inside: as the film starts.

Steady and ominous gray light comes in through an ornate, pane glass window, on a far, right wall. The trees are a dark, vague, bent line, cutting through the gray sky. Iron peephole eyes shut, rolling retina over; a heat warms the inside.

On a movie, a sliding glass door is open and a blanket's out, harboring rain in water and spider eggs, bugs, wood chips, a wheelchair in a mirror. An orange armchair soaking in rain, puddles gathering in the button folds – in the seams of a peat moss pot. The carpet in the house is green. I walk over it, to the glass door, lighting a match and pressing it to a candle, "Hello? Is anyone there?" I say, fumbling with the long wick as someone would a table and chairs, a mouse-tail, or a date seed. Green carpet; wax falls out, settling in through the fibers. The boy sits in the woven lawn chair, careful of the tea bag (if it's wet or not) and he notices the forty different peepholes on the door; the iron eyelids shut around the   obelisk. Pennies melt into the carpet from a wax candle.

All framed in movie screen, I say my line. "Death is subtext death is dream, sec is knots, knits, kits, and kites, and kitchens ," leaning to touch the melted copper in the mint green carpet, vomit green edges line the holes, opened by the copper. My next line: "The eyes in the carpet," I feel over pupils, over lids, fiber lashes leading my hands over them, a blind man. these are all watching me from my own mind, these are the Lsd's, the psilocybin, these are the dmt's. "An elf who makes these tricks these   writers who write hallucinations, wallpaper versus carpet here, full eyeball, ll of ees square, brilliants." I say my next line.

I light my cigarette and smoke it fast, closing the glass door leading out to the porch. The cigarettes been behind my ear this whole time, while watching the candles melt. The copper candles –

The schoolhouse glows in dreary afternoon light and he looks out through the paisley, jigsaw puzzle-frame, at the trees blowing dollars off of the limbs and he yawns, covering his tiny boy mouth.

There was this one time I missed the "Lady Fire Eyes" show as my cigarette hid from my fingers under the chair. Outside, my backyard is always full of surprises like this. "Lady Fire Eyes" is supposed to be my favorite show, it is written in the script.

My bladder is full and I got to see "Lady Fire Eyes" or the scene is cut, so, I sit down in the living room and try to remember my cues.

I fiddle with the prop remote and television comes on. That familiar, awful frequency hums the sound of a lucky rabbit's foot on chalkboard. Blinking eyes and shutter show, Lady Fire Eyes.

I'm trying not to show it, but I've got to piss so badly. The urine's burning in me. It feels like it has leaked over in my fat, pooled in the cells. I almost miss my cue and remember to laugh. This is my favorite show. I laugh, completely natural, totally believable. I can't miss it, but I've really got to urinate, badly. That's not in the cues, or the movie for that matter. My bladder is going to turn into an art film: 56 minutes of gouged balloons in an array of medicinal colors, a whole cabinet of anti-psychotic', antidepressants, amphetamines, the "D.E.X" (the red pill pouring from latex balloon skin inside me.) This is what is going through my head as I play my character in "Portal to Humans" a neat, little feature under the direction of D. Lincoln Selma. I can't miss the show; I'll be fired immediately. "Lady Fire Eyes, Lady Fire Eyes, Lady Fire Eyes," I say in my head, trying not to picture leaking valves, Milton Falls, the red pills, pouring out of gouged bladder.

"Cut!"
"Oh, thank God," I shout to a confused group of bustling people. Running through cast and crew, cluttered around back of stage, into the makeshift bathroom in the makeshift house, the sounds of flickering plastic stick to his mind.

Schoolboy, all he sees is the next scene of the movie, after a moment in dark screens, the way they pasted one moment to the next in editing,
door belt having a seizure, white urine drains from my bladder, into the makeshift toilet, while white makeup is put on my wrists and hands.
"Action!" Sitting in the same worn out, foam-green sofa again, I'm dragging my hands through what hair they have allowed me to have, for this film. I say my line: "Where did I put that," I mutter, perfect, subtle tone.

The boy shifts in the lawn chair, studying the screen. I look around the makeshift room, careful not to strain my neck.

Makeshift boys room: posters, video game console set up on the floor, TV, Lady Fire Eyes always on. I act interested. My eyes are focused on, my lips. The camera's go through cues.

::

Opening, the peep hole covers fold off of multicolored eyes in the door.

The boy slicks his hair to one side and looks over at them, scanning his direction; rolling back and forth, the silhouette of his brain exposed in the light comes through a dirty window, where he adjusts his weight in the lawn chair, making squeak sounds and can see himself (through a pair of eyes in the wall) doing that. Silhouettes of his brain cased in clear fluid, clear skin, clear see-through hair, examined with digital numbers. He makes a bunched up face, distraught by this, it appears gray in his scalp, functioning on some kind of faint, oblivious, subconscious level. He sees, as the brain tenses up on the right side, where he'll suddenly move his foot and kick it over the other leg.

There is a pounding sound from one of the walls in the theater. It could be a knocking hand, one that is confused if they are knocking or running, accidentally, into the door. Schoolboy doesn't know. The peep hole covers droop back over, relaxing shut. The lawn chair and the movie screen, the window, ornately carved in paisley and the knocking, a vibration, pounding away like a nail at a construction site, like a nail pounding through iron, explosive and repetitious, but then with no rhythm suddenly. Frozen stiff with fear the little Schoolboy holds his pale, cotton hands together, watching his breath as the room becomes colder.

Cash is sneaking in through the cracks in the floorboards, beneath the wall of eyes. A five-dollar bill passes through the high door seal. The pounding gets rough, violent, abstract, and definitely not human.

A sort of man's voice is heard on the other end, shouting.

For a moment the boy puts his hands to his face and rubbing his eyes, begins configuring a half decent start to a plan. Suddenly the odor of urine wafts into the Schoolboy's nostrils, he looks down, and sees piss darkening his blue suit pants. At the same time, ominous gray daylight and dollar bills rush into the room as the door of eyes slams against the adjacent wall. He recognizes it, a beast he learned of in school. Frozen solid, he gets into one of those "life flashes before your eyes things."

He sees Selma, his decrepit grandmother catching a fish with her bony wrinkled hands, as the large, white bear lunges. He sees Selma pulling the fish from the hook, the poor thing leaking a small drop of dark blood. She just rips the hook out and sets the thing down, like a watermelon, or a potato, hitting the fish over the head with a large, gray rock.

The Bear's fangs are covered with blood and it enters the theater, panting. Standing up on its hind legs and wandering to the lawn chair, it swipes the dinky thing to the side and gurgles. Now hiding behind a black curtain near stage, Schoolboy watches as the great bear ransacks the place, crashing into boxes and swiping them, until crushed thoroughly. Hazelnut wood seal, saturated once on the stage, reflects Schoolboy almost as clear as a mirror. He looks down and sees himself, in a fetal position standing up. The bear growls and scrapes things aside, the lawn chair, boxes, and cans of film stray across the wood floor. He perches near the screen, and sniffs over Schoolboy, pupils the size of its whole eye.

Little Schoolboy can smell his own gaping fear, as it wafts up from a basket of butterflies, near his suede shoes.

Dollars drift in, carried by a careless gust of wind. Suddenly the bear takes a turn that had been unanticipated by Schoolboy, leaving an open shot straight to the door. He watches the polar bear from behind the screen, checking the door, and then runs out, swinging the wall of eyes shut, bear inside.

Over wind tossed piles of dollars, he runs to the swings and rushes a mixed version of the story in his mind, watching his predator's cub lurking outside, near the schoolhouse window.

After mentioning the wall of eyes, he watches the cub climb away into somewhere invisible to his vision and no bears anymore, he glimpses a pile of bones and flesh lying across the street covered in ice and dollars.
A wind shoots through town, picking up fives and twenties and brushing him on the shoulders.

He runs, disappears into invisible, swallowed up from somewhere behind him, to nowhere, and the town is quiet. In the distance, groves of Dollar and Five-dollar trees sway back and forth, subtle shades of green against a wall of painted gray.

For a long time there is the sound of wind coursing through everything, eating up the dirty dollars, from out of the street and spilling them through the air. A segment of discolored lines cuts a glitch out of the chest and eye and tooth level, followed by a missing sound, one that represents the sound in a place where nothing exists, a "nothing" which is even something. Where there is far greater absence than nothing.

This is the fold where
the tape was placed.

(viii.)

Through baggage claim, lost in dry erase markers, through letterhead, pens with airline insignia marked on the side, I scramble to my feet, throw shelves in a frustrated rage – witness the collapse of the luggage conveyor, shake off. And on green tile, the fern tears and trash termite, walk to the exit, following the bend to closed up check, shout.

After a moment open and exit, through cream door in hallway, the entrance, far opposite of the building, I lunge to my following wall
screwing up my neck, shoving my arm in a sharp wall. The pain, I notice rusted, jutting.
Orange light at a white streak passes my eyes. The heavy door pulls me inside, turning closed the wall behind, and wiggling in the pitch black.

Hands and knees chocolate maze, wood termites dark with candy coated antennae, crawl through orange creamsicle steaks in the chocolate clouds, licked away.
By a giant tongue falling from the skin of the heavens, all thoughts – memories to disappeared idea me, the maze turns around a memory from peek attention.
Chocolate York kitten, Toothy, in a room I figured is an attic, crosses me in Burmese body.
The crosshatched iron mesh, old, rusted grate and through machine –
I see him in a room costume, fashion holes, the side the maze lit with flashlights.
Orange smell talks me through the right direction, pours out silhouette, and a small fire ignites.
Singing, putting fingers to the rusted corners, opening them – spreading them apart, Toothy, replaced with flame is the only thing I seem to have resembled again. In the tunnel, absent minded, burning.
The concrete is similar to my brain. As though I am an airport inside of forgetting and it feels awful to crawl toward the fire right into the room, with a tended blaze and the memory of chocolate York's and Burmese kittens fading with the cold, I can stand up and walk around on my termites.
For a long time Sim tries to remember anything at all, but Sim legs are distracting Sim, and Sim finds itself looking into each and every hole, for a termite to peck out and eat half-studied.
Wandering through each particle as the fire burns softly behind, a cat appears from within the cold memory of the tunnels. He circles around very quickly, it sounds like something is worrying him
and he looks frightened watching the fire as if it is doing something to him. When I turn to look at the fire I see that it wasn't at all fire that worried him, but a door in an attic,it is very clearly now at the far end of the floor. Frightened, watching the door at the end of the attic Toothy nudges my head from the ground the way someone does desperate to leave. Dawn comes.

The memory completely re-loads and I forget the termites and the tunnels and the fake memory of the airport. The large fire ablaze behind everything, the other simulation memory, relaxes Sim into the warmth, split with an attic in an old house.

The fire in the airport pulls Sim back out of the attic and keeps it warm. I turn and mutter to Toothy, who rolls over onto his side and then for a moment I peer down through the hole we made in the floor and see a pile of books covered over the living room – the buzz of different lights in the kitchen. It sinks in again.

The little boy with the switch blade hanging with the mask wearing sheep creep somewhere in this house.

They are using an old memory of an abandoned airport they crafted to keep me under, while they locate our point. The room is quiet and Toothy rolls around, side to side, licking at his right and left paws. He has forgotten what our situation is. He has given up, fallen into a simulation memory as I did. Where can he go sleep and be warm inside of, a made up world.

"Wake up!" I shudder, exhausted of my limbs;
large format pictures of termite eaten legs walking tired through Terminals slowly mesh into reference channel one.

I am a nap, a slow air-wave curled by fire. My arms a pillow. My gaze in the distance, wonderful darkness.Buried beneath snow, I dig hallucinations off of me, dueling multicolor blankets of flame-chewing carpet and wood attic.

Broken floorboards, smell of fire carving rooms.

I'm suddenly onto my feet and Toothy flicks his shoulders letting out his raven wings. I see real legs inside of wooden ones speckled with stars.

A shattering door at the end of the room peels into the attic wood, followed by a small creak and Toothy squawking as the little boy in white underwear clutches the peeled skin of something living in one hand, it locates us.

It runs, digests the room. Neon pulls over the lights, at that same moment another strange and quick thing happens, entirely rare, this happens with phosphorous gas and a union brand of pink light, the molecules in the room become apparent,

just like that, a light from out of nowhere cuts geometrically into separate lines on everything. School Boy is seen in his real body as a puffed up, red faced monstrosity with no speed. The thing looks blind on the grid, slow moving beast with four heads and green fur. Apparently I am faster then he is. Toothy has already ditched –

outer-space, auto-pilot.

Left, throwing him off, I follow one of the lines before me leading into the window, straight out of the attic door, I dodge and weave the School Boy,using lines of mathematics route to flee.

The whole town is covered in the lines, pink grid. I peer along the stairway window, floating along the casement lines, and I watch as the grids make up trees, dollars, specks of dirt, all sticks.

A moment will pass, where the thing has no way of locating Toothy and I.

Then speed of giant fuzz, fast on the lines of light. With no trouble at all I follow to the landing, and make it to the living stairs.

Toothy is perched on book shelves near one intersection in a seventy-seven pattern grid.

Handwoven, silk-light leads to the front door, but it is quickly interrupted by a sudden apparition of black sheepskin through streams. Invisible fish swim in the line across us. Double take,too slow. The thing in clutches already feels through my pockets, molesting.

Pink and white gas escapes and the laser grid dissolves at the surface of the front door.

Laser hands clench my legs as tight into a little ball as they were built, pulling me inward as small as I can, I screech the alarm give up in panic, spasming and flipping over.

For a long time I stay like this, until a bout of silence forces me to open one of my eyes. I am the carpet next to the sheep suit, piled around me. Coming from the moisture ball I see that there is a card attached. I start to read.

"Welcome to the grid of life, this suit is strictly known for better coordination of your laser hands within this maze of town, be well my young friend." Bending over and grabbing the suit, I clutch it and run into the woods, toward town.
(i.)

The nurses step out of the hospital, closing a door of Palm fronds behind. White skirts and red hospital logo's embroidered, they bring silver plated trays into a large opening of Palm trees. And set aside the trays. it must be time for tea.

My friend wakes up to a pouring sound on the cold front

porch of the log cabin, tricky trees. A single oak lined path, marble tree limbs, grey skyline mixed until all marble with the clouds. I Remember: woodstove, log cabin blues, orange, tangerine skyline. A perfect still frame smoke caught dormant, now rises out of a fallen log that is turning black and begins rooming mint green, knotted up lichens. Moment of sentiment, trying on the patchwork, iris stocking and fur pullover.

Fear lives underneath the peel of the blooms, and my friend vomits looking at them.

My friend's so happy to be back in town. The pink fur of African Fawns, and a mammal from the Galapagos islands puddled in dollar bills there, arm in sleeve.

Toothy swoops out of the house before my friend x. and the grid appears from beneath the mammal pile. Stained, bone flavor floats in my friend's mouth, adjusting the legs. By the far edge of the log cabin glowing neon lichens now so tall that antelopes are peeking their heads at us around the corner. Last look, the sheep suit in my friend's hand. X. tries not to throw up, again. A density, a crochet, a neon thread converging in rat kings, a relationship they form beneath her.

The suit has been knit in four stitch. Toothy is blur, my friend x, she is 1943 blur on the layer of thread. Her fingers knit parts of the lichen together, every now and then cupping them together, to blow into the recess formed there. The black monkey suit appears from all this knitting my friend keeps doing, her hands pink, cold.The monkeys arrive from inside the lichen sculptures, begin knitting too, little hats with red symbols embroidered on them. And it's into the log cabin with them, while we hide the monkey suit behind a black log, stumble about to fall over. maps of the firmament begin to appear in red laser, crimson sort of string, and this is where the maps stay, lined , and sewn, threaded along the lichens, notches in the bark of the oaks, every speck of dirt glows on the single trail, the log cabin glows, whirling marbled skyline, now black, glows with the lines of maps.

Embedded there, are some of the numbers 3.5 and 7.4, they appear to be woven parts of the sky I had never noticed before. Diagrams. Encryption (3.7) turn to (7.3) as my friend sets her good foot to the ground to walk, (numeric start up, I imagine.) Town shuffles through a booklet of hymnals, and while this is loading, we freeze frame.

I try to focus on the things in front of me. The organization of these very tiny worms ripping through a number of layers in that pink grid all over everything. Upside down 7.3 to 3.7 are focused on with magnifying glass fitted on one rope of the neon map dangling off a tree. Sheets of newspaper heard tearing around the 'room.' (The grid) 3.75 and going fast, pulls into a cavern in my arm. My wrist is fused to a strawberry Blunderbuss. Controls fairly even; I'm shooting strawberries when Toothy perches on my shoulder at the porcelain raven stand. She shakes away deer ticks from her ruffles, (her eyes) glow in a jar, hold her soul. Every strand of grid that makes up 'town' is, for her, a kind of skin . (Pink string) plugged into her back hatch.

Weaving a loading cord, in through her cavities, along a fine length of her chest, the woods reflect black (a motion picture inside of her body) stuck at the middle, garlands and roses.

Error in the past sequence now surrounds a gold leaf picture frame, where I am holding a flower stitched pullover suit and extension cables. Protected by this grid of our lineage, the color of our threads, us. Our direction. Swimming world in tangles because (we are told) a heavy cluster of wire (A):is stopping to perch inside a cable or (B): has built in lines woven to it. Coordinates to the basic designer appear near the trees in my right peripheral.

Toothy pecks a bundle of threads to say 'I don't get it,' and I am pulling apart the fabric of the monkey suit with my pointer finger and thumb, investigating what it wants from us.

She gets a few good worms, shredding out neon hosts as they hide away in the fur of the pullover. Poorly with her talons (The engineer/ programmer) parts the reality. A cute red bike and a parked Oldsmobile, green houses lined by river. I cannot focus my eyes as it comes undone. Examination of these strings shows a bond forming in the suit. Grid lines become parts of the map. Integrating numb data.

After a moment of running lights - the main street of town appears.

A school house building is sewn in, various threads in brown canvas, pink yarns, linen bag, stretched over reality. Stapled into view along olive wood frames.

Town is inside of a cocoon. Mid-winter, Nineteen Fifteen. Photographs had originally been developed with copper plates in a sepia tone developer. The dollars were captured in the photograph using microscopic films to achieve the blowing effect through trees. School house and swing sets all represented digitally, through yarn, copper plates, gels, through wood grain. Through plugs, through wires, through marble.

Cold, pink lines, built of triangles, attachable that evening, settled in the developer. Picture.

I pull a note from a pocket in the black fur suit. Folding it open, and attempting again, some form of understanding, I witness a new marking engraved in the paper, another grid within a grid within a grid, a replica of hand writing. I have seen this in the office before. Hybrid. Russian stirred Mayan.

The note comes into focus: :[enter town (area seven,) by supplementing this body armor in sub-town area five, where area five meets area seven]::

A note draws up light weave here, it is in thin cotton air. Inside the pastel card, letters line in the dimension of rag oxygenate molecules dispersing [e]'s followed by exiting [c]'s. The note is blank. Dollar bills blow by foot, on Toothy. Since before reality, she has been he, and curls around my legs. The black suit is squirmy. Laser hand shuffles settings, in a teal interface.

"Maybe It's demon suit. Lead me astray on the grid, huh Toot?" Toothy shivers, jumps from my foot, shaking dollars off of her violently, letting out a small, perturbed yawn.

"Town, that sews me to the wrong threads! Never in my entire stay have I heard of Town, Toothy?" She shakes her head and sneezes.

"I checked pronunciation." It disappears in digits, no pronunciation! I make out the last E's bleeding a tiny dance, numbers maybe? Temptation is to put on fur, watch thick growing, uncontrollable urge and have strange burdens. That seems to be right, I am by the minute plagued. I linger in the middle of the field, waiting for Toothy to get out of the clutters of her yawn. If I go back to the (cat house) they would know about Town.

Or maybe, you'll just put on the suit. (dead mammal's, raccoon, bear, dinosaur.)No, No, No! No put on the suit! Who said that, Toothy? You say that? The animals fall apart, I thrash them around.

Whispering dollar bills, folding over each other in wind. School boy activates behind me. Somewhere, an array of digital one, zero. Toothy jumps from the dollars, stuck mid-yawn and relapsing to raven, forms wings, perches on and digs into my shoulder. I see it standing in the window of the house for a millisecond. Thoughts spin in its mind. It deactivates.

Now this moment with concrete fingers, I am unraveling the edges of the suit. It executes painful symmetry on my flesh and methodically, loving, inserts tiny knives into the concrete hands.

Put it on now. Screeches from the activity place. Out of a far radio, tucked behind a window, a weapon from five dimensions, intermingled persona, just another item in a sorceress hat collection. Inspecting threads, I get back to work beginning on the loose weave of the three joints making up the knees.

A part between the armpit opens into a tiny threaded hole of raccoon ligaments, I fear the exact mph these holes move in, and see the threads move in order to force shut the air. \A violence in

(*)

mmmmmmm0oim dismemberment

mp,m,,m,m;autoimmune0}

Feeling comes from each thread in black objects, is of excruciating evil, and in no way has place. Throwing suits down in the dirt, I swiftly bury them.

(*2)

]]\{LO)OOOOOOOOOOOOOOOOOOOo009

I wind down to the school house and brush dollar bills from trees as I open the heavy wooden door. A wall of eyes slams behind me and pale light of evening folds slowly in, through the window. A shutter after burial, picturing suits in slow attempts to inject thread in me, I am slithering on the internal lengths of numbers, as to form adjustments with my skin. A second tying of my bone is sinking in the lace of it. The third adjusting of my skin is itself in the fat and the muscle of it. Toothy climbs off of my shoulder and morphs onto an old stage. This time she is a Selkirk Rex kitten, prowling behind thick velvet curtains with an umbrella. She wanders around a wild notion in a state of cat paranoia, while I look for Town. Reestablishing general cleanliness, (as to create a central space,) stacking boxes of code print outs commences in the corner of the room.

(*) TERM Glitch: Unraveling reality taking place within the applications screen.

(*2) TERM Glitch set: Repeated unwinding of data occurs within the standard coding (possible virus interruption by programmer) Also known as playful interaction between the coder and receiver of codes.
Sleep]

Boxes of clues on top of boxes of clues. A map of the woods marked with green dates. Burned copies of the original seep from beneath three yar old drafts. Marks in the wood, three claw marks coded in brilliant textures, And then print editions on sheets of rice paper. Overlapping numbers. Boxes of this:

[,b'/<OK"/]o,o,8u6u89mmmmm mm98umu000000000000] Figures

000000000000000000000000000000mp-;-l866po8p knuckle
0o.llllllllllllln

(II.)

Paper is flipped up in the room. Digital code ink blobs and paper. Neat geometric patterns, rain. I drop near a lawn chair and ponder its existence. Thinking about the patch work and me. Get a shovel and dig a hole near trees where he cannot go. Try. Live there. I want to throw the suit away, get it out of my site. The black fur pulls me toward it,
 each string wants me to regret this if I see to its death. Folding the black suit up into neat fours,
I set it down near the paisley window and sit on the white lawn chair.
.

I get up and shuffle my coat onto my legs, lying back next to her, my vision goes thick velvet, red curtain, thick dark cotton. Shapes hidden behind the paper appear on a low lit stage.

Toothy crashes   her dream into mine, using a face of the most beautiful woman, and in a maniacal giggling manner, whe wraps suddenly across me. We grind and fumble for each others genitals in the noise: muffled peeps recognized by hands pulling my friend x into our session. This process is called deconstruction (undoing of threads.) Being enacted with a set of tools, estrogen, the black monkey suit is slipped over her naked body. Menacing Giggles out in the distance, coming near the paisley window. our bodies merge. I look down at the animal pecking my crotch, it's Toothy as a cat, not x.

 Little curtains of glass, my body has a way of finding ways to turn cold and fill with water, my guts set themselves aside. A breath stays in a lodge to warm up.

Witnessing   the shards of glass melt down and set in a puzzle of mechanics, I stand up in a sudden gliding, red curtains for wings and the clouds, my feet on stage, folding sunshine into a place at an edge of tropical forest for us to float off of the ground while we make love, the birds fly to me and peck into pieces (within a matter of seconds) the old mask I had been wearing.

We're all the same now, gliding low in the sky on a valley, and the trees, oh the trees.
 I grab a hold of curtain in its plush red velvet and arrive at the school, orgasm lifting Toothy, and x. (who turns into a cup and saucer) green tea steaming as I spill some on my leg passing through. A note reads: Don't drink Toothy, unless you want to kill.
At the edge of the saucer curtain, a cat fish comes at me through bubbly. I ask the air in discombobulation of reality if I just... Just...
 Toothy peacock turns to face me in the bubbling light, a glow of random eyes the color of bent glass, sequins, sends me whirling about in theater, in vision of two rows (one theater and one peacock feather) does double in one picture. I see legs as somebody Else's, giant hooves, white fur leading my eye to thick monster wings jutting from within my back.
]

        We launch out in a cloud, wing made of the horizon. Toothy peacock clutches my back wind and warm tastes, like sea water, pushing our wings deep in the salt, the pale blue of sky below whistles up. A puzzle of a town, the land has been tilled and built up on. Wood and layered cakes, bunkers and shops.
We descend in a small area of marble. At the sea's cliff we land on top of a roof, inspecting a tiny glass window in the place. A quint magic shop filled with gnome characters and cast, bearded fishermen. A large gold clock hangs by the window display. It changes times on it. We look away and watch as it changes. No one tends the store.
My hooves rest in compressed sand on the roof top. Sets of stairs going north to the hills up an avenue, dark gray are lined with shops. Tapering to a great dark shade of cob huts along the walls of a neat cave, another set of stairs traverses up along the descending ground of the shop. I trot down ragged slope of the cobble stone near the forest, peeking into the magic shop one last time before Toothy and I make our way along little sunken sidewalk.
Up, on an open grove of trees, Toothy stops short suddenly, calmly glancing back. Her wings open to the direction of woods her neck stiffens with. She releases an irritating sound I have never heard,of a chicken. Building irritation that explodes into noise, a sonic resonance passing into the aqueduct, shooting everywhere at once, echoing.
I notice little figurines of bearded men, standing on the cobble stone street; each a replica of the next. All have the same, casted expression on their hand painted faces.
Bent necks tilt the little gnome faces down at something on the ground that I cannot make out. All have been fired with heads pointed down. Toothy, (not

seeing the figurines) continues her squeaking in the woods. Her feathers brilliant beside the gray Malachite. She folds them down behind her, calm comes over her tiny bird mask. The cobble stone slope to the figurines tapers and then grows. I knock a figure of a garden

elf over and it shatters open onto the cobble stone. The other figurines shift castes, molded looking at my direction. I didn't notice any movement in my periphery.

They congregate around a hole, the gnome people shatter under my giant hooves; I sniff at the darkness and see something deep under ground. Something that comes closer. It gets right up to the cobble stone edge where a patch of moss has grown, and becomes a velvet cloth. I sniff the edge of the velvet. Toothy, (a gray cat) curls around my arm, a long tail flipping up sporadically, her paws on my chest.

Outside, the air is blowing dollars off of a tree behind the theater. Rubbing my eyes, watching them drift passed, I wonder (in my haze of sleep) what the figurines had been, wishing I had wings.

A reason to stand, I'm planning to stand, I don't stand. Nowhere in sight, not found peeling my eyes open, I decide and shut them right away, back to sleep. For a moment I catch glimpses in the window, rain drizzling through bare trees. Wind pushes little segments of sequin beads to the window pane. Where is my friend, x. She was in here, told me a story about this thing, Wednesday, this thing that has something incredible. It was like nothing I could imagine.

I close my eyes, feeling my Rex cuddled under my thighs, slowly a tiny yawn. I readjust my arms around sounds emitting from the cabins accordion vent. A hat sits, perched on a night stand. My hands are freezing, i think. The rain taps on the schoolhouse, Patterns dancing out of the hat into the black forest of my head. Cartoons - a lit up stage arriving on tires. Rain drops dressed in outfits. Puzzle pieces from an elephant puzzle around waists, lights on.

A roaring, crackling open, upstairs window waking my friend to a theater. The stage lifts her head slowly with a streak of orange under her chin. Kitty has already run off, near boxes stacked by the wall. We both look to the ceiling. We stare in panic, in wood grain. There is no upstairs of this building, I am sitting very still, staring at the wood. Dust falls, followed by heavy sounds on the roof. Off the stage, x wanders to a door, watching rabbits jumping through scores of music in her periphery. The symphony moves to a far paisley window, and forms in a spray of the composer ink, into a cluster around the frame. Rain builds a building that looks like dripping track housing, rows of light into pathways, like streets, impossible to see through.

A plastic, sheep mask drops from the edge of the roof, peeking into the theater (its breath already inside) the plastic sheep mask twisting and melting with the lines of rain. Toothy sees it behind the boxes, meows, syllables the thing outside talks through. The plastic mask hangs upside down in the window. I lock the door slowly. The voice becomes clear as Toothy changes form behind the box. More codes, a rambling nothing to say. A program running dashes, periods. Slashes More dreadful, I come from the door into the theater, watching the melting mask. Toothy has gone. Three sixty and the room blurs, stencils of chicken wire.
I cannot stop the grated blur as it spins. I see the end of his tail around the back of one box. It could see me watching it and I see myself in a mirror. The mirror is blending. I used to come here when I was a child, never once a mirror. In it, dark figures stand behind me. Figures dressed in black, eight year old boys. Knocking a lamp and boxes over, the lamp shatters. Shards of glass blend away with beads of water, the wood floor sucks it all through cracks. Boxes stacked in a disarray fall, replaced by the boy.

I hurry to the stack where I had seen Toothy. I see two things: one is Toothy peering from a hole into other parts of the building. The other is a pair of pearls, eyes under a mask.   Directly, for a moment, I notice no hole, the illusion made of corners. I mutter, moving back away from the fallen boxes.
"Toothy?"
"Toothy?
From the boxes black shapes, masked wolf details jump to feet and pause at the door. Pausing in mid air, it scans the room until it gets me in its view. Over a whole stack of boxes it leaps toward me, lands hard and I make out the mask switching through faces; tiger mask made in Taiwan, rabbit mask made in Sweden. Richard Nixon mask.

A scream is heard at the swing sets across the street. An odd silence takes form after, into darkness, night. Hours go undisturbed. The sound of crickets grows as the front door of the old school house opens. A dark figure steps into the night. The crickets quiet to the shape. It looks over both shoulders and walks into the forest behind the old theater.

A door shuts by wind as the suit stumbles through pink lines, soft pink light of the grid. Onto a hillside, the lines following a dark wood behind the school house, the daylight whispering away behind it. Suits pass into an orange pink glow. Bright light grows as it pulls in the first subject (suit.) Neon pink lines over everything, deep.

Forest is mapping coordinates. Deep vortex of shapes emerges. Stepping ladders lead the suit far into the sky. A ship floats in the center of the vortex. Snakes below, wolves above, the suit tries carefully through impeding beasts, to create, the ships horizon sinking into space,

(IX.)

\\\\\\\\\\\

I put the suit on and school boy wanders from the house. He's been crushed underneath something, his hand holds his little head as he wanders up to me. To the suit, he mutters something, signals to the house and turns around, I follow him.

Inside the house, he shows me a picture album of myself, and aggressively points to me and Toots. He makes a signal, moving his hand across his neck, as if to imply that I should cut my own head off.
He pulls out another album and points to the photograph of the old, abandoned silo, tucked deep inside of the forest.

I haven't been to the place in years, he wiped it from the forest centuries ago.

I nod my head, implying that I will be there. He holds up an old clock; the time is 1.43. I watch the numbers rearrange to 3:21 am. He points to this set of numbers and takes me to the kitchenette where an old fashioned calendar, taken out of the nineteen fifties, shows pictures of women dressed in house outfits. They smile, but their eyes have been rubbed out with something. He points to tomorrow and writes something with a small apparatus.

Wipe all their data. I nod gently and school boy evaporates into his grin.

I beckon Toothy, who swoops out of the house in haste behind me. He whispers in my ear. He heard everything. The grid appears from behind the dollar bill trees, by a far edge of town, closing in over the last point of the forest and looking down at the sheep suit covering my hand, I see that it's glowing in a dense crochet of neon pink threads. They seem to be connected, they have to do with each other. It is as if the suit had been hand knit.

Tootsie and I are a blur, running our hands through the layers of thread, mapping lines across the firmament, between everything, and he turns to look at me with his eyes glowing pink.

The oranges and every string of grid line begin to grow brighter until we are swimming in pitch black, using the lines to coordinate our direction, with deep, black strength, the swimming world of glowing tangles becomes a heavy cluster of wires.

Stopping, to perch somewhere inside a cable line, Tootsie pecks a bundle of threads and I begin pulling apart the fabric of the monkey suit with my pointer finger and thumb. I cannot focus my eyes as it comes undone and through examination, the strings form a bond from the suit, through the grid lines, becoming part of the map. I have become like him, a virus attaching to this town. After a moment the main street of town appears. Some of the buildings drawn up in pink threads, the rest is a mid-winter picture of dollars blown in the wind. The school house has become the library this whole time. Swing sets are all represented digitally, in cold, pink digital lines.

A representation of school boy hangs in the swings, built up of such triangles; evening is settling over Acacia as I pull a note from the pocket of the suit, folding it open and attempting again something of understanding. A new thing has been engraved into the card paper, a replica of the same hand writing in different context, and bringing the note into focus I read on:

For directions to the library, please animate the schoolboy figure guarding the door with this pass code, he will come to life and find documents you will need. "Owl enter Atlantis town." If you forget to say this three times, Schoolboy will instantly reanimate in different stages, so be careful. Do not stutter. -A Pearl Night (area six), please re-a line this Perle Pl ex night jump suit original with your body in sub-town area five, where area five meets area six, there after you turn back around, you will now be in Atlantis town (area six instead of your before area five.) Please leave sub town. Please remember to drop the purple flex jump suit off in the box labeled purple p Lexi in sub-town area five.

I ponder the note for a moment, watching dollar bills blow by at my feet, piling onto Tootsie, I have got him. I nudge Toothy to get into the suit. He stares up at me. I grab him and pull him in. He reads the note and calms back into a patch box, near my hip and we walk up to school boy, guarding the entrance to the library.
"Owl enter Atlantis town, Owl enter Atlantis town, owl enter Atlantis town," The body jerks to life and turns to us, mechanically staring for a long moment. His eyes are pure white marbles, a fear comes over me and I begin to move away. He grabs my arm and pulls me over to the library doors across the Boulevard. I am careful not to speak. Toothy squirms inside, but the machine guard sees nothing. He walks us to the first aisle of manuscripts and shoves his hand into a box next to the door. The box glows blue light and the machine boy casually shuts down, head bent down onto one shoulder, hands draped at the sides.

I haven't been here in a long time, but things are exactly as they were before. The labels have been taken down thoughtfully. He doesn't want anyone to learn, so that he can keep control over the town.

Codes, I need codes, mostly programming prompts. I need his most influential code book.

Someone watches me from outside of the windows, watches me from behind my shoulder-blades.

Toothy nudges to get out and I push him back, but he will not stop and wiggles his way out, dropping onto the floor of the library. I peer back at schoolboy, who is passed out over the box next to the doorway. Toothy cleans at his feathers and looks around, flapping his wings. The sound echoes through the stacks of books and reaches the schoolboy, guarding the door, who slowly animates back to life.

Toothy flutters around to the other side of the shelves and clutches a book from the low shelf near him; the book hits the floorboards and the sound reaches the schoolboy guard, who shuts back down, now stale, he stands at the doorway, entering a slime covered hand back into the box.

The cover of the book is blank and I lift it, open it and readjusting myself, I realize that he has found a book on recoding animals. The page with ravens on them has three lines of reference for the original DNA, cattle being one of them. A cat and female human the other two. I remember her now as I look at this. My wife. She had been beautiful, long locks of gray hair, she had been old at the time of our parting, I am at the beginnings of a new set of memories. I look down at Toothy. She looks at me and squawks. "Shh," I hold my hand over the suit and the schoolboy comes to animation at last in the door way, walking swiftly to the aisle.

I grab another book and slam it against the floorboards, but schoolboy doesn't stop, instead Toothy comes out into the aisle and squawks at the machine, and then it comes around to where I am. School boy charges at me with a strange vacant look on its face and then reaches to a book at the top of one shelf, pulling it down and handing it to me. Charging back to the door, he shuts back down, hand in the box.

I open the book to the first page. These codes are unrecognizable, they are not even in language, pictures or codes, but dots, a series of large and minuscule dots.

I flip throughout, scanning thousands of pages of the same kind of dots set up in a variable of patterns. This must be something, but what. I set the book down next to the other and shuffle for more, pulling down a book with the words reference printed onto the spine. On the cover is a engraved circle, there is nothing inside of it. I open the first page and see that the same dots are being explained. Four large dots seem to be an equation. I scan for a similar pattern as the complex ones in the other text, finding even more complex equations. These are labeled by setting. There is one for each part of a simulation of a town. This is it. I begin decoding some of the other book. "The forest takes over the old factory." Is all that I can make out. I take the two books inside of the suit and grab Toothy, my wife into the pocket. We will not have any reason to meet in three hours underneath the old factory. I leave the library, watching closely the figure standing empty in the doorway. "Bye." I say. No response. I dig into my pockets, inside of the suit and they are there! I cannot believe it, this all really did happen. I make my way into the forest behind the exit of town and kneel down before a five-dollar tree where I gather dry dollar bills into a bundle and tear pages from the book.

I crumple them up and create a ring of pages around a circle and pull out the matches my Simulation had found while in the airport, striking one. The flame rises, starting the dry sticks and dollars. The pages begin to start up. Little dots of code move around, lighting and turning blue and then finally a deep black, eaten by the flames. A part of the forest goes back in the distance and the flames rise, intoxicating. I tear more pages from the book, throw them into the fire and the swings dissipate. The green grocer that had been there twenty years ago reappears. People from town begin to emerge from inside. They are looking around, have just been born. I tear more out and then finally throw the book

COLD MACHINE ANDROID GOD FLYING COURSES |

(Vii.)

"Welcome home!" A voice shouts from a recorded tape behind the cream counter.

Other than this it is bleak; a pink rabbit suit appearing from out of nowhere on a long, red clothes line.

I peek around the office, glimpsing printed matter from the nineteen eighties folded, flying to a stop. I notice that it has been freshly washed and on the recording, that or a hidden persons voice. The stale man says to put this pink rabbit suit on.

He's getting impatient and I reach, in a reluctant way, through the waiting area desk,clutching the light, soft fur into my hands. Pulling the bizarre suit down off of the clothesline, it drops in easy form, and I pull it through a small hole in the double thick glass. The edges of the suit catch on the clothes hanger, and I struggle with it for a moment (my back turned to the doors.)

Noticing a small rectangular business card in the left hand pocket, I Press my fingers inside the fur, and pull it out in a flashy blur of bar codes.
I study the emblem inscribed over the top left corner. I do this quickly, reading the strange words out loud: Welcome home 50311305! Please put on this suit and wear it at all times when aboard. instructions and your partner are awaiting you in Sector three, office room G." The room begins feeling cold, outer-space lows.
Turning twice, the room stays the same gray cement, now encased in aluminum framed doors. A sign above one of the rusted exits reads
the sector number, starting at zero and going to four.

I stumble into the legs of the pink bunny suit, tripping as I get all the way into it and lunge through the empty room to the giant, rust stained door where I stop, sniffing strawberry short cake.

A list of vermin who knew Lexi have been stapled together and run slightly across my vision: a puzzle of the eaten aluminum.

I shove my bunny slipper at the door, a ricochet passes through rooms,
signing a flight of decayed brass stairways ahead, one after another.
I pass cases of books that have been stacked in a large numerical eight, put to rest on one side,
stairways cross infinite lines of text around me, leading up three stories into the past, away a hundred years.
∴

It smells like I'm aboard a submarine, the detergent they used to clean the suit smells like strawberry cake. Strawberry submarine, great mix.
I pinch my nose closed and walk passed hazard signs lined along a broken fence.

I go not down, not up, but to the right and then to the left along a figure-eight. Through the steps, it follows sideways, pink in my bunny suit.

Wandering through dozens of stairs, until I breach some end, I get to a door with a number on it: Sector Three. This is the place.
I open the door and walk in. Empty replica of the same office as before.
The sun comes in through one large double paned glass window.

Broken pieces of frozen cow lay in one corner, a diamond necklace skewed on top. "5031305, welcome." A man with black eyes appears from behind a black door. He looks like good 'Ole school boy from the school house downtown, his slick black hair in a comb-over,
pale skin, bags under his black eyes, a crooked smile.

Pointing over to the pile, frozen and crumbling scraps of my old partner,
Lexi, he says: "She needs a repair," he hands over a slim, manila envelope and turns back to a blackened door, in an apparition symbol collage, disappearing.

"Introductions are inside there," he says, smiling another lost, friendly smile and then leaving the office for good.

The black door slams and I walk over to Lexi piled in the corner, peering into the solid chunks of her muscle exposed under the flickering phosphorus.

The fog comes out of complexities in the room, either from the vents in the office or it's coming out of Sarah Lexi, weaving above me. This room,
patterns, too many rooms. I say aloud that the room is in doubles, wording it to sound like you would, shouting through a window to someone on the other side.

I duck my nose beneath the zipper flap in my pink bunny suit and take a deep breath, clutching the yellowed instructions close to my chest and blowing cold air through the pink fur. "The nameless old man is reflecting in the window past layers of low cloud coverage. The steel floor is wearing a Fedora hat, tilted to the faceless blur (…)"

"--Sarah Lexi is in a pile on the floor, my old pal who took her time through vague smoke if we were ever trapped, like now..." They must be implementing gas.

I must hide deep inside my bunny suit from the smoke: a dense, yellow fog, casual as it enters.

The gray door next to me, I grab its handle. The peep hole I had in my vision, but never noticed, until now, shining clear, and the man in fedora hat peeking in from the other side.

I push the gray door open and fall into another room, into the lingering smell of submarines.

The fog wraps around me and goes straight for my kneecaps. Hovering through my strawberry cake bunny suit. Slamming the door, I notice other fingers grasping the door jamb. Then I stop, freezing from the cold, my muscles tighten, suddenly still without time, standing in painted replication on panel.

Watching as the fog follows a hand, a group of fingers as they lift a fedora from his head, the attack moves toward the body of the cow, setting down in the corner.
He makes the motion by the enormous pile of molding cattle parts. "They changed me," he says. By my enormous pile of molding socks. "It's good to be back." I cough. I cover my face from it and feel disgusted by this.
Sarah's diamond necklace curls in animation around his neck.

The nurses walk to a large, woven table. A boiling Calderon, placed on palm fronds, steams. One of the nurses bends over and gets a ladle full of the tea, pours it into flower print tea cups. A group is called in scrubs to the table to sit. It is time for tea.

Hiding in the pink fuzz, I suck on the black plastic zipper.
"Have you been able to read the instructions yet?" black eyes asks, looking at the yellow envelope and then itching his scalp. "Uh, yeah," I say.
         "Okay, good," he closes the door, making the attack fog die back into the office. Above is the sign for this sector, printed in harsh Russian hybrid. "That

fog is weird, pulled me right out of there," he says as we walk into the drone of steps, echoing sideways in long hand across a figure 8.

Through submarine scraps, "What do you mean," I say, clutching the handrail as we roam down through industrial chrome, woven along a strange area of laughter that is the sound of our steps. Apartments and gravel roads –

"I mean this fog brought me back Apple Jack— Why are you being like this," I look at him and pull the bunny ears down, inspecting his dark, black eyes in the dim industrial light. "No! put that back on," black eyes shouts.

I quickly do so. "Okay then, if you are her why don't you go ahead and tell me something about yourself only I would know." I stop, smug feeling angry someone would play such a strange trick on me. "Why are you being this way Jack, this isn't like you," he looks down at his tan loafers, he seems to be thinking about crying. "You didn't read the instructions did you," he says, his lower lip quivers, slow at first, then quickly.
"No," I mutter, "What are you gonna cry," I say, crumpling my brow. He shakes his head, no, sniffles and then begins to break into tears before me. Lips quivering, sobbing.

(III.)

Wire graphs spiral the surrounding black suit – closing pink spider legs in a

slow mutated hand reaching for vines draped in space. Grasping spiders, I see pop-ups. Forced momentary glimpsing back to town - I linger, look through a window of thee abandoned house at the far edge of Acacia. Turn the heads on a coin and there's the office. I'm sitting in a chair in a suit, waiting. Halogens flicker above rooms, singe the green window. A lever is pulled deep in the ship and ricochets on the elongated track. A pink bunny suit melts down, a hanger rushes to the window, slams to a halt, and I have the disjointed feeling this is happening before and after I receive a glimpse. I cannot place the notion, I wander to the glass.
A dread falls, collapsing through me; tumbling rod down a flight of stairs, abstract rhythm over me, the weight of rhythm cursing the metal dents.
I reach through a hole six inches wide and tug the pink suit down over the rusty hanger. The line hurries back from where it came and loud horns blow in the depths beneath me.

310

I pull out rabbit suit, an older hanger lines up at a window next, there is no suit on this one. Pieces of paper fall from the pockets. Black ink – a note explaining the other hanger.

Return it.

I flip off the hood, undress from it, and stumbling in my clothes, the black suit is shoved through the six inch hole.

Flipping pieces of paper over, I get lost trying to read. I see there is language written, the pink mask and suit must be worn for a duration on the ship, this I already know but some pieces of the puzzle are missing –

The black suit rearranges itself folding up along the window, mutating in a snake slowly, an amoeba black wiggles on the hanger.

Line pulls quickly into darkness and a moments pause, climb in, setting strawberry shortcake on my shoulder I am pressing the mask down.

A tiny green light flipping on one of the walls near the waiting room chairs, reveals a low rumbling, chair glued to a section of floor. World of the ship, wires, lines of grid crisscross and vertically everything. Handwriting emerges all. Frozen for time, in an attempt to decipher fuzzy words, everything points once the marks have been in my brain.

The hood down, the mask examining this place to be without, words some madman disappears. The rabbit mask down, frustration flowers, stems, petals and I can make a tower of the distance, tied in metal rope and catwalk twines. The strawberry ice cream is overwhelming.

The creosote steel of steps in maze lines. The rubber mask on, I must emerge, become obvious face and my right index finger in the eye hole -

flip on and pull down the rubber inside a snag, the little hairs on my forehead; now stepping into the metal woven ship, I pass staggered circles. The grid around me begins pink, fuzzy slippers over my feet. Intersecting lines send me through sound, organized into directions, recently scouted. The front door looks at me the way a castle looks at me,

with a homemade hat that pokes in a coal chamber. Created solely in the grid, a tiny Rex comes under a tall, coal hat looks much like Toothy, younger, a tabby. Delicate, I reach down, but the little bugger decides

to crumble, appearing elsewhere. Strawberry cake wearing off inside the rubber lining -

"Toothy! I missed you -" I try and say. Rubber gloves make it like I am in a space suit, it comes out muffled under rabbit mouth.

Grinning through rabbit mask at Toothy, I pet his kitten fur and watch him wipe his cold nose over the wrist of the pink fuzzy. He smells the strawberries. The smell slows down his face eyelids stick on eyelids.

He winks at the castle walls appear lit from within, and he freezes on the ground, pawing smolders over diamonds. A packet of pop rocks is unearthed from the

black coal chunks, Toothy kicks Pop rocks to me. I open them, "this is the first
thing I've eaten in a long time." I think. He unearths a bee's hive and picks at it.
Gathering bits of honey, the retractable claws, slowly grow saturated in dripping
gold. He licks the honey away and snatches bee's from in the air.
One falls to sub-diamond flooring in the shape of a laser disc.
Little chrome being. Strawberry and creosote wafts out of the suit.
Spaceship within the chrome disk folds one of its walls to us dark tunnel, built
into now, the engine pumping, the computer running.
The sense of smothering in face pillows,
lounging in an air conditioned room, we pass deep ship and looking out of the
windows, mere circles near the low walkway, purge castles in giant caverns of
my brain.
I see airport –
crafts landing
from the careful Toothy ship's
bay.
          He is giving out orders –
 foreign registry books, a
realm I cannot understand,
at the door way,in my pink rabbit fur, peering through
caverns.
Coating tubes with conduit, the ivy of technology that makes my stomach growl,
maybe the pop rocks.
Toothy Mohawk straps in, connecting his ship.
It begins everywhere, electricity up and pops, short blue flames in the atoms, the
way that the Pop Rocks done in my mouth.
Toothy loses contact, slams down his front paws
and meows
foreign tongue.
He turns bird wing, turns raven, flies.
I wonder, are we are still ship, because the water can effect that.
Rain hits hollow echoes all of the rooms – ship rattles.
Toothy flies in other rooms, I follow, now I feel its effects, lag of legs, ongoing
torso, bunched up rabbit suit crossing the deck.
Another eyesight, ship toy, built (and I know it) a giant monster, all pink,
hands bigger than door, look killer.
And huge, wandering feelers and octopus, through foot tentacles –
the tunnel curving long, dark, back fifties friction move.
All gray in the big fat brain of pink bunny.
The dust, flecks of rabbit paw and see where we are.
I am looming Toothy in watered down dripping of wires.
Up vines, animal angry and I get back in the ship, strawberry smell,
the suit, replaced now with odor wetness.

In time wet everything will smell like mold everything. I come in contact with black shit.

Down in a chair to the size of the far window and shaken from waiting to be normal, I settle and listen to the crickets chirping ship, softly a rhythm Toothy flies in, the ship tight, flying again, the wire branches on the outside craft and we are a network of stars, a constellation attach in the

brain of the ship, leading around deep sense, our meeting of bodies, the closest chrome, merging metal flesh ship, senses.

Movement left, fly left, ship senses, down, we fly down. Crafts buzz fragile next – merged bodies appear culminated. Further darkness, more ship senses. Our direction vibration, a meeting place in a broken hive. Far edge of darkness, the top of a castle.

Craft tips on the other surrounding us, followed

all lines up into order. To change formats, that digital analogues, swarm of bees settled in the hive.

.

B ees. Just bees setting up the hive, in our origin form, about school boy

and wonder Lexi, were crawling in deeper, near bee triangle, I peek. Through window and watch, a people in rabbit and exits.

Toothy back cat and wanders from ship, a thick liquid.

He swims in meowing, and pad metal cross in the black,

where he turns to then shakes, to then violently.

Liquid long time settle his wake and in pocket, I feel crumpled instructions.

Good to be back in size, at least think to normal size skin loose as would slip right if too fast.

Luggage float in black, as to how I will cross.

Factor in luggage, walk to the liquid, bend down and touch it.

Conveyor pulls me in abrupt, throwing legs to the air and pushing through water, out doing anything, suddenly under, I see Toothy looking

worried from the shore, being swept away.

Brown in swirled gray

over shoulder of the suit, all I notice

mounds of luggage, the dark water stream

the light from the sun, cases travel on the

outside of the glow, near my twisting, slowly.

Dry and sat propped to the

Toothy replica. I've arrived at metal beach.

Watching

waves, a mechanic ocean pulls bags through,

up cases, segment,
systems, ocean organizer,
all Toothy shakes off irritated.
wet a little
we watch the mechanical sun rise on pulleys,
toward the ceiling.
Near that barely people, rising
as well all across the dome construction,
other humans in bear suits unpacking from the swarm.
I wonder about Lexi, if she might be on one of those ships,
if they are using her for her milk.
It makes me suddenly very sad to picture her
in a room being robbed of her milk for her calves.
I see the rubber housing of the tubes
coming from the suction apparatus
giving her infections.
I see the infections closely from here,
her eyes caked with
tears from being forced to give away her freedom.
Her back has been broken
by those animals,
I just know they are hurting my Lexington.
If I could wish one thing,
one thing right now,
I wish Lexi would be safe.
I picture her as a woman,
she has long brown hair and blue eyes,
peeking over the edge of the rabbit suit at me.
She winks and touches my hand softly, saying she missed me.

In time lapse video, a lavender seed grows along a shady patch in the old cotton
sun. A few months later I am half alive. I am waiting for a memory of Lexi, in
clean, lavender skin. Cotton turns around a line of trees, reaching a silk vine.
I unfold my lavender wing, absorb her, a distant memory of her, memory that
almost has no meaning.
The native figure comes outside and finds a
rooted lavender within her hay, poking a calyx through a rigid lock. Calmly, she
unfolds my arms from the latch, not break me in half.

Memory is gone. Dollars drift by outside a window, covering the forest floor
behind the house.

(xiv)

A ring of hair, within the peach curtains, coils over my shoulder, curls into numbers. Sharp bone fragment, on an x-ray, punctures seven eights of an inch into the stratum corneum, spinosum and stops at the dermal layer,scrapes a nerve. An authority voice whispers. toothy's familiar squawk in my left ear shakes me from the rigor Mortise; I run, lose balance near the stove left abandoned, dodging it by the hair of my right leg,(on an x-ray.) I stumble with Toothy, digging his claws in, entirely over a nail out of the wall, I almost land with it in me.
Toothy launches across, ending tangled in light fixtures on the ceiling. Over myself, near the edge of the basement, I fall. Hanging over a light switch, I land in a pile of books and foreign newspapers. Trash confuses my feet, I continue running. Bags. The tapping at the window has legs, moves through the kitchen continues and I wait for the thing to be at the landing. A sheep suit, mask wearing, psycho maniac, sighted in the darkness at school boy's house, a picture of an old man hanging crooked on the wall?
Holes in the wood lead dusty light into the basement. I think eyes will come to those holes and look away quickly, trying to clamor to my feet.
Sticking to the floor, janitor suit and nails puncture, but no matter, I've landed, frozen with fear, seized or punctured on the landing of stairs to the basement. I am able to wrap four fingers over a book of matches in my pocket. The railing is what I am grasping. For a moment before doing so, I realize I will have to check on my hand to know for-sure. I only have enough courage to protect my body from the darkness beneath.
The fifth floor of terminal B, dead escalators, around the silent parking lot, to the sand, I begin to believe that my house is built there. I crawl into a closet, there is evidence of paying. I am inspecting the bones of my own hand as they sweep through me, chiseled hand of fear.

Suddenly dawns on me, I have gotten lost in thought. I am someones dream, termites eat my legs tearing holes through their nightmare transport; there is the hammer and there is the boy, near the green tools glowing. The blue jungle someone is building from televisions , outer space computers. There on a table – glowing beakers; probably hallucinogenic drugs. Tarps hanging under a bridge, things unattended.
His stitches glow, his eyes stitched together in the background, He leaks out time/space.{Softly absent time of oblivion the broken steel of night – straight lines, dessert trays, broken gray and ominous fort of windows, blurring in the wind. Because, sand throws its particles of beating in a rage of nails into the tool bench -}

Boy was he there (…) A basement has a lot of funny things that appear to be boys. That's not him, he's chopped into a thousand different pieces and spread over the entire house like cow manure.

It was only – me.

I thought the coat rack was him. Just the play of light in a far window, limping through an ivy patch outside. Wind has chiseled past with a knife, the animal.

Black dogs near the house taken up, into the wind; perforates sand alloys, something ink stained in the for rent signs. A cabin, recently whitewashed, dog hair. A sheep suit stands in a corner, shaved with trimming sheers, sound of fur's falling.

"Toothy!" I shout, waking a cat on my shoulder to jump. The shape of absent moaning. Fuzz leads the kitchen tiles to me, Toothy forces on, holding his wings down. I peek him, half cat in one eye, half bird in fifteen other eyes, running down his shoulders onto the small of his back; puzzle pieces flying from his shoulder, (blue pictures. Eyes.) The cat dissolving the ravens in a puddle of concrete shapes, leaving Toothy, the York cat in these eyes, in these (blue bottles) his eyes hanging on for dear life as they fall away. We race through the kitchen, I see school boy outfits melting in the oven.

School Boy, naked perches over the stove, oven open, cooking his suit; turns paper white, aluminum pokes through, switch blade implemented to flip with. Instinct gets me. Mothering tries to stop me, but fear of the little knives clenching my movements makes me laugh hysterically and run in haste. I run to the living room, fall over books on the floor. In the corner, over toothy's perforated eyes, a black mask shapes itself under the mantle piece, bending out of sight in slow motion near a stack of books.

Black sheep suit disguises itself in the books, through the spines, toward us.

In the kitchen, the little boy runs with a steak knife. He already cut himself with it, and wields it maniacally. Death smears over blades my way, lifts off the ground and crashes us into the attic, landing in the rafters.

Rafters switch to arrows, pointing to the simulated area, a set of stairs at the end of a gray corridor emerges. Sim has just been born today. Rooms in a mixture of focuses and greens surface along the edge of a rectangular grid, then concrete is poured in. Focus systems are still a bit fuzzy; Sim grows. Small code in the corner of Sim vision (A_90) a mouse.

Lights twitch, string of numbers (//32.51.//34)

flicker out to a darkness of loading more equations.

Green, neon, blue; arrows take shape, complete their edge, then die back in thin digits. A numerical sequence occurs (8///1).

At a start screen in this game the simulation settles itself numerically and appears before seamless signals flashing "GO."

A mouse crosses, then dissipates behind a counter inside the doorway of a destroyed room.

Sounds clanking around the mouse, like the stopping short, heard the simulation toward the room and paused. Silence deep as echo, there is no way around it.
Strung together code (A_90) starts settled
versions of mice and ears.

Flicker inside the storage room now, beyond the entrance of A_ terminal, Simulation finger's hunt
through signature napkins (5) with airline logos printed on the outer edge of them,((9.1)) packets of soap and dishtowels. (632)
It fingers through complimentary boxes of signature toothpicks, (87.3) mint candy, (//0.00) towelette boxes (779)the mind is blank canvas.
Dust (0.1)fluorescent light and stains and shadows:
(//32.) (8.7.51) (3.3) & (777.1)
Jutting organizer shelves ^(625) shadow and paint, (77.1) (.0) shadows of memory. (77.1) (.002+)Sim doesn't remember everything, storage closet, all it can see. Only memory begins fumbling.
Sim fingers through cases of abandoned junk, becoming aggressive,the shelves fall off of shadows, revealing a nest of code.
Rats see Sim, and the rats scuttle into a hole.
Sim stumbles in codes
(//32.5)   (77) & (7(8))
(5) ((9))   (A_90)
(//0.00)(A_90)
(0.1) (A_90) (A_90) (77) (7(8)) (A_90)(2213.2) (213.1)(A_90)((8.3)A_90) .
(563)   (A_90)(A_90)(A_90)   (779.)
Sim hands the Sim air, a balancing tool. The last paper towel to search the carpet. Sim blends others familiar with it.
The complimentary packs of sugar, cream (221) (213.) The thank you cards (563) of the unknown airlines. The wall, coated in shadows (77) (7(8))
The printed matter of Sim mind, shelved,installed in Sim memory, built to shelve centuries.
Body steps from closet and recognizes something:
Birch wood and termites in Sim legs. Bashed counter; Sim rests a moment, processing its entrance terminal above the stairs.
Sim takes looks through holes in the counter, sees (A_90) mousy looking back. Seems to make sense, but Sim remembers something else, something deeper in Sim memory the mind has been programmed not to look at something.
Shoulders wander, deep hallways, scattered bags of trash, and wire, in snags around a hole,
the airports abandoned guts.
Sim descends a broken escalator, (De javu (1_.7_7_51_._0__)
Sim's termite eaten feet echo in the holes of terminal walls.
Descends, taking caution in the space surrounding. Downstairs, great darkness and wire.

Sim has to adjust its eyes to see the long
case of metal, sticking from the ceiling.
Sim leads eyes to the floor. The body has been here,in this airport a long time.
It got here exactly and from here it came. Lost in Sim, in a dark room. Wires
hang from electric boxes smashed open, ripped by thieves. Huge chunks of carpet
torn back reveal bundles of cable, shredded in the floor. Ceiling sags,
yellow damage, thin half inch luggage drop rots   near a door; deformed ice
growing a line at the bottom. Bits of computer show through and then, leaving a
thin line of glowing mold on the base of a fern. A home in the mechanisms of the
luggage belt form and out pops (A_90's.)
Broken window tailors Sim through mud, luggage belt, a face, body reflecting on
a wall.
Mold has formed illusion of mouth from rotten rubber.
Jumping the strips, through mechanics, black mold another storage room, the
exact replica of the first area comes to Sim light.

(iv.)

I see Laser hands in front of what used to be me.
They are sifting through dollar bills and the weight on my middle back forcing
me to flex.
Suddenly, sound is heard, it filters into my ears, a cattle stampede miles away.
Screeching draws directionally to a furry, pink bear legging. Silver chaps bent
around my side, sharp pain climbs my neck. Clutching big wads of dollar bills,
flung backwards and pulled into an upright position while shown rope, long
knotted, once in silver, once in black, threaded twice.

Try to stand, followed by cackling woods.
Sticker bush of hands. She turns me to face her,
deep, beneath the fur of this bright pink bear suit she's got on. Nothing moves, a
flicker
of silver gloss lipstick she wears over her imperfect, white teeth; a cleft of
seducing silver lips.

Black and silver rope tied around
parts of her, inside of my pink bear suit.
With microscopic tools, I might see a pack of circuitry,a ceiling of wires, a floor
of confusing visions sprayed through table cloth,
doily; I may see red glass within a wall, red stained glass. Flight plans.
::

Her make up is done nice tonight, a mere red line over two white doll eyes. Filters are important, blankets and paint (…) Non affiliates, joint marketing, schizophrenia.

She's got me by the mind just found in a card – I give her Ginkgo from my skin - medications while she jumps back onto my waist for instance and kicks my ribs described above.

"everything is wrong, everything is wrong. But I love you. But I love you."

A Rope attached to my cock, with your life you need, just go for it. And the little one (your opt out choice) covered in the bear costume kicks ABA machine down the mattress,

the chaps – my life muzzle become too dry over my shoulders, since I can't move, too moist, and flavor grown thighs organized by region relish around the back of my head shatter.

High quality, heavy weight stock paper dots are cut brilliant from the fifth dimension sheets, landing edges on a postcard photo of acid castles, until completely covered in them,

\\\

[The winter eats red dots from the installation guide,
 cut into hills.]
[The sky is cut out until they
take anyone, animals, circles. They cut away the rocks.] Medicine woman. Hole punched, paper dots guide and punch and stiletto holes and angel hair century. Cut.

"Smack!"

I hit my chin across the dream of a monkey bar, my neck pushes my eyes into the sky. It's green before light of countless, fuzzy edges.

(Xi.)

I keel over, wrapped inside
a blanket woven in darkness
that is dappled with stars.

Threads, once symmetrical,
lead an area of light

from my vision – coated thick
in fur – to the frayed
edges of the blanket.

Eyes
that see beyond there, the
frayed edges, gather warmth.

Another star-speckled darkness,
one generated of space,
is touched by the cold mucus
which drains from my nose
to low metal, represented by
a frequency,
nothing solid aloud to exist,
yet,
anything complex as an elemental
metal appears behind this,
this blanket of darkness.

There is what I gather as me
(a stream of consciousness made
up of darkness, absence of light,
color, symbols, strung along an axis of light).

A frequency is barely legible inside nostrils to Sumerian steel.
A frequency evaporates in the verbal iron, creates a darkness from its behind,
evaporates in frequency, created, it propels me forward in a wonder worm. The
long, dark moments warp and turn to no.

The white paper of no [This nothing] this absence of darkness, white black, the
vice-verso, crumbling forward. Frayed blanket, stars, white paper.

There is still what I gather to be me, could come close. White, still thing, no.
What comes before the [no] is still a thing - something, the anti absence of a
thing. Infinite no – This kind of nothing before no one, before the infinite no. It
looks like something. It is white, it is on a plain
and it surrounds me.

Seventy miles away, on a strange arctic island in the Gothic
Town of Acacia, there stands in a far reaching section, these Ivy eaten mansions,
one of which Schoolboy lies in segment (One part being an ear
in the basement, one part eyes in the attic, scalp and hair in the upstairs
bathroom.) Resting, (his mind in the living room, sitting out in a china dish,
floating in warm fluid, his arms in the sink in the kitchen, his legs resting on the
stairs to the attic). Pelvis in the love seat, spleen in the shower, lungs out back in
an old chest, under the falling leaves of a Willow tree. Teeth in the downstairs
bathroom, placed in a row of
dentures inside the crystal grandmother glass. The rest of the Schoolboy's face
has been separated from his eyes, teeth and scalp viewed in "the process of
elimination" and set up on the fluffed, blue pillow in the boy's radio flyer
bedroom. Along with his suede shoes, blue uniform with a button attached, which
reads "sleeping baby."
The 1950's version of the phone rings,
green lacquer finish vibrating side to side,
"bring bring bring.." It rings,
next to a pair of segmented hands, resting on a doily, under the old phone.
From the wrist to the finger tips, the hands shiver to life, (slowly at first)
flailing into the receiver and then lifting the antique phone off of the base.
Dropping the phone accidentally to one side, resting near the base of the phone:
with no eyes, mouth, teeth or brain, there is no way to respectfully answer.
Cloud
coverage against the sun bent
sky prints clouds on my
blanket, cut out to fit
my fumbling body within.
(Now back to life in
my laser
suit) with my rubber grips
around the fire
of a small sun, at the frayed
edges of darkness-
The phone receiver lies on one
side, green against woven cream doily.

BEEP, BEEP, BEEP, BEEP.

Many layers of sky turn into the wire and down, through the phone, as a series of
beeps, representing a dead line:

BEEP, BEEP,BEEP, BEEP.

One of the segmented hands clutches its finger's over the receiver,
picking it up, under the gray light of day, coming through the living room
window, setting the phone on the green base and resting again, over the doily on
the wood end table.

::

_____

Sting from above,
where the clouds turn to
water,
I wake in the rain,
falling slow from space.

The metal underneath me soaks
into my thighs, butter on
butcher knives as I crash
through
the third floor, somewhere.

An abandoned house lingers in fog,
near a grove of dollar bill trees.

Lashings of submerged white
light strobe before my eyes,
blocking my view.
I pull my hands to
my throbbing head,
watching white light pulsing in
me
and as it exits through
somewhere
inside my head,
casting shadows over the area

before me, I can't feel pain, but see that shards of the rafter wood stick through me, holding me by my thighs. There is a lot of blood taking trails down the broken beams, puncturing the floor of the house.

Overcast sky from the gray outdoors
is the light, it comes in, through the
hole in the roof, where I must have
landed, from a fallen picture
in the sky, pouring into the earth
like a concrete statue of a man
(except for one that is lit on fire.)

I can't tell if it's a song I hear in the distance, over the grove of trees, or if this is just sharp buzzing inside my ears, inside my head, ringing in an elaborate orchestration of impact.
(Hitting down so hard,
I should be dead).

Where did I even come from?
I wish I could move.
These beams!
I try tugging the splintered dust and old, spider infested wood from my sliced butter thighs, but they don't budge.

Long awaited and secretly tombed
screams of ancient tongue barrel
out of the lung case,
below a strained chin and
chipped tooth. The far edges
of dry space lips crackle
under the Berlin wall, crumbling
down in the rubble, in
the far reaches of white
time.

It's as if I'm watching all of this on video tape set inside a memory. I remember standing in a box, inhaling my future into a scattered sidewalk, all darkness and that one light from the door, drifting
in through FYI rain.

(Mountain peak – peeking eyelids) A stop
light peeking into my open
box, out from where I am standing, some side
street, passed out nine ways
from narcoleptic steps, the stop light between my lips turning into crumpled
paper, ashes. Waves of fog rolling over me, a random memory error from
over-stimulated brain shell.

I strain to get up and peek
the mountain, thoroughly from the snow simulation, even down to the
compacting of the snow, the thing gets it right.

Some one on foot approaches me from the north. The fog, it invites itself into the
room, past my shoulders, it
weaves quickly through my
hair and hands me wounds,
the temperature drops.

Another, long awaited shouting erupts, from within the lung case below,
shattering the fog over my head, where it fills back in again. A bottle of fresh
latex paint surrounding my body and closing in around the thigh fillet is poured.

Outside the house, on Halsey Boulevard, near the schoolhouse, wind is pulling
down one dollar bills from the dark, black trees.
It carries them into the air, above the swing sets and places them down, in a bleak
forest, near the Schoolboy's residences. The forest follows suit, dropping fives to
the forest floor. Tens and twenties pile over ones and fives, folding over in a
dreary dance.

A violent breath cuts through the woods, sending dollars deep into the blurring
distance. A kind of chase, occurring at some base level, a newspaper
consciousness, farther and farther away from the main Boulevard; the crisp
dollars, freshly fallen from their branches, fly fast into a great darkness, lingering
at the edges of trails.
From the attic window, I peek, watching as the wind tosses thousands of dollars
into a dark ravine of ivy eating trees.

My jeans are soaked to the outside and watching, I see blood drift down through the open hole in the roof. It covers me, so that now I do not recognize where my legs are and some hundred thousand office buildings make up the gray space. My mind is purposefully filling it all in.

Chambers, caved into thin rectangle shafts, pass over fog, turning slowly before a base sphere that appears. Revealed, only from its emanating light sources, there within the sphere of all future office buildings spins slowly in the fog. Attachments are long and thin from the most impossible facets. Chambers, emitting light, pass by, in front of my vision, and the fog dissipates softly as the offices slow to a stop before me. There, ever so slightly the fog closes in, over parts of the mechanism, like clouds turning invisible. Speakers sound, buzzing into stagnant air. Compact, leaking symbols of foreign scribble enter the air, move away, fog yellows the glow in my vision. Glitches pass over the whole generated town – over the symbols – over the fog and homes, the lights in the offices burn out at once.

It's muggy, uncomfortable, and stale. I sit here, noticing my feet have healed back to normal and my thighs are no longer punctured through. My hands are working properly within the rubber laser gloves. Some large, dark window screams: "5013100," the voice sounds taped. In an office. It's cold, stale and uncomfortable in here.

I move extra quick, glad to have agility back in my legs, and I rush toward the window, where the voice yelled the number. Tripping, I land on my laser suit jacket, with all these papers I am carrying flying out from under my flailing arms. The papers cut through the room, landing shelter svelter before me, foreign symbols and shapes cover the sheets; I crumple them all up, throwing them half-hazard into a tan leather bag I seem to have acquired mysteriously, presenting my self to the window.

(Xii.)

T OOTHY SHIFTS, morphs the Negro Rio into chocolate York, a

larger division of English bovine. Toothy shifts attribute,

eyes categorical in "views" over part of a metal beach. The bees
swarm from a broken hive in Bulgaria, through Moscow, through the fuzz
their bodies crossing.

I see her – God, principally. She winks, licking the hive honey, as
mechanics of ocean organize luggage valiant around us.
She illustrates her 'fuck' tongue in different degrees, licking the hive

clean.

Lex stands in her ever-growing numbers before me, avidly pursuing

studies and athletics – An awkward, Romanian expression accustomed

to her face rises, she eats honey away from the bees, staring into satellites

– or an active development, perhaps tucked inevitability where a star fell

out.

I see a diamond falcon over her broad shoulders, heavenly tufts of
white hair grown in savage defeat, maple trees I grasp, tugging down
on, pulling myself closer, barging through the "evil" distance, both
companions infinite. The smell of mustangs, the lamb and the wild rose. I

hug the Balkan countryside tight, get the image of a strawberry patch Lex

got into.

The honey, drooling off of her ear flips back and forth. Tears turn to

paint laughter, as I fight my material universe and feel the silent dances

overwhelming embrace of peasant girls.

A small shudder echoes through scarcely altered tradition, and covered

with glowing frescoes, she stops eating, stares at waves.

Sun, a mechanical giant fit by an artist to the sky, a glowing ball of

flesh, a welded achievement, fit into place on a sheet of cold silence.

Blankets on our beach climb down, austere. I study mosaic, clutch the necklace firm, altered scarcely, watching her eyes dance to the clouds (made of shaved alloy.) They press on, depicted Byzantine art, overhead they lift Greece through paintings: pulleys and ropes. We watch, self confident in vision, sky folding down an area of rich warehouse, mosaics, frescoes, symbolic embers and Lex turns to. A universe bird, performing nearby lake Ohrid, in the Raska area, she flies to the monastery darkness, circling Bulgaria in a thousand private flowers and ornaments, landing on my lagging shoulder, squawking a Romanian hello. Nudging my reclusive cheek, once, in a loving manner.

We walk the metal beach, the festival of strip, tourist cabarets in the summer, into the collapsed sheets of the sky. Enclaves of the ceiling are large, broken pieces of old skies they abandoned in this sector. The floor unclogs in a place and the ocean drains out of the building.

As we walk, inches of Kosovo gray water dwindle golden, down a drain. Lex nudges my suffering chin.

Lex tugs at me, until I fall out from a vanished splendor, a spot I had been hiding in. She shakes her head, no. Then squawks Swedish-Belgian loudly; pointing her emerged beak behind me. I turn and see them. Giant, exalted blue crystal, soft at the edge of my shoulder blades, the
 wing span of a giant bird crossed my
relaxedy arms. The crystals jut out seven feet on both sides behind me. A

force pulls me up, off of the beach. Air moves through the fibers of my

bones, lifting me into the air without effort. Ruffling her wings, Lex flies

ahead, leading the way through the warehouse curtains, to Transylvania,

over the alloy clouds, across the pounded copper beams. She turns to me

as I lift the clear wings over my head.

A sort of natural movement I've done before comes second nature.

I inhale quickly next to her, exhale and push down on the wings, rising

higher toward the buildings ceiling of stars (light bulbs in rows) theater

inhales move me up, exhales create a glide. Next to her, I let my eyes rest

over the beach, now a concrete island in a great concrete swimming pool

without water. Her eyes reflect the light bulbs. A smell of ozone blends

together and I follow as she leads over a section of buildings on the other

side of the sky. Caverns made of Plexiglas fly underneath, giant castle

walls come into view in front of us.

I touch the wall as we swoop down, touching a memory. Lex perches in

the steeple at the top of one building, and her wings relax next to her.

I enter a memory I stored inside of the walls years ago. A bright light, a

small boy standing in front of the mirror.

I let go, and swing to the perch next to her spasming squawks. She points

her beak at the stars and looks for a long time at them. Down at the
ground, I watch a boy in the memory growing from the castle into the dirty
street run. Lex stares into the stars, stops to clean her feathers

and trembles. She gets herself snug underneath the bell. It starts to snow,
Mismatched in the satellite, the last form of the boy is seen running into
a subway underneath the city as we fall asleep. We wrap up in our wings,
dozing off for the wishes and the last form, the descending red of a plant
axis.

∞

Florida, 2014

OLD HIGHWAY

Over in the venus fly trap, the long, black finger-nail-needles, 10mg xanax prescriptions, and a shit pipe -

I am in a room of eyeliner, cover up, and lipstick- four of the windows are my white sleeved waiters. Under cherry tree, and red oak doors, dancing to the foot stickers, dance by number, and a map tacked in the back of the room, I've no comparisons.

The numbers, filmed behind fog that play on reels of dream before the butterflies, eyelids, boxes of computer parts, broken fans, torn out hard drives, they have been
left here, standing between this megalithic static, built in the sky as a gymnasium (on the one hand, I can literally fork lift mashed pieces of the static inside of a television apart from that skyline,) on the other hand, sweep pill bottles, oh, from the mountain, to find an ocean in a speech I wrote for people dressed in rags.

I am "octal-coil-line-dancing," to carve my way along a narrow highway, in a red velvet cake, mask covered chin - carrying strawberries for breakfast. I think "they" should have a healthy fear of me- late at night, in the road, a healthy respect for any manic or grim reaper passing along the coast.

WAVES

Humans are nesting in flat tires, free box clothes, in a frozen waterfall, beneath an iced over maze. Dmitri -- who emerges dainty, (fully equipped kitchen in his hands,) time traveling with his knife collection -- Dmitri's fingers cut at the hair of sleep group no.5, 7, and 23, handling the tissue paper moon as delicate as hair, right before breakfast. BUTTON the dark coma, it pours syrup from little glass bottles, pours red mouths

this early in the house. I, version three hundred, have person-
ally served benadryl to this Sickness for a very long time. I've
been With the result there and weaving whistles to Irish wing-
span, angelica, rosaries spinning in the home! My fingers are
like ropes this morning, and your fingers are like Rosemary
bundles lapped in 1965 waves. A doll comes now, so galactic
it unravels a girlfriend naked onto the wooden floors, and our
window sill.

BUSES

Shállow, sat by the sidewalk, whistles two queens and eight hats
from his lungs, dervish a whirling dervish in the mind of an
abracadabra tuesday.. joining two sets of hair in a long braid of
whimpering orgasm quartets, the hurried juniper solar system
which won plaid and dusk, a fine ghost now draws the lines
with a white house, and woke with stick around like necklaces,
of course. Juniper is a small galaxy, the roots are rooms sweating down the bright handlebars, a dinosaur the lenses length,
abracadabra ropes and ribbon future long, joining the coastal
kinky brown ligaments, juicing roses, weekend, understand the
need to be held in secret, all these flurries the distortion wheels
if midnight in Texas, I lay under that chandelier turnkey, at 11
Christmas bulbs, turnover, gorgeous boats in the willow trees
floaty aboveground, I am closing my eyes, juniper trees lining
the shore.

VISTA

I have elaborated chambers of my body that took 200 tetras,
October 30th, and not a human face, but a momentum to
land in "moment umbrella." Ethereal, and steering the passage,
arm in arm to cavities. I keep contact ingredients for diamonds
in my faith pocket, and let dusk (a healthy relationship be-

tween you and the long drive away) save my life to search
a PhD in library science. In my mind is helium, and I felt the
gorgeous, marble entry to the abandoned houses. WANTED for
latching onto a museum like a tick. Chanelle comes in waves,
shifts a satellite radio to wormholes. In a depth of yarn, lengthy
hearts remodel the universe for a canœ. Just P. M. Creek,
apples chanting strawberries. Dawn, you look lovely. Grow god
inside mismatched sweaters, any roomy reward. I've forgotten
the make up, so tediously inscribed in the mirror, and woke
eating storm cake. Roped in roots is the world, unfolding poly-
amorous.

Fin Sorrel was born February 9, 1985, in California. He was raised in Oregon, and as a teenager, he dropped out of high school to further his personal studies in black and white photography, he learned how to hop freight trains, and studied anarchist literature at an info shop on 3rd and Burnside, in Portland, Oregon called liberation collective.

His first adventure on trains led him to begin writing in a journal which was lost in a drunken bar fight on a road trip through northern California. He didn't give up, and began keeping journals of "pœms" written using random newspaper articles, bits of conversation, and sketches. Living on the street, in squatted abandoned buildings, or on friends couches, Fin learned the hard lessons of life, which would be some of the later inspiration for his first short stories. After an incident where he was homeless traveling through Santa Barbara, Fin was hospitalized for a severed blood vessel in his septum, which led to his death. The clinic in Santa Barbara were able to recover Fin, and he lived through the incident. This would be the inspiration for such stories as Teacup Galaxy and explosion no. 1.

Still traveling, Fin is working on his next collection of surreal tales for his first novella: Adams st.

He runs MANNEQUIN HAUS, where he now publishes Avant Garde/ Surrealist fiction and plays. Exploring the country side from out of a backpack, ghost towns, and abandoned buildings fascinate, and inform his surreal style. Contact him via mannequin haus: infii2.weebly.com

Pski's Porch Publishing was formed July 2012, to make books for people who like people who like books.
We hope we have some small successes.
www.pskisporch.com.

323 East Avenue
Lockport, NY 14094
www.pskisporch.com